FAMIL

By Ki

Table of contents

Copyright
Authors other works
Foreword
Chapter one
Chapter two
Chapter three
Chapter four
Chapter five
Chapter six
Chapter seven
Chapter eight
Chapter nine
Chapter ten
Chapter eleven
Chapter twelve
Chapter thirteen
Chapter fourteen
Chapter fifteen
Chapter sixteen
Chapter seventeen
Chapter eighteen
Chapter nineteen
Chapter twenty
Chapter twenty-one

Chapter twenty-two
Chapter twenty-three
Chapter twenty-four
Chapter twenty- five
Chapter twenty-six
Chapter twenty-seven
Chapter twenty-eight
Chapter twenty-nine
Chapter thirty

Kim Hunter

Copyright © 2015 By Kim Hunter

The right of Kim Hunter to be identified as author of this work has been asserted in accordance with sections 77 and 78 of the Copyright, Designs and Patents Act 1988.

All rights Reserved

No reproduction, copy or transmission of this publication may be made without written permission.
No paragraph of this publication may be reproduced,
Copied or transmitted save with the written permission of the author, or in
accordance with the provisions of the Copyright Act 1956 (as amended)

This is a work of fiction.
Names, places, characters and incidents originate from the writers imagination.
Any resemblance to actual persons, living or dead is purely coincidental.

OTHER WORKS BY KIM HUNTER

WHATEVER IT TAKES
EAST END HONOUR
TRAFFICKED
BELL LANE LONDON E1
EAST END LEGACY
EAST END A FAMILY OF STEEL
PHILLIMORE PLACE LONDON
EAST END LOTTERY

Web site www.kimhunterauthor.com

FOREWORD

The world is a dangerous place to live; not because of the people who are evil, but because of the people who don't do anything about it.

Albert Einstein

CHAPTER ONE
Bull Bay Jamaica 1990

Mercy Higgins made her way home from school, she had just two weeks left until she saw the back of the place and she couldn't wait. Her long legs and small waist were to be envied and with perfect cheek bones and huge brown eyes, she really was a beauty. It was the height of summer and the sun was still hot at four in the afternoon. If she could get her chores done early enough Mercy hoped that her mum would allow her to go to the beach for a swim. The Higgins's were respected members of the community and although not rich, they had far more than most. The small three bedroom wooden bungalow was freshly whitewashed and everything sparkled inside. Tandy Higgins ran a tight ship as far as her home and family were concerned and when Tandy spoke, everyone listened. As Mercy reached the front gate, her younger brother Matthew barged past her, he was the bane of Mercy's life but in his parent's eyes, could do no wrong. What Matthew wanted he got without question, even if it meant Mercy having to go without. Suddenly her mother's voice could be heard booming from inside the house.
"Mercy is that you girl? Get your backside in here now; there are chores to be done."
Not daring to keep her mother waiting, she climbed

the three wooden steps onto the porch and was about to turn the handle of the front door when someone waving caught her eye. Junior Williams was leaning up against the fence that separated her house from the vacant plot next door. When she looked in his direction, he winked in a way that sent shivers down her spine. The same age as Mercy, Junior was not the kind of young man that her parents would approve of. There were no other words to describe him apart from he was a thoroughly bad boy who had rarely attended school and who spent most of his spare time down at the beach drinking beer with his friends.
"Hey Mercy, come over here."
Torn between wanting to chat and the wrath of her mother if she didn't go inside, she decided to take the telling off and spend a few minutes with Junior. The pair giggled and smiled at each other and Junior began to flirt. Taking her hand, he teased Mercy about her school uniform. When Tandy's voice could once again be heard bellowing out Mercy knew that she really had to get inside but as she turned to walk away, he again grabbed her hand.
"Meet me at the beach tonight."
"I can't my parents would go mad."
"They don't need to know, wait until they are all asleep and slip out. I'll be at the reggae shack for most of the night."
As Mercy pulled away he planted a kiss onto her

cheek before running off down the road. She could feel her face flush and prayed that her mother wouldn't suspect anything. Entering the kitchen she saw Tandy at the stove and just by the way her mother stood, told Mercy that the woman was in a bad mood. In her right hand she held a giant wooden spoon and Mercy Higgins knew that she would probably end up being hit with it.
"And just where have you been missy?"
"I aint been nowhere Mama just walking home that's all."
"Well you took too long about it."
With that Tandy swiftly flicked her wrist and the wooden spoon smacked the side of Mercy's face with a whack. Holding the palm of her hand up to her cheek Mercy tried not to let the tears fall but her face hurt and she couldn't stop them escaping.
"Now get the table laid, your Papa will be home soon."
Doing as she was told Mercy removed the plates from the cupboard and after putting them onto the table, went to fetch the cutlery. Her hands were full with knives and forks just as Matthew ran into the kitchen and not looking where he was going he barged straight into his sister. The cutlery clattered to the ground but he didn't say sorry or help her pick them up. Instead he went straight to the cookie jar and grabbing a handful, began to shovel them into his mouth.
"You clumsy girl! now look what you've done, they

will have to be washed again and don't take too long about it."

Just as Mercy stood up she felt the full force of the wooden spoon as it made contact with her back and this time she cried out in pain. All the while Matthew stood watching and when his mother lashed out again he sniggered loudly.

"That's for being so careless girl, now get them all washed up."

Just as she'd finished her father entered and walking over to Mercy he gently lifted her chin and placed a kiss on her cheek. Instantly he noticed the swelling on the side of her face.

"What happened to your face baby girl?"

Mercy took a sideways glance at her mother and Tandy's eyes narrowed when they made contact with her daughters.

"Oh nothing Papa, I just walked into the door that's all."

Winston Higgins studied his daughter for a few seconds. He didn't really believe her but he didn't want to push the matter any further. His wife could be a nightmare when you got on the wrong side of her, so it was best just to let the matter drop. After he had washed his hands the family all sat down at the table and tucked into ackee and salt fish with rice and peas. Tandy Higgins may have been a tyrant but she was also a very good cook and the food went down without any complaints. Mercy was left to wash all the pots, while the rest of the family went into the front room. By the time she had finished it was past eight o'clock and after saying goodnight to everyone, she went to her room. Leaving her door ajar she sat on the side of the bed waiting for them all to retire. Matthew followed about an hour later and by ten she heard her mother and father go to bed. Quickly changing and applying a little lipstick, she placed cushions in her bed so it looked like she was asleep and then opening her bedroom window, climbed out onto the back porch. Mercy was so desperate to get to the beach that she didn't see Matthew looking out of his window. He smiled to himself, whatever his sister was up to, he would make sure that she paid dearly for it.

The walk down to the beach took five minutes, it was pitch black but she knew the terrain like the back of her hand. Mercy's heart was racing, would Junior be there or was she wasting her time? Approaching the old bar that was referred to as the reggae shack, she needn't have worried. Bob Marley's 'Could you be loved' was loudly playing and there were three or four other lads standing with Junior. Walking over Mercy suddenly felt nervous and for a second wished that she was back at home in the safety of her bed. When Junior saw her he smiled and beckoned for her to come over. The smell of ganja was heavy in the air and the look in his eyes told Mercy that he had smoked more than his fair share. He passed her a beer and as she swallowed her first alcoholic drink, he handed over the joint he'd been smoking for her to try. Mercy Higgins placed the joint between her lips and then inhaled deeply and she immediately began to cough, much to the amusement of the boys who had been watching her. Suddenly she felt light headed as her body began to dance to the music. Junior took hold of Mercy's slender waist and pulling her in close, slowly began to smooch to the music. The sea air was fresh and the sound of the water breaking onto the golden beach had a calming effect. They danced for a while and to Mercy it felt as though their bodies were one. Junior Williams was everything she had dreamed of in a boyfriend, fit, strong and with the most handsome face she had ever laid eyes on. His beautiful smile had her mesmerized and when he spoke, she felt as if she was in a trance.

"Come on, let's go for a walk."

"Where to?"

Just down the beach, it'll be nice, you know romantic."

Mercy smiled, she couldn't resist him and the alcohol and ganja made her feel as if she was under his spell. As they walked off into the dark the other boys could be heard laughing and it bothered Mercy.

"Why are they laughing?"

"Don't take any notice of those fools, they're just jealous that I've got such a beautiful girl on my arm."

It seemed that Junior knew exactly where they were heading and when they reached a deserted spot, he stopped and took her in his arms. Kissing her passionately, Mercy felt as though she was going to pass out, her whole body was tingling and even though she had no experience with the opposite sex, she knew this was right, this was how it was supposed to feel. Lust began to take over and as Junior moved his lips along Mercy's slender neck, she could feel his hard penis pressing against her. Placing her palm over his denim clad crotch, she began to gently rub, unsure of what was happening, she also knew that she wanted him here and now. They both pulled at each other's clothes and Junior guided her down onto the cool soft sand. When they were naked he studied the beauty before him, from her perfectly formed breasts, to her hips and her wonderful long legs. Junior was finding it hard to control himself and as he lay on top of her Mercy began to kiss him passionately. He moved his body in such a way that her legs slowly opened up for him and Junior entered her for the first time. The initial few seconds were electric and even though the pain of losing her virginity hurt more than she had imagined it would, it was a strange pleasurable pain and it felt so good to have him inside of her. Junior's strong actions were intense and as Mercy placed her hands onto his buttocks he jerked and his whole body seemed to go ridged as every muscle

tightened. For Junior Williams it was now over, his seed was inside her and he felt totally relaxed.
"Oh baby, that was amazing."
Rolling from her, he laid out flat onto the sand and for a few minutes neither of them spoke as they stared up at the sky and stars above.
"Do you love me Junior?"
"Yeah, of course I do, didn't I just prove it."
Mercy smiled but as she rolled over to cuddle him, he suddenly seemed different. She couldn't put her finger on exactly what it was but there was definitely a change in Junior. Laying her head onto his chest, Mercy drifted off into a beautiful sleep. When he heard her softly sigh, Junior slowly moved away and after grabbing his clothes, walked back to the shack to join his friends.
Waking up in the dark Mercy began to panic, she was alone and had no idea what time it was. Due to the ganja and alcohol she was still a little worse for wear and as Mercy walked along she was slightly unsteady on her feet. At last she managed to make her way home and after several attempts, climbed back into her room through the window. Falling into bed, she didn't even undress and it wasn't until her alarm went off that she fully remembered what had happened just a few hours earlier.
The first one to wake in the house, she made her way to the bathroom and when she saw the blood in her underwear, realised it was the result of losing her virginity, she also knew that if her mother found

out there would be hell to pay. Cleaning herself up she headed into the kitchen and began to prepare breakfast for the family. Matthew, who had crept downstairs, now stood watching his sister. A bitter spiteful boy, he didn't have Mercy's good looks or any of her kind ways and he resented her for always getting attention whenever they went out. As she turned around Mercy was a little startled when she saw him.
"What's wrong with you?"
"Nothing, I was just wondering how much my silence was worth?"
"I don't know what you're talking about, now out of my way little boy I have to lay the table."
"I saw you last night climbing out of the window."
"So?"
Matthew wore a smug grin and Mercy was starting to get worried, if he said anything to their mother then Mercy knew she was in for a thrashing like never before.
"What do you want then?"
"For a start I'll have your allowance when Papa gives it to you, the rest I will have to think about."
Deep down Mercy wanted to wring his scrawny neck but instead she smiled sweetly and nodded her agreement. It was a Saturday and as usual not much was happening, the day was taken up with housework and when Mercy had finished one job, her mother found her another. She wasn't allowed to hang out with her friends or go outside like her

brother but she never complained and carried out her tasks to the best of her ability, which most of time was never good enough for her mother. All day long she had hoped that somehow Junior would contact her but there was nothing. Again she waited for her family to go to sleep and then escaped via her bedroom window. Making her way to the beach, she saw Junior with his friends but unlike before, this time he didn't beckon her over, in fact he totally ignored her and Mercy realised she'd been used. It broke her heart when she thought of how stupid she was and what she had willingly given to someone who cared little about her. After slowly walking back to the house she made her way to her room and sitting down on the bed, sobbed her heart out. It was the worst feeling she had ever felt but nothing could prepare her for the following morning when the family were in the car and heading off to church. Junior Williams and his friends were standing on the street corner and as the car passed they all began to make lewd gestures and it didn't go unnoticed by Tandy. Turning in her seat she gave her daughter a look that told Mercy she was in real trouble. After the service was over and when Mercy was helping her mother to prepare the lunch, Tandy began to speak.

"If I find out that you've been up to no good with those boys I will beat you until you are black and blue, do you hear me girl!"

Mercy could only nod her head and prayed that her

mother would never find out the truth. She was ashamed at being used by Junior but the thought of her mother finding out worried her even more.

The weeks soon passed and Mercy had left school and was now working at the local department store, a job that her father had secured for her and one that she hated. The days were long, and in the past week the air conditioning had stopped working making the place feel like an oven. Trying to carry out her duties was proving difficult with all the heat and when she fainted one Wednesday afternoon, her mother was called. There was no fuss or compassion, Tandy just drove her daughter home and when they were safely in the house, she turned on the girl.
"Are you pregnant?"
"What Mama?"
"Don't act all innocent with me girl, I saw the way those boys looked at you and what they were doing. Lift up your dress."
"What?"
"I said, lift up your dress!"
Mercy Higgins did as she was told and at the same time saw her mother make the sign of the cross.
"God give me strength! You dirty little whore, you're with child."
Mercy knew exactly what her mother was saying and she began to shake uncontrollably.
"Get to your room, your Papa's going to go mad when he finds out."

Mercy did as she was told and her whole body continued to shake as she sat on the bed waiting. It was a further hour before her Papa came home and when he walked into her room, she didn't expect the reaction she got. Winston had tears in his eyes as he asked if what her mother had said was true. Mercy could only hang her head in shame and nod.
"I thought he loved me Papa and then I found out he just used me."
Winston Higgins sat down beside his baby girl and took her in his arms.
"We'll sort something out, don't you worry girl."
Days passed and with them Mercy's stomach began to swell and swell. Finally she was called into the front room and told to sit down. Matthew had been sent to a friend's house and her father sat in the armchair with his head in his hands. As usual Tandy was taking charge and now stood in front of her daughter with her hands on her hips.
"You have brought nothing but shame upon this family and before anyone finds out what you have done, we are sending you away."
"But where Mama I don't......"
Tandy's hand swiftly moved and slapped Mercy with so much force that the girls head was knocked sideways. Winston flinched but he didn't dare go against his wife by offering any comfort to his daughter.
"Don't you dare even speak to me you little whore. As soon as we can arrange it, you will go to England

and live with your uncle Donavan. My brother isn't a soft touch unlike me, he will make sure this never happens again."

It would be a further four months before all the paperwork and documentation was arranged and in that time Mercy was still expected to work. Each morning her mother would bind her stomach tightly with bandages and threaten her with a beating if she told anyone she was in the family way. The days were long and hot and by the time her plane ticket arrived, Mercy couldn't wait to leave. Her parents drove her to the airport but there wasn't one show of emotion or even a farewell from her mother and when her father's eyes welled up, Mercy could only hang her head in shame. Tandy thrust a scrap of paper into her daughters hand which had Donavan's address scrawled onto it. Winston gripped Mercy's shoulder as he wiped away the tears from his eyes but then shaking his head, he turned and walked away. Tears streamed down Mercy's face and when her mother spoke for the last time, she couldn't believe what she was hearing.

"From now on we no longer have a daughter, do you hear me girl? Don't ever contact us again." Tandy turned her back and walked out of the airport leaving Mercy holding her luggage with floods of tears streaming down her face. She knew it would be futile to run after her parents and beg their forgiveness so she headed towards the departure gate. The feeling of loneliness filled her heart, it was the first time she had ever experienced this emotion but Mercy had a funny feeling that it wouldn't be the last. Her father had pressed a few Jamaican dollars into her hand along with one hundred English pounds that he had managed to convert without his wife's knowledge. To Mercy it was of little comfort and buying a coffee and a chocolate bar, she took a seat and waited for the call to board the aircraft. It was just after six in the morning when the plane took off and it felt as if she'd been awake for ages. The baby was pressing heavily on her bladder and no matter how much she wriggled in her seat, she couldn't get comfortable. When the tears again began to fall she suddenly became angry, angry that they had abandoned her, her own flesh and blood had actually turned their backs on their only daughter. Mercy wiped the tears away with the back of her hand, this was a new beginning, the chance of a fresh start and she wasn't going to allow them to spoil it for her. From now on she was on her own and Mercy swore that no matter what, she would make a good life in London for herself and her unborn baby.

CHAPTER TWO

Ten hours later and just before four pm British time, flight BA126 landed at Heathrow airport. A heavily pregnant Mercy managed to find her way through passport control and then on to baggage reclaim to recover her solitary suitcase. Passing through 'nothing to declare' she expected or at least hoped, to find her uncle Donovan waiting to collect her. Maybe he would hold up a cardboard sign like you saw in the movies but there was no one to greet her. Pulling the scrap of paper from her pocket she studied her mother's writing but she didn't have a clue how to get to the address. A kindly porter noticed the confused look on her face and asked if she needed any help. Mercy felt nothing but pure relief and after taking directions as to which underground she should use, set off on her journey. London was nothing like Bull Bay and even though Mercy had seen photographs they hadn't prepared her at all. The buildings were so tall; there were so many people and the noise, she had never heard anything like it, it sounded as if everyone was talking at once. There and then Mercy Higgins decided that she wasn't going to like this country and the worst thing of all was the weather. Before she had left Jamaica her father had purchased a coat but it was nowhere near thick enough and she could feel the chill as it gradually seeped through to her bones. Trudging on with her suitcase in hand, it

took her over an hour before she finally emerged out of Brixton road tube station. Stopping at a Spar shop to ask for further directions, she was eyed suspiciously by a group of young boys. One in particular shook his head in disgust. Spitting to one side while not once taking his eyes from hers, was his way of showing distaste at her predicament and she clearly heard another's remark.
"If they're old enough to bleed, they're old enough to breed!"
The boys began to laugh and after the shopkeeper had told her which way to go, Mercy almost ran from the premises. She could feel her cheeks flush with embarrassment and the wetness of tears on her face as they began to fall. Right at this moment all she wanted was to be back at home with her family and for none of this to have ever happened but she knew in her heart that it could never be and she just had to get on with her life. Wiping her cheek with the back of her hand, she straightened up her back, took in a deep breath and continued to walk along. It only took her a few minutes more to reach Ferndale road and her Uncle Donovan's home. Staring up at the house, it looked cold and grey and nothing like the brightly coloured houses of Bull Bay. As she opened up the front gate Mercy sighed heavily with relief, at least she had arrived safely. Gently tapping on the door she hoped to be greeted with open arms but when Lady Morgan, Donovan's wife opened up, she looked Mercy up and down

and then turned around and walked back into the hallway leaving the door wide open. Mercy slowly stepped inside and after closing the door, she entered the front room. She spied her uncle seated in a huge leather armchair watching a television that was so large, Mercy couldn't take her eyes off of it. Lady was just standing with her arms crossed and she didn't look happy at having a visitor.
"She's here."
For a second there wasn't a response and then slowly Donovan Morgan eyed the girl but there was no loving embrace, true Mercy hadn't seen the man for a number of years but she still hoped to be welcomed into his home. It was the Jamaican way and his disapproving look hurt her deeply.
"So your mother tells me you have a bastard in that gut of yours, you've done nothing but bring shame on your family. My sister is a sweet, kind woman and you must be some sort of evil child to burden her with so much grief. I said I would take you in but you are going to have to pull your weight around here and do a fair share of the work. As soon as it's born you can get a job and pay for your keep. In the mean time you will help your aunt Lady around the house and you hadn't better slack, because child or no child you will still get a beating."
Mercy didn't dare answer or stick up for herself. She wanted to scream at the man that it wasn't her fault that her mother wasn't a kind woman but

instead she remained silent.

"Go with your aunt and she will show you to your room. Don't come back downstairs; you can stay up there until the morning. Have you eaten?"

Mercy vigorously shook her head; she was so hungry after the flight and hoped that he would now offer her some food.

"Well that's your fault; it will do you good to go hungry and teach you a lesson."

Lady Morgan roughly grabbed Mercy by the arm and pulled her into the hallway.

"The room at the top of the stairs will be yours and you'd better not make any noise. I expect you to be in the kitchen by six in the morning to prepare our breakfast. Well! Go on then what are you waiting for?"

Mercy climbed the flight of stairs and the sight that greeted her behind the closed door made the tears start all over again. There were no curtains at the window and no heating, the mattress was old and stained and there were no sheets or pillows. A solitary sleeping bag had been thrown onto the bed and it was all there was to keep her warm. Climbing inside, she lay down and prayed that tomorrow would be better, because how she was feeling right at this moment, it couldn't get any worse.

      Daylight flooding into the room woke Mercy and she hoped that she hadn't overslept. She didn't have a watch or bedside clock so she really didn't have a clue what time it was. As quietly as she could Mercy opened the door and went into the bathroom. Her aunt and uncles bedroom door was still closed so she reasoned that the time wasn't an issue. Walking into the bathroom she sat on the toilet to quietly pee and after splashing her face with water, headed downstairs. All the ingredients had been left on the side to fry up a hearty breakfast but there was only two of each item and Mercy realised that she wouldn't be allowed to eat the juicy sausages or bacon. Quietly she sighed and then got on with the task in hand. By the time Lady and Donovan entered, the table had been set and she was just placing the plates down. Apart from barking an order to make a pot of tea they didn't speak to her. Mercy stood and watched them devour the food and she slowly rubbed at her grumbling stomach. When they had finished, Donovan got up, kissed his wife on the cheek and then left for work.

"Right! Clear this table and get the pots washed up. When I come back, if you've done a good job and only if, I will find you something to eat."

Mercy smiled and nodded her head in the hope that her aunt would warm towards her but there was nothing. The teapot was still hot, so after glancing at the door to make sure there was no one coming, she poured a cup and added four teaspoons of sugar. It wasn't much but at least it would dull the hunger pains for a while. When her aunt returned she only glanced around the room and nodding her head in approval, passed Mercy two slices of bread and some butter.

"Eat this and don't make a mess. I'm going to the market with my friends. While I'm gone you can clean the house and no short cuts or you'll feel the back of my hand when I get back."

Mercy quickly ate the bread and just as she'd been told, thoroughly cleaned the house. By the time she'd finished she was exhausted, the baby had decided to have a game of football inside her and all that Mercy wanted to do was lay down. Intending to only have a short nap, by the time she woke she could see that the sky was a lot duller and time had flown by. Making it down into the kitchen, she was relieved to see that her aunt still wasn't back but a few minutes later the front door could be heard opening.

"Mercy! Mercy where are you girl. Get in here and help me with these bags."

Carrying the shopping back into the kitchen she was instructed on what was to be prepared for the evening meal. This time as her aunt and uncle sat down, she was allowed a little of the food but she wasn't invited to sit at the table and had to stand and eat.

Three months later and in the middle of the night, Sonny Higgins came kicking and screaming into the world. As her labour escalated, Donovan drove her to the hospital but left her alone outside the accident and emergency department. Apart from the presence of the midwife, Mercy was on her own throughout the birth. There was no one to offer comforting words, in fact the midwife was actually angry with her as Mercy hadn't attended any antenatal classes and screamed out in agony instead of panting throughout the contractions. The pain was horrific and went on for hours but finally when her child emerged it was instant love as soon as she clapped eyes on him. Mercy and Sonny Higgins returned to Ferndale Road two days later and if Mercy had thought that the regime was tough before, nothing prepared her for what was to come. Neither her aunt nor her uncle even bothered to look at the baby and Mercy was told in no uncertain terms that it was now time to find a job. Reluctantly Lady Morgan had agreed to look after the child in the evenings but throughout the day Mercy was expected to carry out her household duties. It didn't take long to find work at the local shop which opened from six in the morning until midnight. Mercy's shift began at six in the evening and she just had time to prepare the meal before she had to leave for work. If she was lucky, a few scraps would be left out for her when she got back but more often than not she would go to bed hungry. Sonny was a contented baby who allowed his mother a chance to sleep but the long days and shifts at the shop were beginning to take their toll on her. It seemed to be a nonstop round of cleaning and washing and as hard as Mercy tried to make time for Sonny, it was so difficult. She hated leaving him each night but had no choice in the matter and when her shift finished, she would run home so that she could spend a few minutes with her son before she went to bed. When Sonny was approaching his first birthday things finally came to a head. Mercy had left work early due to a bad headache and as she placed her key in the lock at just before eleven she heard her aunt screaming at the top of her voice. Quietly creeping in the house, Mercy made her way up to her room and what greeted her made her blood run cold. Lady Morgan was leaning over the side of the cot screaming at Sonny and calling him all the names under the sun.

"What the hell are you doing?"

Lady stood up straight and marched over to where Mercy stood. With her open palm she slapped Mercy as hard as she could on the cheek. The blow was so strong that it knocked Mercy sideways and for a minute she stood in stunned silence.

"Don't you ever speak to me like that again do you hear? Now I want you and your bastard kid out of my house! I never wanted you here in the first place."

Suddenly Mercy found her inner strength and lashed out at her aunt. She didn't know where her anger had come from but a mothers bond with her child was definitely not to be taken for granted. A vicious assault took place as Mercy grabbed Lady's hair, pulled her to the floor and punched her several times in the face. Lady was so taken aback and surprised that she offered little resistance. Mercy was like a wild cat fighting for her baby's life and even if Lady had tried to fight back she would have been no match for this girl. As quickly as her frenzy had begun it stopped and after giving herself a moment to calm down, she picked Sonny from his crib and held him tightly to her. Lady Morgan staggered to her feet and with her face bloodied and her pride dinted, made her way over to the bedroom door.

"I want you and that little bastard out of here now!"
"We will leave first thing in the morning, now get out of this room and don't come back or I'll do you some real damage!"

Out of fear, Lady did as she was told and Mercy heard the woman washing her face in the bathroom. She half expected her uncle to come after her but he didn't and Mercy could only surmise that Lady hadn't told him what had occurred in the bedroom and she would at least wait until Mercy had gone. Lady would later inform her husband, that his niece was possessed by the devil.

The following morning and long before the Morgan's woke, Mercy packed the few belongings that she owned, wrapped Sonny in warm clothes and left the house never to return. She didn't have a pushchair or buggy and had to carry her son in her arms but it wasn't a struggle. Mercy Higgins knew that she could carry the world on her shoulders if she had to, anything as long as she and her son were free. The Social Services Department didn't open until nine am so for over an hour she stood outside the building and cradled her son in her arms. When the doors finally opened she smiled at the security officer and let out a sigh of relief. Being the first client of the day she was seen quickly and when she told her story and explained that she wasn't yet eighteen, things moved fast. Within the hour she was driven to a mother and baby refuge just outside of Brixton. The room she was given was large, warm and very clean. It was explained that this was only temporary until permanent accommodation could be found. Mercy actually spent two weeks at the refuge but she didn't mind, she was safe and there were other single mums to mix with. Finally Anita, her social worker, telephoned with news. A small flat had become available and they would like Mercy to take a look. At four that afternoon Anita collected Mercy and Sonny and drove them over to Lambeth. On Fitzalan Street, a large block of flats that towered five storeys high loomed towards them. There was a lift but Anita explained that most of the time it was out of order but it didn't faze Mercy in the least. The flat on offer was on the third floor and as she entered the small two bedroom apartment, she let out a gasp. Every room had been freshly painted and all the carpets were newly laid. There were

blinds at the windows and when Mercy walked into the small kitchen she couldn't believe her eyes. It was modern and clean and there was even a cooker and fridge.
"So what do you think?"
Mercy began to cry and placing Sonny onto the floor she covered her face with her hands.
"I love it. Thank you, thank you so much."
Anita placed her arm around Mercy and gave her a hug.
"You deserve it sweetheart. Now you will have to stay at the refuge for a few more days until a crisis payment has been organised. Once that's through I will take you to the second hand warehouse to get furniture and any other items you might need."
Mercy was speechless and three days later after Anita had rushed the crisis payment through, Mercy and Sonny were safely installed in their own little flat. It wasn't plush but it was home and the payment had even stretched to a small television which Mercy cherished on the long lonely nights. It took her a few days to stop grinning at her own good fortune, it seemed that finally their luck had changed and the future looked brighter. From now on things could only get better, or so she hoped.

CHAPTER THREE

TWENTY ONE YEARS LATER

"Will you get your lazy arse out of that bed right now!"
Mercy had been calling Sonny for the last twenty minutes and if she didn't leave soon she would be late for work. Her shift at the local supermarket started at eight thirty and she wouldn't finish until two. After returning home for a few hours she would then be off to her second job of the day cleaning the council offices on Norwood High Street. Her working day would finally come to an end after working from seven until ten at Barry's fish bar on Lambeth Walk. Mercy worked two of the jobs for six days a week and the long hours were starting to make her feel drained. Every day she was feeling more and more physically drained and the added stress of having to constantly be on her son's case, had her feeling that she couldn't carry on much longer. It was probably one of the reasons why she got so angry when Sonny laid in bed all day.
"Right! This is the last time; if I have to come and get you out boy, you'll be sorry. Today of all days you had better not be late."
There was no reply and raising her hands in a show of submission, Mercy grabbed her bag and coat and

left the flat. Old Mrs Bateman who lived next door was just picking up her milk as Mercy closed the front door and she smiled at the woman as she spoke.

"I tell you Gladys, that boy of mine could test the patience of a saint and no mistake."

Mrs Bateman laughed but Mercy could see the hurt in the woman's eyes. Gladys had been a good neighbour and for years Sonny had stayed at her home after school so that his mother could go to work. Mercy paid Mrs Bateman a few pounds a week but in all honesty Gladys would have looked after Sonny for free. When he reached fifteen things suddenly changed, Sonny refused to go to Gladys's and instead hung out in the park with the other youths from the area. When she questioned him, all he would say was that the old woman stunk like the old books Mercy picked up on the second hand stalls. There was no persuading him otherwise and she knew full well that the boys were up to no good but there was nothing she could do about it. The wages from her three jobs only just paid the bills and gave them food. Clothes came from jumble sales or charity shops, something she knew her boy hated but she had little choice in the matter. As the years passed Mercy had hoped that things would get easier but with the constant price increases on food and heating, if anything it was now even more of a struggle. When Sonny Higgins came home wearing the latest designer trainers and a sports jacket that it would have taken his mother a month to pay for, Mercy knew that he was on a slippery slope and suspected he was doing something illegal. There was no other explanation for him being able to afford the things he was bringing home and she was worried sick. He no longer went to church with her on a Sunday and his language at home was foul. Mercy had erased every part of Junior Williams from her life but the one thing she couldn't erase was the fact that Sonny had his father's blood running through his veins and it was bad blood. Twice Mercy had been called home from work because Sonny had been arrested, true they were only minor offences but even then she knew he was destined for a life behind bars.

"Is it today Mercy?"

"Yes Gladys and my stomach is in knots already."

"You going down to the court?"

"No, there aint no point and to be quite honest I can't afford to lose any more money. That sounds horrible doesn't it but it's the truth and besides, I really don't think he wants me there."

Gladys Bateman picked up her second pint of milk and pulled her dressing gown together.

"Sweetheart, no one could have been a better mother than you and don't you ever forget it. I know in my heart that deep down Sonny's not a bad boy, just a bit misguided. I'll be praying for him darling and I'm sure he'll be fine."

Mercy smiled and nodded her head as she walked

away but she wasn't so convinced. Back inside the flat Sonny at last decided to get out of bed. Today he was nervous and it wasn't a feeling he liked. Hanging around the flats with his mates Sonny was the big man but today he would stand in front of a judge feeling small. His mother nagging him so early in the morning hadn't helped and now as he tried to eat a bowl of cereal he started to feel sick. It wasn't supposed to have turned out like this and if that stupid old fool Harold Wells had gone down the pub like he normally did, then none of this would have happened. Sonny had been cajoled by his mate Pingo to break into the old man's flat, saying he was an easy touch. Unbeknown to the pair as they were rifling through the drawers of the wall unit, Harold had woken up. As the old man confronted them he began to shout and Pingo lashed out. There was a heavy thud as Harold fell to the floor and hit his head but he had already recognised Sonny Higgins and within twenty four hours Sonny had been arrested. His solicitor managed to get him bail but the temporary reprieve was about as good as it would get. Advising his client to plead guilty, Adam Moore told Sonny that he was definitely looking at a prison stretch and with his past record, it could be anything from six to eighteen months. Well today was the day and he might as well get on with it, so dressing in the clothes his mother had laid out for him, Sonny set off for the central criminal court building in the heart of the city. Taking his solicitors advice, Sonny pleaded guilty in the hope of receiving a lighter sentence but that wasn't to be. His reluctance to name Pingo hadn't gone down well with the police and they had produced a damning report at the hearing. When all sides had put their arguments over and when old Harold Wells had given his victim statement, the judge retired to ponder on the sentence. When he returned to the court thirty minutes later, his face was stony as he began to speak.

"Sonny Higgins you have carried out the most heinous of crimes against an old man who wasn't able to defend himself. I commend you on your guilty plea but the fact that you refused to assist the police with their investigations wipes out any leniency I could bestow on you. I feel I have no other option than to make an example of you and hope that it will be a warning to others. You will go to prison for three years and I hope in that time you will reflect upon what you have done and change your ways. Take him down."

Suddenly there was mayhem in the room, all of Sonny's friends from the flats, including Pingo, began to jeer and shout obscenities at the judge. Looking at them, Sonny Higgins grinned and shrugged his shoulders like he wasn't fazed in the least. The Judge slammed down his gavel and asked for order but the lads in the public gallery totally ignored him. Pingo began to kick out at the carved wooden panelling in front of his feet and soon the rest joined in. Suddenly five policemen came rushing in to take control as Sonny was taken down into the holding cells. Upstairs in the courtroom he had shown bravado in front of his mates but inside he now felt alone and dejected. His hands were shaking and as he was led out to the waiting prison van, Sonny looked up to the sky and wondered how long it would be before he felt the sun on his face again. The van was separated into small units each housing a single prisoner and as he was pushed inside he instantly felt claustrophobic. There was no point in shouting out or complaining, so taking a seat he closed his eyes for the entire journey and tried to think of better times but it was hard as only thoughts of how stupid he had been invaded his mind. It would have been a lot easier if he had just given them his friends name but Sonny couldn't even contemplate grassing someone up, so now he had to take his punishment like a man, the only problem was he didn't feel anything like a man. Prisoners were all calling out to each other and from what they were saying; Sonny guessed it wasn't their first experience of being incarcerated. The windows in the van were high up and he couldn't see when the vehicle passed through the iconic arch of Wormwood Scrubs Prison. The rear yard was grey and gloomy and as he stepped from the van, he stared up at the large brick building wondering what was about to happen. Being led into the reception area with the three other new arrivals, Sonny was handed his prison issue training bottoms, sweatshirt and shoes and told to get changed. When all of his personal possession had been logged, he was at last escorted to a single cell. It was common practice on the first night so that he could be monitored. If he was deemed to be no threat to himself or any other inmates he would be moved the following morning to a shared cell. The cell was cold and as he lay down on the bed, he could feel every lump and bump in the mattress as they poked into his back. The night was long and the incessant noise didn't seem to ever stop but Sonny finally managed to drift off to sleep although it turned out to be a fitful night of unrest.

At six in the morning he was woken by the door being opened, the constant sound of clanging keys being placed into locks seemed to go on forever and hauling himself up he got washed and cleaned his teeth. As he was taken to the dining hall he instantly heard the jeering from the old timers; it was always the same when anyone new arrived especially if it was your first time. Sonny ignored them and picking up a sectioned tray, stood in line to collect his breakfast. The food on offer looked disgusting but he knew he had no choice but to eat as much of it as he could. A prisoner dressed in chefs whites approached from behind the counter and threw a piece of toast onto Sonny's tray. He then dolloped a ladle of porridge into one of the food compartments but before Sonny had a chance to walk away, the server hawked up a mouthful of phlegm and gobbed it into Sonny's porridge. Staring at the man for a second, Sonny Higgins didn't utter a word and then made his way over to one of the vacant tables. After eating his toast and having a quick swig of tea he looked around at his surroundings and sighed deeply As he hadn't shown any suicidal tendencies and had been deemed fit to mix with the other prisoners, behind the scenes plans were being put into place to move him onto the wing.

Later that morning Sonny was escorted to his new cell. The room was slightly larger than before but whereas he had previously had the space to himself, this time he would be forced to share with two others. There was a set of bunks on one wall and a single bed on the other. At the end of the room was a stainless steel sink and toilet and Sonny could only shake his head in disgust at the lack of privacy. A large man with facial tattoos stood up from the bed and introduced himself as Damo. Lying on the bottom bunk was Chris who only nodded his head. The cell door closed and Damo explained that was it for the day, if they were lucky they might get a few minutes exercise later but it was very sporadic and in all honesty highly unlikely.

"The rest of our meals will be brought round on trays so I suggest you get comfy mate because the

days in here can seem really long."
Sonny climbed up onto the top bunk and the three men chatted on and off for the rest of the morning as they got to know each other. Chris would add a few sentences here and there but for the most part he remained silent and let Damo do all the talking.
"So what's it really like in here Damo?"
"Like a living hell. Anyone who plays up more than a couple of times are treated to the liquid cosh and believe you me, they soon quieten down after that."
"So what's that then?"
Damo was now in his element, he loved teaching people. He saw himself as having a superior intellect and would show off at every opportunity. Out on the wing he was comically called 'The Knowledge'. He had always thought the name was a reflection of his intelligence but as with most nick names, it was nothing of the sort and was more of a piss take than a term of endearment.
"Well, they normally use amytriptylene or perphenazine although there are several other drugs available."
Chris suddenly butted into the conversation and Sonny was a little shocked as the man had hardly spoken a word until now.
"For fucks sake Damo get on with it will you, the boy don't want a fucking lesson in pharmacy."
Sonny giggled but it didn't make Damo smile, in fact he was quite put out at being interrupted.
"As I was saying, oh fuck it Chris you've put me

right off my line of thought."
"Thank fuck for that."
Again Sonny started to laugh but was stopped when Damo held up his palm.
"Do you want me to explain or not?"
Sonny tried to keep a straight face as he nodded his head.
"They are all psychiatric drugs which in here are inelegantly termed 'the liquid cosh'. Screws manhandle a hostile prisoner down and forcibly inject them. You aint never seen anything like it, a strong hard man is reduced to a docile dribbling fool and it aint a pretty sight. A lot of them hit the hooch and go crazy."
"You mean there's alcohol in here?"
"Of course there is, we often ferment our oranges, don't we Chris?"
Chris didn't reply which was nothing out of the ordinary and it seemed that Damo didn't really expect him to.
"Now I'm going to try and have a kip so if you two can keep it down it would be highly fucking appreciated."
Chris and Sonny looked at each other and grinned but neither said a word. The hours passed and Sonny was constantly glancing towards the door but Damo had been correct, the door didn't open again that day and the time really did drag. There was nothing to do but think, Sonny had no reading material and even trying to sleep was impossible as

there was so much noise on the wing. Finally at ten o'clock the lights went out but as Sonny lay in the dark with just the glow of the moon shining in through the window, it seemed like the loneliest place in the world and it made him think of his mother and all that he had put her through. Feeling the tears begin to flow, he turned over to face the wall so that Damo and Chris didn't know he was upset and couldn't see him crying. He must have eventually drifted off to sleep because he woke to hear a strange moaning sound. Turning over in the bunk he looked down to see Chris on his knees in front of Damo. Sonny couldn't believe his eyes, the man was actually giving his cell mate a blow job and the moaning sound was Damo's grunts of ecstasy. Sonny turned his back again and placed his fingers into his ears as he tried to block out the vision and noise. The sight had made him feel physically sick and come hell or high water he would make sure that tomorrow he got moved.

Waking to the sound of doors banging, Sonny instantly sat up on his bunk. For a moment he had forgotten where he was and the realisation made him lay back down again with a thud. Suddenly he remembered what he had seen last night and he looked at his cell mates with distaste and distrust. When the cell door opened he was off of the bunk in a second. Still fully clothed from last night, he went over to the sink and quickly cleaned his teeth. Damo was now awake and still in the

single bed, Chris was lying on the bottom bunk but both were still unaware that their antics had been observed last night. Damo stretched out his arms, yawned and then farted loudly as he spoke.
"Morning Sonny boy!"
Sonny didn't reply and silently the other men took it in turns to wash and use the toilet. Sonny Higgins couldn't bring himself to talk to Damo or Chris and only nodded his head as he walked out onto the landing. The dining room was as noisy as yesterday but thankfully he didn't receive the same reception on his second day. Standing in line to get his breakfast, Sonny came face to face with the same server from yesterday. Holding his tray up, he leaned in close as he spoke so that he was near enough to the man without being overheard.
"Gob in my food again cunt and I will cut you open like a fucking stuck pig."
The server looked shocked, he also didn't want to take any chances, at least not until he knew who he was dealing with. The man gently scooped the porridge onto Sonny's tray and nodded his head. As Sonny walked towards an empty table he now knew that trouble would soon be following him and his over show of being a hard man had to be upheld. Eating his food as quickly as he could and after clearing away his tray, he went over to the guard on breakfast duty and asked to see the wing Governor. Luckily for Sonny, Graham Stevens was one of the most lenient officers in the prison.

"What's the problem?"
Sonny leaned in close.
"My problem is that I'm black and you calling me a fucking nigger don't sit well. Now if I don't get to see the governor, I'm going to shout that accusation out loud and clear and you'll have every black fucker in here on your case, get it screw!"
"Now you listen to me sunshine or whatever your fucking name is. I don't take threats lightly so seeing as its your first time inside, I'm going to forget what you just said but if you ever try that again your feet won't touch the fucking ground. Now as for your request to see the governor, I'll see what I can do."
Sonny could live with that and turning his back, made his way onto the landing and his cell. To his relief Damo and Chris were still at breakfast, so climbing onto his bunk he laid down and waited to be summoned to the Governor's office. When his cell mates returned the atmosphere was strained. Damo didn't know exactly what the problem was but he had a good idea. Chris Mann was a homosexual, whereas Damo wasn't but time dragged in this place and if someone offered him some comfort, Damo wasn't about to refuse it. He was concerned that it had upset the kid but it was dog eat dog in this place and for his own sake, Damo hoped that Sonny would quickly learn that fact and accept it. He didn't want any trouble, so picking up a magazine he gave Sonny a wide

berth, well as wide as he could in the ten by eight space.

Mercy had received a courtesy telephone call from Sonny's solicitor and when he told her the sentence she flopped down onto the chair and began to cry. She just couldn't work out how it had all come to this. Mercy thought back to the day when she had first set foot on English soil and all the dreams she'd had. Life had turned out the complete opposite and everyday it seemed to get harder and harder. Pulling on her coat she went outside and tapped on Gladys Batemans front door. When her elderly neighbour finally opened up, Mercy began to sob.

"Oh love, come on in and tell old Gladys all about it."

Placing the kettle onto boil the two women sat at the small kitchen table and Mercy told her neighbour that Sonny had received three years. Gladys stood up to make the tea and removing a small bottle of rum from the overhead cupboard, liberally laced each cup.

"I know it sounds a long time sweetheart but if he behaves himself he could be out in less than half that time."

"I know but what worries me is the fact that he won't behave himself, he could come out even worse than he was before he went in."

"Now you don't know that Mercy. What's the point in fretting over something that hasn't even

happened yet? You have to support him and be here waiting when he gets home, now drink up your tea before it gets cold."
Mercy took a sip and as the rum fumes entered her nostrils she began to cough. The liquid warmed her and although she was normally teetotal, she liked the feeling the tea was giving her. The women talked for over an hour and by the time Mercy put her key into the front door lock she was starting to feel a bit better. Gladys was right; there was no point in worrying, well at least not at the moment.

CHAPTER FOUR

Graham Stevens came through for Sonny and less than an hour later the cell door opened and he was escorted down the stairs to the ground floor. The Governor, Gordon Hargreaves, was a hard but fair man. He also knew when someone was trying to pull the wool over his eyes and he was wary of every prisoner that asked to see him. That said, Sonny Higgins was new in and he deserved to be seen as it could be something important.
Experience told him it wouldn't be but none the less he would grant the young man's request to see him. Officer Stevens tapped on the door and they both entered when told.
"Come in Higgins."
As the door to the Governor's office closed behind him, Sonny walked over to the desk and without being asked sat down. Suddenly a voice from the back of the room shouted out.
"On your feet Higgins, now!"
Sonny did as he was told but felt uneasy with two prison officers standing behind him, who were obviously there to restrain him if he kicked off. Last night when he'd been talking to Damo and Chris they had told him all about the liquid cosh treatment that was a regular practice in the Scrubs for anyone that didn't toe the line. Sonny had visions of being injected from behind at any

moment, it wasn't about to happen but as with all twenty one year olds, his imagination was running wild.
"What is so important that you need to see me Higgins?"
"It's my cell."
Suddenly he received a prod in the back from Steve Monroe, one of the officers standing behind him.
"It's about my cell Sir!"
"Sorry, it's about my cell Sir. There are three of us in there and the other two are faggots. Don't get me wrong, I aint homophobic or anything. Look what I'm trying to say is that I don't want to have to watch a bloke sucking off his cell mate in the middle of the night."
The Governor sat behind his desk and for a moment didn't speak as he studied a folder that was on his desk. Gordon Hargreaves rubbed his chin for a second while he gave the situation some thought. True it wasn't a very nice image but this was prison and the young man needed to toughen up. Looking directly into Sonny's eyes Gordon began to speak.
"Higgins, I'm afraid that it's all part and parcel of prison life and you're just going to have to get used to it. I know it's disgusting but we are all jammed in like sardines so I'm afraid there's nothing I can do. That said, I can see where you are coming from and I understand that as this is your first time in one of her Majesty's Prisons it can be an ordeal but it is exactly that, a Prison. I cannot just pamper to

everyone's needs because something or someone has upset them. The scenario you describe, much to my distaste, is a common event here and you will have to learn to live with it. As soon as another space becomes available I will consider moving you but until then, I'm afraid you will just have to accept things the way they are."

"But Sir I....."

"Out Higgins, the Governor has said all he's going to."

"Then I can't be held responsible for my actions Sir!"

It was no more than Governor Hargreaves expected, they were all trying to be hard men instead of the silly little boys that they actually were.

"Are you threatening me Higgins?"

For a few seconds Sonny just stared at Gordon Hargreaves but he was quickly brought back to reality when Steve Monroe roughly grabbed him by the arm and pulled him towards the door.

"I said out Higgins, now!"

The other officer immediately stepped forward and taking an arm each, they frog marched Sonny back to his cell. This new inmate was starting to get a lot of people's backs up and if he wasn't careful there was going to be trouble. Sonny wasn't stupid and he knew he had talked the talk but it was now time to walk the walk, that or they'd make mince meat out of him. As the officers opened the cell door Sonny placed his arms and legs out so that they couldn't push him inside. It took several seconds of

wrestling before he was overpowered and thrown down onto the floor in a heap. When the door slammed shut, Damo who was sitting on his bed, could only shake his head but he did jump up and lift Sonny onto his feet.
"You alright mate?"
Sonny shrugged away the help but still nodded his head; he felt like a fool and was embarrassed.
"Let me give you a bit of advice kid, you're on a hiding to nothing if you think you can beat the system. If you kick off on a regular basis, you're going to end up getting the cosh and believe you me pal it aint nice."
Sonny climbed up onto his bunk and Damo proceeded to tell the story of his first time in prison many years ago. The regime was harder back then and he suffered terribly until he learnt to toe the line.
"The thing is kid, like I said you won't win, slowly but surely they'll grind you down. God knows I was the same and if you take my advice, you're better off being a model prisoner, then you won't bring any trouble on yourself. If you carry on the way you have been and piss the screws off, they'll take it out on all of us. They know full well that if everybody suffers, then someone will finally get pissed off and sort you out good and proper and I should know it happened to me years ago."
"Yeah well it would wouldn't it; you're nothing but a queer cunt! And just where the fuck do you get

off giving me a lecture?"
"I'll tell you something boy, if you don't change that attitude, you might not get out of here period."
"Is that a threat?"
"No, it's a fact. I was about to educate you and tell you a story about a young kid similar to you but to be honest I don't think you're ready. You'll just have to make the same mistakes as every other cocky little cunt that comes in here thinking he knows the fucking lot."
Damo had just been trying to help the young man by giving him some friendly advice but Sonny didn't see it that way and after a few seconds he had blocked the man's words from his mind. Damo might as well have been talking to himself for all the good that it did. So far Sonny's impression of prison wasn't as bad as he'd expected it to be but the screws were complete and utter bastards and he was quickly becoming fed up with them. He was in no doubt that there would be trouble on the horizon but he was going to toughen up and face it like a man. If the system wanted to play with him, then as far as Sonny Higgins was concerned let the games begin. By early evening you could cut the atmosphere with a knife and Damo had just about had enough. Standing up his face was level with Sonny's who was still lying on his bunk.
"I think the three of us need to have a chat if we're going to stay roommates."
For a moment Sonny wanted to laugh when Damo

said the three of us as Chris hardly ever uttered a word.
"What about?"
"Don't treat me like a cunt; you know exactly what I'm talking about. I know you don't like what goes on in here but it's not like we're asking you to join in now is it? Fuck me mate, you really are going to get some serious shit if you keep judging people."
Sonny didn't reply and just rolled over in his bunk, a gesture which told Damo to give up as he was wasting his time.
Earlier that day and unbeknown to Sonny, the wing Governor had made a rare visit to a cell, the cell of one Frankie West. When his door opened and as the Governor walked in, Frankie who was sitting at a small wooden table looked up from his papers. As a model prisoner he was one of the few inmates allowed a single cell.
"Afternoon Frankie."
"Governor."
Gordon took a seat on the bed in a way that told Frankie West this was a relaxed visit.
"So how is the studying going?"
"Pretty good thanks, I've got one more exam to take before my degree."
"And what do you hope to do with it once you are released?"
"I aint really thought about it Governor, it was never about that. I just like to keep my mind occupied and this is as good a way as any, I still

struggle with those computers a bit though."
Governor Hargreaves laughed, he knew exactly what Frankie meant and he often wished that they could all just go back to good old fashioned pens and paper.
"Now I suppose you're wondering why I'm here?"
"Well it has to be something important for you to make a house call."
Governor Hargreaves gave a wry smile which told Frankie that the man was about to say something he wouldn't like.
"So what can I do for you Sir?"
Gordon shifted uneasily in his seat. He could just order the move and the man would have no say in the matter but he never liked to rock the boat if it was avoidable and in any case he wanted Frankie West on side and not as an enemy or all of this would serve no purpose.
"There's a young inmate who came in a couple of days ago, it's his first time inside. He's full of attitude and bravado but it's nothing either of us haven't seen before. He's celled up with; well in the boys own words, a couple of faggots. He came asking for a move but as you know only too well, we're chock-a-block at the moment. I know it's a lot to ask but I wondered if you might take him under your wing so to speak and show him the ropes. I think if he's left to his own devices he's going to bring a lot of trouble upon himself and if there is just the chance of saving the lad from a life of going

from one prison stint to another, it's got to be worth a try."

Frankie West thought for a moment before he spoke, he liked his own space and peace and if he had a youngster bunked up with him, then that would all go out of the window. On the other hand the kid might turn out to be fine and cause him no aggravation whatsoever.

"I aint totally against it Governor but if there's any chance, I'd like to monitor him for a couple of days without him knowing."

Gordon Hargreaves nodded his approval.

"That's a good idea. The wing has been quiet of late so I think a little reward is due. I'll have one of my officers make sure he's out tomorrow evening when I'm going to grant some association time. By the way his names Higgins, Sonny Higgins."

The Governor stood up and after a grin and a nod that silently said 'thank you', he left.

The next day, Frankie West tried to knuckle down regarding his studies but no matter how hard he tried thoughts of this Sonny character kept invading his mind. Frankie had two years and six months left to serve of a fifteen year life sentence. The judge had set a term of fifteen years in nineteen ninety nine and he'd spent the first twelve at Belmarsh as a category A prisoner. As his behaviour had been exemplary and he was no longer regarded as a danger, he'd then been moved to the Scrubs to see out his sentence. Frankie West had murdered a man but in reality there had been four deaths, although he was only ever charged and convicted of one. If his true crimes ever came to light and were proven, he would end up spending the rest of his life in this godforsaken place. Now the days were being ticked off but in all honesty he didn't know what he would do when he was released, he didn't even know if he would be able to survive on the outside as the world had moved on and he felt as though he'd been left behind. Well within his rights, Frankie could have applied for parole years ago and in all probability it would have been granted but Frankie was content to do his time and take his punishment for the loss of the lives that he'd taken. He was only thirty seven years old but mentally he felt much older. Some of the things he had been witness to while incarcerated were truly horrific and would stay in his mind forever. That said he still felt safe in here and the Scrubs was far better than Belmarsh. In that particular establishment there were many men who would remain incarcerated for their entire lives, men who had nothing left to lose and who would happily kill or maim another human being just for looking at them with the wrong expression on their face. Frankie had always kept his eyes fixed on the ground and never looked anyone directly in the eyes, he had seen too many lose an eye or an ear for the slightest reason. Paedophiles would be beaten within an inch of their lives if other prisoners got the opportunity and that opportunity would often be laid on a plate for them by the Screws. Frankie had always sworn that he would never become institutionalised but that's exactly what he was. It had happened slowly at first, so slowly that he hadn't even noticed and now he was content to have everything provided for him and to do as he was told. He could remember a time when he was a free spirit and would take on the world if necessary but now all he wanted was to be left in peace but there was little chance of that in a place like this. All in all prison was a dangerous, volatile environment and Frankie knew that he had to at least try and help the young lad. Deciding to put all thoughts of the boy to the back of his mind and get back to his studies, he glanced at his bedside table. The clock said two pm and he reasoned he had a good couple of hours before tea was served and the cells were unlocked for association. Then there wouldn't be time for studying but in a strange way he was looking forward to his new challenge.

CHAPTER FIVE

The cell door was opened at five thirty exactly and as Frankie West emerged he realised that he was the first to be let out. A chair had been placed outside his cell which directly faced the pool table. Taking a seat he opened up his newspaper just as the room began to fill up with all manner of prisoners. Muslims gathered in one corner to study and chat about religion, young lads congregated around the pool table and a few of the old timers had started to play cards at one of the tables that had been set up. Frankie didn't have a clue what this Sonny looked like but the Governor had informed him that he was sharing with an inmate by the name of Damo who was heavily tattooed on his face. A couple of minutes later and Sonny, Damo and Chris were led in and Sonny Higgins made a beeline for the pool table. A game of doubles was already in motion between two youths from Stepney and a couple of older men from Liverpool. Sonny thought that if he struck up a conversation with the coloured lads they might be friendly but nothing could be further from the truth. When one of the scouser's, Big Ray Magann, potted his opponent's ball they began to argue.
"You cheating cunt!"
"What the fuck are you on about nigger, don't you know how to play the game?"

Sonny butted in, he hoped to settle the matter and possibly get a game.
"Excuse me mate but I was watching and it was definitely a foul."
Suddenly Big Ray turned on Sonny.
"Who the fuck are you talking to, new boy! If I wanted your opinion I'd have fucking asked for it so keep your black nose out of it."
All the while Frankie was listening and watching from over the top of his newspaper. Damo and Chris, who were leaning against the wall, knew there was trouble brewing but neither offered their cell mate any help. Big Ray turned back to the table just as Delroy Grant picked up a ball and placed it into one of the pockets.
"You fucking cheat!"
"Who the fuck are you calling a cheat, honkey!"
Suddenly a pool cue whizzed through the air as the young man swung it with all his might, hitting Ray on the side of the head. His eyes were wide and staring like saucers and Frankie West knew that it was all about to kick off big time. Ray Magann bent down and with all the strength he could muster, grabbed the underside of the pool table and flipped the whole thing over. Delroy Grant dived over the upturned table and punches were flying out from all directions. Before he realised what he was doing, Frankie was out of his seat and had grabbed Sonny by the scruff of the neck. Almost lifting him off of his feet, he dragged the young man

backwards and into his cell.

"What the fuck!"

Frankie slammed the door closed and held his finger up to his lips. In seconds the association area was flooded with Officers who were all carrying batons. It was nothing short of a mini riot as people who had nothing to do with the skirmish now joined in the fight. The men were soon overpowered and a lot of the prisoners were physically thrown into their cells. When the wing governor walked into the area, the place was put on a complete lockdown and Sonny found himself stuck in Frankie's cell. It would all get sorted out when they did a head count but until then he had no choice but to sit it out and wait. Even before it had a chance to get started, the two day monitoring that Frankie had asked for had come to an abrupt halt and everything was happening a lot faster than he had hoped. Shrugging his shoulders, he took a seat at the table and as he'd always been a great believer in everything happens for a reason, decided to just go with the flow.

"What'd you do that for?"

"What?"

"Drag me in here; are you some kind of nonce? If you are then I'm telling you, you aint going to get a go at me without a fucking fight Mister."

Frankie began to laugh; it did nothing to sooth the tension and he could see the anger start to build in Sonny's eyes.

"Look, I was just doing you a favour. All those fucking idiots out there will now get time added to their sentences, is that what you want?"
"Well no but..."
"Just sit down and shut your trap until they come for you alright?"
Doing as he was told, Sonny took a seat on the end of the bed. Frankie continued to sit at his table and began to read an exercise book. He wasn't concentrating but only waiting for Sonny to start up a conversation. It took longer than he thought it would but finally Sonny Higgins asked a question.
"So what's that you've got there?"
"Study books."
"Study books! Well what a fucking waste of time they are."
The conversation was interrupted when the cell door was unlocked and two officers walked in.
"Higgins you're bunking down in here from now on. Get your arse off that bed so we can replace it with a bunk."
Sonny didn't argue, he was more than pleased but the same couldn't be said for Frankie. He had hoped to get to know the boy a bit first but it had all been taken out of his hands and he now had a cell mate whether he liked it or not. Sonny climbed up onto the top bunk without asking which one he should use but Frankie didn't comment as he wanted the bottom one anyway. A couple of times throughout the evening he tried to engage in a

conversation but Sonny wasn't very responsive, so in the end he gave up trying.

When the door was at last unlocked at seven am the next morning, Sonny was the first out and headed straight for the dining hall. Big Ray was in solitary so Sonny knew that he was safe for the moment. Collecting his breakfast without any hassle, he made his way over to Damo and Chris.
"Mind if I sit with you two?"
Damo just shrugged his shoulders, this show of friendship came too late and in any case he suspected Sonny wanted something.
"So how's it going with your new cell mate?"
"Funny you should ask that, I was about to ask you if you knew anything about him, why he's in here?"
"That's strange because I had an inkling you were going to ask me that."
Sonny furrowed his brow which told Damo that the boy hadn't got a clue what he was on about. Damo didn't answer the question for a few seconds and he knew it was winding the lad up; finally when Sonny was fit to burst Damo at last spoke.
"Murder."
"Fucking murder!"
"Yeah and even though he only got done for one rumour has it that there was a lot more bodies."
The colour visibly drained from Sonny Higgins face. Now he was in a real dilemma, he'd asked to be moved but now wanted to be back with the two faggots. This new bloke could be a psycho and slit

Sonny's throat while he slept. Sonny's eyes were wide and he rubbed at his brow in an agitated manner. Damo wanted to laugh as he thought about the saying 'be careful what you wish for'.
"Cheer up mate; he's on his last bit of a very long sentence so I can't see him risking that by topping you, then again....."
Sonny knew that he was being wound up or at least he hoped he was and standing up he gave Damo a contemptuous look and stormed off back to his cell.
Frankie had decided to skip breakfast and was already deep into his studies when his new roommate walked in. Glancing up he could see the look of worry on Sonny's face and placing his pen onto the table, turned to face the troubled teenager. Rather than ask the young man what was wrong, he asked about Sonny's life.
"So tell me, what do your parents think about you coming to Jail?"
Sonny climbed up onto his bunk and was about to tell Frankie to mind his own business when he had a change of heart. If he talked to the man and they built up some kind of trust, then at least he would feel a bit safer.
"There's only me and my Mum. My old man still lives in Jamaica but I aint never met him."
"So why did you get into trouble or are you one of the innocent miscarriages of justice like the rest of the idiots in here?"
Sonny felt as if the man was mocking him and he

didn't like it.

"What like you? You aint no different."

"No sunshine that's where you're wrong. I'm the only guilty man in here, well at least as far as the others are concerned. I deserved what I got, it wasn't a mistake and I'd do it again. What about you?"

"Not if I have to come back to this shit hole but there aint much choice for young black kids in Lambeth. The pigs are always on your back and no one wants to employ us, as far as they are concerned we're all muggers and gang members."

"Bullshit!"

"What?"

"Look kid, life is what you make it no matter where you come from and if you keep using excuses like that, then you'll never amount to anything. I'm almost at the end of a degree and if it wasn't for my past, would probably be able to get a good job that pays well. You're still young enough to achieve the same but without a murder conviction following you around. Keep hanging out with the gangs and you'll end up back in here time and time again. On D wing there's actually three generations of the same family, now to me that's fucking nuts but they never seem to learn. There is no free ride kid and if you want to get anywhere in life you have to make it happen yourself."

"It's so easy for you to spout all that crap but you aint black."

"Maybe I aint, well not totally anyway but I think there may be a little of the old jungle blood in my veins. Putting that aside, I didn't have a good start. My old lady was a Brass and a drug addict; she couldn't look after herself let alone me. I get the opinion from how you spoke of her, that your old lady is a good woman."

Sonny thought for a moment and yes his mother was good and now he wished he'd taken her advice and lived a clean life, God he missed her and her nagging ways. Sonny laughed to himself when he thought of all the times she'd dragged him to the church on a Sunday morning, now he would gladly go if it meant getting out of this place.

"So didn't your mum want you Mister?"

"The name is Frankie, Frankie West and in answer to your question, I don't know much about her, only what I've been told. I gather that she loved me to bits one minute but the next would have sold me to the first paedo on the street when she was desperate for a fix. Anyway, she died when I was two but by then she'd already handed me over to her boss."

Sonny looked shocked and imagined the man's next words would be how he was sexually abused. Frankie could read the boy like a book and laughed out loud.

"Not like that you Muppet. Harry West ran a club, a pub and god knows what else over on Chalk Farm Road in Camden. My mother, by that I mean my biological mother, did a bit of exotic dancing so to speak in his club. After a while the dancing got less and less as the need for drugs took over. Anyway, when he saw she wasn't coping he offered to take me in. Harry West the notorious villain became my father and life saver."

"Villain?"

"Well yeah, he was a villain alright, I mean you don't run joints in north London without knowing a few faces and mixing in dodgy circles but on the whole he was a decent bloke, at least he was to begin with."

"So what's he think of you doing time."

"Not a lot, he's dead and the family cut all ties with me after I was sentenced. It's no good crying over spilt milk, I deserved it. Enough about me tell me what you did."

Sonny described the robbery in detail and what had happened at old Harold's flat. He kept referring to Pingo as his mate and Frankie couldn't for the life of him understand why.

"So you were there but it was this Pingo kid that knocked the old man over?"

Sonny nodded.

"So why are you still calling him a mate. The cunt let you take the flack and didn't have the fucking balls to stand up and be counted. If someone ever did that to me, they wouldn't rob anyone else I can tell you. What are you going to do when you get out, hook up with that toe rag and end up back in here again, do some more bird for him no doubt?"

Frankie's words suddenly made Sonny think, all this time he had kept his mouth shut and where had it got him. Frankie was right, Pingo was a cunt and Sonny didn't know why he hadn't seen it before, he always thought he was being a good friend but all the time the others must have been having a right laugh at his expense.
"You know something, when I get out of here I think I'm going to move away from London."
"Oh yeah and where will you go, Essex?"
Frankie began to laugh and it instantly wound Sonny up.
"No, I'd like it if me and my mum went to Jamaica. She's still got family there but she aint seen them since before I was born. She used to tell me all about Bull Bay and a little shack that was down on the beach. A long while ago it was a bar and I think I'd like to work somewhere like that, you know, next to the sea with the sun shining all day."
"Well good on you, getting a stretch has at least achieved something. Now shut the fuck up and let me get back to my books."
"Aint you going to tell me about what you did? I mean it's only fair, I told you my story."
"Maybe tomorrow, anyway if I tell you it all it's going to take hours and I really need to get on with this. It wouldn't do you any harm to look at a book, that's if you can read?"
"Of course I can fucking read you cheeky fucker!"
Frankie West smiled and at the same time picked up

a book from the pile in front of him and threw it up to Sonny. He didn't look at it straight away but an hour later when Frankie lifted up his arms to stretch, he glanced up at the boy and saw that Sonny was already several chapters in. Maybe he could do something to help the kid and even if he couldn't he had to at least try. Wasting his own life was one thing and even though he'd met hundreds of kids like Sonny over the years, if he could stop it happening again then maybe prison, in some strange way, would have been worthwhile.

By early afternoon the next day and just before they were supposed to have tea, all hell broke loose in the centre of the wing. It was on the ground floor but whatever was happening, Frankie knew it was bad. Sirens were going off and he could hear several cons shouting and screaming which started the rest of the wing off. Still contained in their cells, it didn't stop them calling out and banging anything to hand on the steel doors.

"What's going on?"

"Your guess is as good as mine son but experience tells me that we won't be let out for quite a while. This place is always on a knife's edge and those daft cunts on the lower landing cause trouble for the least little thing. They smash up their cells and we all have to pay the price, last time I didn't see the outside of this room for three days."

Sonny thought for a moment, he was intrigued with this man and wanted to know his history.

"So why don't you tell me about your crime?"
"Sonny it would take too long and besides it was years ago now."
"So? And it don't matter how long ago it was or how long it takes to tell, we aint exactly got anything else to do now have we?"
Raking over the past always caused Frankie West a lot of pain and that's why in the last few years he'd tried to blot it all out. It hadn't worked but the memories weren't as frequent as they once were, now he was being asked to relive it all again but then it was only fair, the boy had told his story when asked and he hadn't held anything back.
"Ok but if you get fed up just tell me and I'll shut up. It all happened a long time ago and I suppose I need to really start from the day I went to live with the West's."

CHAPTER SIX
SUMMER OF 1975

It was ten o'clock in the morning when Harry West and his minder Kelly Graham walked along Chalk Farm Road in Camden. The sun was shining and Harry felt happy to be alive, Bella his wife, had cooked a fabulous meal the night before and desert was her dressed up in a bright red baby doll nightdress. Bella always knew how to please her husband and last night had been fantastic. At home there was only ever one cloud on their horizon, Bella's inability to conceive a child, still Harry knew how lucky they both were, business was booming and material wise they wanted for nothing.
"Look over there Harry, aint that one of the girls who used to work for you at the club?"
Harry West glanced across the street and saw Dilly Mallow pushing a pram that had seen better days and really belonged in a skip. Kelly walked on but stopped when he noticed his boss wasn't beside him. Turning around he saw Harry manoeuvring through the traffic trying to reach the woman on the opposite side of the street. Kelly watched as his boss began talking to her and was about to join them, when he thought better of it. You didn't poke your nose into Harry's business, not if you knew what was good for you and for all Kelly knew, the kid could be more than the child of an ex employee.

Kelly wondered if Harry was in fact the father but he quickly put that idea to the back of his mind, Harry wouldn't be happy if that little bit of gossip began to circulate around the manor and getting on the wrong side of his boss was the last thing Kelly wanted to happen.
"Hello there Dilly girl, how have you been keeping love?"
Dilly Mallow looked up into Harry's face and he could see the dark circles under her eyes and the premature lines that marked her face.
"Not so bad Mr West thanks, a bit tired but you know how it is. His nibs here keeps me on my toes, bless his little heart."
Dilly pulled back the covers to reveal her son and began to coo and fuss as she did so but it was a poor attempt at coming across as the doting mother. Harry looked into the pram to be met with a beaming smile looking back at him. The child couldn't have been more than a year old but Harry knew that with a mother like Dilly; his future was already mapped out.
"What's his name Dilly?"
"Frankie and he's a real handful I can tell you. I dearly wish I weren't on the stuff Mr West but I need it see, and Frankie was the result of my desperation. The punter offered me good money not to use a Johnny and the golden brown was beckoning if you get my drift."
Dilly now lived in a squat on Jamestown Road and

to say it was run down was an understatement at best. Harry hadn't set eyes on her since the night he'd been forced to sack her but he wasn't an uncompassionate man and right at this moment he felt nothing but pity for Dilly Mallow. The baby began to gurgle and laugh and Harry West instantly took a shine to the youngster. The little chaps face was dirty and his once white romper suit was now a drab shade of grey. Looking back at Dilly his heart went out to her, he'd always liked the young woman and at one time she had been one of his best dancers. Even when she started to experiment with drugs he'd allowed her to carry on working at the club but when her arms began to show needle marks, it was the last straw.
"You alright for money love?"
Dilly's eyes filled with tears as she slowly shook her head.
"You know me Mr West, I've never got any cash and when I do get some it goes straight in my arm. Having a baby wasn't fair on me or him but there aint a lot I can do about that now is there?"
Stuffing a twenty pound note in her hand, Harry began to walk away but as he crossed the road, called back over his shoulder.
"Come by the club later and I might be able to help you out in some way."
As Harry reached the pavement Dilly could be heard calling out 'thank you Mr West, thank you.'
Harry was a well know face in Camden, he'd ran

Rosie's night club for the last decade and a couple of years ago he'd also purchased the pub next door which now went by the same name as the club. Both businesses were profitable but it didn't stop Harry West from dealing in anything and everything that was illegal. He'd known Reggie and Ronnie Kray on first name terms and had shared a few pints with them over at the Blind Beggar pub or in their nightclub The Regal; at least he had until their arrests. The men's acquaintance had made for a good working relationship and everything ran smoothly and without any aggravation. Harry had also known the Richardson's well but had avoided mixing in their circles as he didn't like the way they carried out their business and preferred to keep his own dealings private. Still he had shown the men respect whenever he was in their company and that respect was returned. Now trouble didn't seem to follow him unlike the other known faces but he was still glad that all the aforementioned were no longer on the scene. Harry's club was one of the first to introduce exotic dancers and in the sixties it had drawn in large crowds. Married to Bella for the last fifteen years, Harry idolised his wife. He put her on a pedestal and gave her everything her heart desired, everything except the one thing she really wanted, a child. Over the years, it was the only subject to mar their almost perfect marriage and one that had caused the couple immense grief. The recent move to a large house on Primrose Gardens in Belsize Park had softened the blow for a few months but after Bella had furnished and decorated, the old yearning quickly returned. Seeing Dilly with her little child had given Harry an idea and it was one he knew that the girl would go along with, if not today, then as soon as she was desperate for her next fix.

Entering the club's foyer the two men were met by a doorman/bouncer who took Harry's overcoat and hung it on the rack that stood under the stairs. Making his way up to the club, Harry poked his head around the doors that led into the clubs dance area. In the cold light of day the place was drab and smelled strongly of stale alcohol but Harry loved it with a passion. The large seating area was covered in scarlet velvet with low glass tables in front. The dance floor wasn't a bad size but on busy nights it wasn't even visible as so many people would cram onto it. Harry didn't follow the rules of not overcrowding and would never turn away a paying customer but the more people that came to the club, the more its reputation seemed to spread and in the early seventies it was the in place to be seen at. Nodding his head that everything was as it should be, Harry proceeded to his office and took a seat behind the desk. Removing a large leather diary from the drawer, he studied it carefully as he looked at his agenda for the week which had already been mapped out. Bob Reynolds from over in Shoreditch was coming in as he had a proposition to put to

Harry and Lucky Wilson was due in later with a large quantity of knock off alcohol. Last night's takings had to be counted and banked and any problems with the staff sorted out, so all in all it was going to be a full day but it was nothing out of the ordinary, at least for the moment. In the next hour everything would change and for once Harry would put all thoughts of business to the back of his mind. Right in the middle of working out the barmaid's rota's, there was a knock at the door and Kelly Graham poked his head into the office.
"|There's a visitor downstairs to see you Boss. It's that girl from this morning; want me to tell her to sling her hook?"
"No no Kelly, bring her up."
Doing as he was told, Kelly led Dilly up the stairs and as she entered the office her usual loud bravado had disappeared. Little Frankie was perched on her hip, he'd been crying and trails of green snot were running down and into his mouth. Harry stood up and grabbing a handful of tissues, walked around the desk and at the same time gagged and retched.
"Fuck me Dilly! Look at the poor little sod."
After Harry had wiped the child's nose Dilly sat him down on the floor and then flopped into one of the armchairs that sat facing the desk.
"I know Mr West I know but I just can't cope with it all. I'm thinking of putting him into care, as much for his own safety as it is for my sanity. You know the kind of life I live and there's no way that's going

to change, what chance will the poor little mite have?"

Harry noticed the fine beads of sweat that were beginning to form on the young woman's brow and he knew it wouldn't be long before she was offering for sale anything she had and that could well include her own baby. Things were happening a lot faster than he'd expected and he had to tread very carefully.

"Look Dilly, since I saw you this morning I've been giving your predicament some thought. Why don't you let me take the kid so that you can get on with your life? There will be a few quid in it and I'm sure it would be best for all concerned."

Even though Dilly was starting to cluck she still had her wits about her and eyed Harry suspiciously. The offer of money was very tempting and she knew deep down that in the end she would accept but just at that moment her motherly instincts cut in.

"Beg your pardon Mr West, but you aint some kind of fucking kiddie fiddler are you?"

Harry wanted to laugh and at the same time he was angry but he didn't let it show. If anyone else had asked that question they would have received a serious slap but this situation had to be handled with kid gloves if he was to get the result he wanted.

"Don't be fucking daft of course I aint. Look, as far as I know my wife can't have kids and we could

give little Frankie here a good home and a good start in life. Don't you want that for your boy?"
"Of course I do, my boy means the world to me. So, how much are you offering?"
"A monkey and another ton each month until he's sixteen but I warn you Dilly don't try and squeeze me for more or you'll pay the consequences. Now they are my terms so take it or leave it."
Dilly Mallow thought for all of ten seconds before she nodded her head. A hundred a month would keep her comfortably in gear or at least go a long way towards it and the added bonus of the initial five hundred was like Christmas and birthdays all rolled into one. Harry walked over to his wall safe and removing a bundle of notes, counted out five hundred pounds. Seeing the cold hard cash, Dilly Mallow's was on her feet in seconds and stood holding out her hand. Heading for the door, she didn't even kiss her child or say goodbye and there were no tears shed as she left the room, something that cut Harry West to the quick. Picking up the baby he laughed out loud as Frankie gave him the biggest smile imaginable. Calling out to Carol Milligan his secretary and bookkeeper, Harry gave her a wad of notes and told her to go out and buy everything the child would need.
"Tell Kelly to take you in one of the vans, oh and Carol, only the best for my boy."
Three hours later the woman returned and informed her Boss that everything was loaded and

"Aint you happy darling?"
"Happy? Of course I'm happy, you've made my dreams come true but how did you manage it, whose baby is it?"
Harry explained all about Dilly and assured his wife that there would be no repercussions regarding having to hand Frankie back. When the baby woke and Bella gently cradled him in her arms Harry knew that this was the best decision he had ever made in his life.

Over the following few months Harry continued with business as usual and nothing gave him greater pleasure than when he got home at night to find his wife lying on the sofa with little Frankie cuddled up next to her. Harry still had the odd moment of worry about Dilly, especially if he saw her on the street and she called out to him but he finally stopped fretting when shortly before his boys second birthday, Harry received news that Dilly Mallow had been found dead in a squat on Whitehorse Lane over in Stepney. None of the other residents she shared with bothered to ask what had happened to her child and as far as Harry West was concerned, from now on nothing could ever threaten his little family again. The true facts of the tragedy wouldn't emerge for many years but in intimate circles rumours were rife that Harry West had ordered the death of Dilly Mallow.

CHAPTER SEVEN
14 YEARS LATER

With his jet black hair and hazel eyes, Frankie West was growing up to be a handsome young man. Many times over the years Harry had studied the boy when he was doing his homework and unaware that he was being watched. Harry had a sneaking suspicion in the back of his mind that his son was of mixed race. Without any details of exactly who Frankie's father was, the boys ethnic genealogy would always remain a mystery but it still didn't stop Harry wondering. Although he wouldn't admit it to anyone, Harry West was a deep rooted racist and the idea that his son could be anything other than one hundred percent white, played heavily on his mind. On the other hand Bella adored the boy and from the tender age of four, he had been enrolled into the best schools that money could buy. There was nothing in the world that could have stopped her loving him and Harry was well aware of that fact and it was for that reason only, why he had never shared his concerns with his wife. Frankie adored his mother but there was always a distance between him and Harry that he couldn't bridge and for the life of him he didn't understand why. Harry had tried to be close to the boy, tried to make himself have feelings but they just weren't there. He even introduced Frankie to his passion, boxing and took him along to the local boys club. Frankie West soon became one of the best amateurs in the area and all to please his father. When he lost the ABA national semi finals tournament, his eyes had gone straight to his dad who had sat cheering from the front row and he couldn't be off noticing the disappointment in Harry's eyes. The defeat only spurred him on and the following year the title was his, which was a testament to his skill, ability and desperate need to please Harry. For once Harry West was proud of his son and along with taking him to training three nights a week, he had a state of the art gym installed at the house. School holidays were spent with his father at the nightclub and it was the only time that he loved being in Harry's company. He instantly dropped the posh accent of his public school education and mixing with the real Londoners that his father did business with, was a real eye opener to the young boy. Frankie loved the way they didn't mince their words, he liked the swearing and the camaraderie that they all seemed to have with each other. He loved all the known faces, faces that scared most people but to Frankie were just uncle Bob, uncle Fred or whatever their first names were. He adored the staff that worked at the club and pub and they also seemed to take an immediate shine to young Frankie West. On one particular day, Bella had arranged a dental appointment for her son and it was agreed that he would meet up later to have

lunch with his father. Frankie's treatment had finished earlier than expected and making his way over to the Club, he was stopped in his tracks as he climbed the stairs. Blood curdling screams filled the stairwell and for a moment Frankie contemplated leaving but something deep inside wouldn't allow him to. Reaching the top he slowly walked towards the office door that had been left slightly ajar. Harry's right hand man and accomplice in crime noticed that the door was open and as he made his way over to close it, saw the young boy standing in the corridor with a face as white as a ghost. Kelly Graham grinned in Frankie's direction but his expression was more sinister looking than one of affection. Stepping outside, he pulled the door closed behind him.
"Hello there Frankie boy, what's up?"
"I'm supposed to meet my dad for lunch."
Kelly slowly moved his head from side to side and at the same time his grin disappeared.
"Not right now kid, best you make yourself scarce for a while, go for a walk around the block or something. I'll let Harry know you were here."
Inside the office, Dean Wilmot was in unimaginable agony. He had just had the fingers on his right hand smashed with a hammer, hence the screams Frankie had heard. Dean held his hands together in an attempt to ease the agony he was in but it didn't work and he began to shake from the pain. He tried to explain, wanting to buy some time but he was

blubbering as he spoke and saliva dribbled from his mouth, making him difficult to understand.

"Please Mr West, I told you I'd get the money and I will, I promise."

"I know you did Dean my old son but you knew the score when you took out the loan and you also knew my terms. Now if I don't get what you owe plus interest, that little display of punishment will seem trivial to what's coming your way. You have two days sunshine and if you don't come up with the reddies plus interest, which has now been doubled for the week, me and you are going to fall out big time."

"But Mr West I...."

"I don't want to fucking hear it Dean! Look son, I like you but business is business. Now on your way, see him out Kelly. Oh and Kelly, bring me a coffee back would you, there's a good lad."

When the door was closed, Harry once again continued with his work. Violence was part and parcel of his world and dishing out punishment, had over the years, become second nature to him. After what he'd just witnessed, well actually only heard, Frankie knew something bad was happening and decided to do as Kelly had told him in the hope that when he returned things would be back to normal. Ten minutes later and as he approached the main entrance, he was met by his father who was just leaving.

"Alright Boy? Did you get them gnasher's sorted

out?"

Frankie was about to reply but as usual his father cut him off.

"I aint got time for lunch today son and besides your mother wants us to go out tonight to some fancy restaurant. You can help out in the pub, collect some glasses and restock the shelves or something until I get back. Just keep yourself busy and don't give the staff any lip or get into any bother."

With that Harry West jumped into the passenger side of his Jaguar saloon and was driven off at speed by another employee Jimmy Saunders. To all who knew him, he was Jimmy Fingers, Frankie didn't know why the man was called that but he was wise enough not to ask questions, even if the person being asked was his father. The earlier incident would never be mentioned again and Frankie could only guess that Kelly hadn't told Harry his son had heard what was going on. The next four hours were spent laughing and joking with the regulars and staff alike but when the door opened at just after four, the laughter instantly stopped. Harry walked in with a face like thunder and everyone in his employment recognised the signs and knew it was best to keep their heads down, his own son included. Frankie joined Harry in the back of the car but as Jimmy wove through the traffic, not a word was spoken. Entering the house, Harry's persona instantly changed as he

tenderly kissed his wife on the cheek.
"Had a good day babe?"
"Really good, now upstairs with the pair of you and get washed, the table is booked for six pm. Oh Harry I forgot, did you ask Jimmy to drive us?"
"Yeah he's coming back about five thirty, anyway what's the occasion?"
Bella laughed as she playfully scolded her husband and son for being nosy and then told them again to go up and get changed. At five thirty on the dot Jimmy Fingers rang the bell and waited for the West's to come out to the car. As soon as the front door opened he was out of the driver's seat and opening the back door like a professional chauffer. It was always this way when Mrs West was in their company and Jimmy wouldn't dare do any different. Harry sat up front and Frankie joined his mother in the back and for the entire journey, Bella continually squeezed his hand and smiled. Pulling up outside the Royal Hospital Walk restaurant, Bella West let out a sigh of pleasure and at the same time she heard her husband groan. Harry hated anything posh and this was about as posh as it got, still he didn't say a word, what Bella wanted Bella got without question. Once they were all seated the waiter came over with the wine list and Bella ordered a bottle of bubbly and an orange juice for herself.
"Are you feeling alright darling?"
Bella West couldn't contain herself any longer and

as soon as the champers arrived and had been served, she asked for her husband and sons full attention.

"What I'm going to tell you will be a little shocking but I hope, shocking in a happy way. I've been feeling a little under the weather lately, so last week I took a trip to the doctors."

Harry grabbed his wife hand and squeezed it tightly. As Bella looked into his eyes she could see fear and knew that for all concerned, she needed to put them out of their misery. Her husband was one of the hardest men in London; he could also turn into a blubbering idiot when it came down to anything concerning her. Bella West was in the middle of her menopause and had been suffering terribly with a hormonal imbalance. Her periods were erratic and when she started to gain weight, had put it down to her time of life. A visit to the doctors a week earlier had seen her receive the most shocking news of her life.

"I'm pregnant; in fact I'm nearly six months pregnant. In just over twelve weeks we will have another addition to our little family."

Before anymore could be said and just as she was dreading, Harry turned into that blubbering idiot who constantly embarrassed her but who she also adored. Turning her gaze towards Frankie she looked for any reaction and when he burst into a wide grin, she knew that the news was the best she could ever have given them.

Almost three months to the day of her revelation Bella went into labour. It was a little early but her consultant said it was nothing to be alarmed about and after a speedy labour of only two hours; a blonde haired, blue eyed, Helena West came kicking and screaming into the world. The whole family were elated and none more so than Frankie, but he would quickly find out that his life was about to change forever. Bella's feeling hadn't altered towards her son but as she was so busy with the baby, they didn't spend as much time together. The same couldn't be said of Harry; now that he had a child of his own he couldn't be bothered with Frankie at all. Any spare time the boy had, would see him sent down to the pub or club to work. It seemed as if Harry didn't want Frankie having much contact with Helena, almost as if he now contaminated the happy family unit in some way. One Sunday morning, just as Helena was approaching her first birthday and Frankie his sixteenth, Harry called the boy into his study for a chat. As relations had been strained between father and son for several months, Frankie hoped that a nice long talk would put them back on an even keel but what he was about to be told would turn his world upside down. The room was completely panelled in oak and a large partner desk was positioned in the middle. A deep buttoned sofa and strategically placed chairs gave it the feel of a gentleman's club.

"Take a seat Boy. Now I've been giving things a lot of thought lately and I can't see any real benefit for you to stay on at that school with the rest of them Toff's. It was always planned that you would eventually join me at the club so it might as well be sooner rather than later. You can learn the pub trade first and then we'll take it from there."
Frankie didn't dare interrupt but he desperately wanted to protest that he had hopes and dreams of his own, he longed for a career, he didn't want to work at Rosie's Club or be a part of the family business. Biting his tongue, he listened as more bad news emerged.
"There's a spare room over the pub and I think it would do you good to live on the job and get some real hands on experience. Until you're old enough to serve behind the bar, you can tidy up and collect glasses, stock take and fill the shelves, you know what to do. Right I'm glad that's sorted out, now I need to talk to you about your mother."
"Mum! What's Mum got to do with this?"
Harry's eyes were cold and hard and something made Frankie feel that his father was really enjoying this, almost as if he'd been waiting years for this day to come.
"I don't mean Bella, she aint your real mother. Your old woman was a dirty druggie brass who used to work for me from time to time. When she couldn't handle you anymore I stepped in, lucky I did as she snuffed it soon after. Don't look so fucking shocked

boy, I mean it aint as if you look like us now is it? Personally I've always thought you've got a bit of black or Asian in you somewhere along the line." Suddenly everything fell into place. The reason why for all these years he hadn't been able to get close to the man who he thought was his father. Now it all made complete sense, Harry had never kept his racial views quiet and it must have driven the man crazy having to have someone like Frankie living under his own roof.

"So why tell me now?"

"Because I have my own child and you're...."

"I'm surplus to requirements?"

"You can put it that way if you like. Now I don't want you to upset Bella, so this was all your idea alright?"

Frankie was beginning to get angry and Harry could tell that the boy was about to blow up.

"Don't fucking cross me boy! You've had a marvellous education but now the free ride stops. Go and pack your bag and say goodbye to Bella and Helena, Jimmy Fingers will be here soon and he'll drive you over to the pub."

Frankie stood up, he knew when he was beaten and there really was no point in trying to persuade his father further. As he turned the handle, Harry informed him of one last thing and it would be the final nail in the coffin that would see his once happy family disintegrate before his eyes.

"From now on you will refer to me as Uncle Harry,

now hurry up before the car gets here."

It had taken several days before Frankie could settle into his new home and he would never be able to get used to the constant noise that came up through the floorboards from the bar below. Months later and the feelings of anger and bitterness still hadn't subsided but he never let it show to the other staff and when he'd referred to Harry as Uncle, no one had questioned him which he was grateful for. To begin with, Bella West had constantly telephoned asking him if she had done anything wrong and with each call it had broken Frankie's heart when he had to tell her that she hadn't and that it wasn't anything personal, just something he wanted to do. He had asked for her to allow him to grow up and spread his wings and his request was eventually granted. Six months later she brought Helena to the pub and hardly passed the time of day with the boy she once called son. Frankie put it down to the fact that all her time was taken up with the baby but deep inside he knew it was just a case of once again being pushed aside. Somehow this time it was harder to take than it had been with Harry because unlike with his father, Frankie had believed that Bella actually did love him. There and then he decided that he wouldn't allow another human being into his heart unless he was absolutely sure that they would never leave him. If he was ever lucky enough to find that one special person, then Frankie West knew that he would die before he would allow anyone or anything to come between them.

CHAPTER EIGHT
EIGHT YEARS LATER

Never actually working with his father at the club, Frankie West along with a handful of staff, now ran Rosie's pub on Chalk Farm Road. He loved the area and would spend as much spare time as he could down at the Lock just soaking up the atmosphere. All creeds mixed together with not a sign of tension but Frankie knew it was just because of where it was unlike other places in London which were much different. Back then Frankie West was a people person and could talk for hours to anyone about any subject. Harry hardly ever came into Rosie's and was more interested in the club and all the illicit trade it had to offer. The pub earned a respectable amount for its owner but nothing near the profit that the club was making. Frankie enjoyed his job and hoped that one day Harry would leave the place to him but deep down he knew that it was just wishful thinking as all the man ever talked about was Helena and what a blessing she was. The West's doted on their daughter, who was turning into a complete and utter brat and it was obvious to all, that one day she would be a very rich spoilt young woman. Whenever Bella wanted to go shopping she would drop the girl off for the staff to look after and everyone at Rosie's detested those days. Helena would go around barking her orders and not one person dared to go against the wishes of a nine year old girl, all except Frankie that was. One particular day things came to a head when just before opening Bella and her daughter walked in. Frankie was out in the back office when Karen Jones, the longest serving member of his bar staff, poked her head around the door.

"Sorry to bother you Frankie but it looks like we're on babysitting duty again."

Frankie rolled his eyes upwards which usually made Karen laugh but not today, today she was angry.

"Ok I'll be out in a minute."

"I'm sorry Frankie but it's not just that. I've spent the best part of this morning washing down the floors and Miss West has just tipped two whole pots of sugar all over them. I'm never going to get it cleared up before opening."

"Miss West?"

"She's insisting we all call her that from now on."

"Is she now?"

Frankie pushed his chair away from the desk and walked out into the bar area with Karen following in hot pursuit. Helena, who was holding up a wine glass and was about to drop it onto the floor began to giggle loudly, as old Markey Taylor, the part time pot man, was hopping from leg to leg in an attempt to catch the glass before it shattered and sent shards everywhere. Everyone stopped dead in their tracks including Helena West when Frankie's voice bellowed out.

"Put that down at once young lady!"

Helena looked up and with one shrug of her shoulders, dropped the wine glass. Holding her open palms in the air she tilted her head to one side and smirked directly at Frankie. Keeping his calm and picking up a small dustpan and brush from the top of the bar, he made his way over to the girl. Grabbing her arm Frankie forced the brush into her hand.

"Clear that up now Helena!"

Instead of doing as she was asked, Helena looked into Frankie's eyes with the same cold hard stare that he'd seen so often from her father.

"Get your hands off me; you idiot! You just wait until my mum comes back! And you call me Miss West from now on just like the rest of the hired help."

Still holding the girls arm, Frankie bent down low so that his face was level with hers.

"The only thing I will call you is a brat, now clear that up or I'm going to lock you in the office until your mother gets here and believe you me you won't like it one bit. I saw a spider in there the other day and it was as big as a rat. Well, what's it to be I haven't got all day?"

The fear in the girl's eyes was evident and she immediately began to sweep up the mess. When she'd finished she was told to help Karen clean up the floors. About to protest, Helena was silenced when Frankie once again threatened her with being locked in the office. The lunch time trade passed quickly and each time Helena had completed a chore, Frankie gave her another. By the time Bella returned at just after two, her daughter was wiping down tables and seemed as happy as Larry. Spying her mother, the girl's mood instantly changed and she ran over to Bella screaming and crying. In just a few seconds, Helena West had relayed all that the wicked man had made her do and was demanding that Bella sack him. All the noise that the girl was making brought Frankie through from the back and when Bella set eyes on him she smiled warmly and winked.

"That's him mum, that's the bully who grabbed hold of my arm and threatened to lock me up with the spider. If I tell my dad he will shoot you!"

Bella West placed her designer shopping bags onto the floor and walking over to Frankie, lovingly placed a kiss on his cheek and hugged him tightly. "Thank you Son, you've managed to do what no one else could."

Helena couldn't believe what she had just heard and started to protest that if her mother wouldn't do anything then she knew her father certainly would. Bella marched over and grabbed her daughter by the shoulders, something that had never happened before and it stunned the little girl into silence.

"You will keep your trap shut young lady if you

know what's good for you. I've been to soft on you Helena but things are about to change. If you go running to your father, I assure you that there will be consequences. Just you remember missy, you spend a lot more time in my company than you do in his and I might just ask Frankie if I can borrow that spider of his if you don't start behaving yourself."

Bella then picked up her bags and walked out of the pub with her daughter running after her promising all sorts as long as her mother didn't get the spider. When the door slammed shut, all the staff began to laugh and old Markey Taylor even gave Frankie a pat on the back.

"Now back to work everyone, we have a pub to get ready for tonight. Karen, I need to finish the books so no more interruptions please. I'm sure after that little madam's side show there won't be any more problems to deal with."

Scanning the room, Frankie noticed that a lot of the advertising mirrors that covered most of the walls were about ready for a good clean. It was a mammoth task and one that the staff hated. Frankie was tired and the last thing he wanted was a staff revolt on his hands so he decided that it would have to wait for a while. After having to put up with Helena's antics today, he wanted to get everyone back in a good mood and handing out extra cleaning duties would never accomplish that.

The next few weeks passed smoothly. Helena West never told her father what had occurred and on the odd occasion when Bella dropped the girl off, she showed nothing but willing and her behaviour was impeccable. The regulars all loved Frankie and trade was growing but he never received any praise from Harry, even though the takings were up by fifty percent. In the evening the pub was filled with customers all getting tipsy before they headed next door to the club and even the midday trade seemed to be busier as more and more of the shop workers and office girls called in for food and a lunchtime drink. Frankie West was real eye candy though he never saw himself that way and if any of the girls began to flirt with him, he would quickly disappear into the back office. It made the female bar staff howl out with laughter and for the life of them they couldn't work out why he was like he was, still Frankie was a good boss and the girls wouldn't have him any other way. At one time or another they had all had crushes on him but not once did he allow himself to be anything other than professional, much to their disappointment.

About to pull the bolt across the door after a particularly manic lunchtime, Frankie was relishing the thought of a few hours rest when a gentle tapping could be heard on the glass panel. Opening up, he was about to say we're closed when he was met by the most beautiful pair of smouldering hazel

eyes, the kind of eyes that can mesmerise a man.
"I'm sorry to bother you but I was wondering if there are any cleaning jobs available. I'm hard working and a good time keeper and ."
Frankie smiled and held open the door for the young woman to come in. Once inside he then pulled the bolt across which startled her.
"Sorry I didn't mean to scare you, only if I don't lock this place up we would never close. Good for business I suppose but it wears you down and a break between shifts is a must. Please take a seat, would you like a coffee?"
The young woman shook her head and softly said 'no but thank you anyway'. Frankie was gasping, he hadn't had a break since ten this morning and he was ready to drop. Walking over to the coffee machine, he poured himself a cup of rich dark Brazilian blend and asked the woman about herself. Adeela Makhdoom told him her name and that she lived in Walthamstow but she didn't once look Frankie directly in the eyes. Her dress was casual jeans and a T-shirt, and on her feet were a cheap pair of trainers, she had the blackest hair that Frankie had ever seen and even though it was scraped back and she didn't wear a drop of makeup, Adeela Makhdoom was stunning.
"So tell me Adeela, why do you want a job here?"
"I attend the Birbeck University studying accountancy and I could do with some extra cash, books and paper don't come cheap."

"That's true but why pick this place?"
Adeela shrugged her shoulders and smiled.
"Close by I suppose and I was just passing so I thought it wouldn't do any harm to ask."
Frankie placed his cup onto the table and took a second or two to think. They had been extra busy lately and Karen was struggling to keep on top of the place on her own. His other bar staff didn't help her much so he decided to make an executive decision.
"I can give you two hours early mornings and I do mean early. You'll need to be here at seven thirty and then one and a half maybe two in the afternoons but you'll have to be out of here by the time the early doors drinkers arrive at around five. It's only a fiver an hour I'm afraid, the boss's orders and I can't do anything about that. I suppose now you've heard all that, you're not interested anymore?"
"Oh I am and thank you very very much?"
"Frankie, everyone calls me Frankie."
"Thank you Frankie and when would you like me to start?"
"Tomorrow?"
"Tomorrow would be perfect."
With that Adeela was on her feet and heading towards the door. Standing on tip toes she was just able to reach the bolt and as she pulled it back, the door opened and Harry West walked in. He didn't acknowledge the woman and Adeela was to

desperate to be on her way home to let it bother her.
"And just who the fuck was that?"
"Someone after a job and it's nice to see you to Uncle Harry."
Harry ignored the sarcasm and walked through to the back office. Taking a seat behind the desk he removed the sales ledger from one of the drawers and was in the middle of inspecting the takings when Frankie appeared with two cups of coffee. Placing one down onto the desk he remained silent, when his Uncle was studying the accounts you never interrupted him, not unless you wanted an ear bashing.
"Well, the books are looking healthy, seems you're good for something at least."
Suddenly Frankie exploded, he didn't know if it was because of how he'd been treated by Harry over the years or if it was a case of he was just tired of fighting a battle that he knew he couldn't win.
"Will I ever do anything that's good enough for you? You know something Uncle Harry, I'm tired of all this. I never asked you to take me in but I've suffered for it for the whole of my life. You discarded me when something better came along, namely Helena. How did you think that made me feel?"
"Look boy, I gave you a chance when no one else would have. You had a good education, what more do you want?"
Frankie placed his mug onto the table and headed

towards the door.

"A family would have been nice, the family you gave to me and then took away without a second thought for how it would affect me or make me feel!"

Without waiting for a reply Frankie West made his way into the bar. This scenario had happened many times over the years and the outcome was always the same, within a few minutes Harry would appear and force a wad of twenty pound notes into Frankie's hand. There were never any apologies or explanation and to begin with Frankie had refused to accept the money but as the years passed, he had begun to finally think 'why not'; although that wasn't the reason he had just revealed his feelings. All he really wanted was for Harry to explain things but hell would freeze over before that happened, so in the meantime Frankie didn't see anything wrong with building a nice little nest egg. A few minutes later and Harry entered the bar, placed his cup down onto the highly polished wood and turned to face Frankie but he ignored Harry and continued to count the bottles of fashionable larger that lined the shelves.

"I've been thinking, maybe it's about time you got more involved in some of my other business lines. Bella is always going on about including you in the family business, so what do you say?"

Frankie knew that Harry had been planning something big for the last couple of years. It was all

very cloak and dagger and he had only picked up a few snippets of conversations here and there, but it was enough to know that Harry was talking about a lot of money somewhere along the line. This was Frankie's worst nightmare; he could just about tolerate being in the man's company a couple of times a week, but work alongside him? Not in a million years.
"Thanks but I'm fine where I am. I love this place and even if I do say so myself, I do a good job. The takings are up and I get along well with all the staff and regulars, so why rock the boat?"
"I aint arguing the fact but when it boils down to it, this place is mine and you will do exactly as I say or you can sling your fucking hook."
With that Harry West walked out of the front door, as far as he was concerned the subject was closed. Frankie sighed heavily, why did everything have to be a battle where his uncle was concerned. Turning around, Frankie saw the bundle of notes that had been left on the bar and picking them up, he wearily made his way upstairs.

CHAPTER NINE

Heading for home, Adeela stopped off at Camden lock and made her way to the basement of the stables to use the public toilets. Years earlier, the building had once been a hospital caring for the horses that pulled the Pickford's distribution vans and now it housed the only toilets on the lock. Pulling her traditional hijab headscarf from her bag, she spent the next two minutes putting it on and making sure that it was fitted correctly. Adeela hated this part of the day and she could feel the anxiety begin to build in the pit of her stomach. It was the same scenario from Monday to Friday and when the hijab was on, she knew it wouldn't be long before she was once more confined to the house and a life, at least as far as she saw it, of slavery. Wanting to rip the thing from her head, she could feel the onset of tears but the fear of someone seeing her without her headwear and telling her family, was stronger than her desire to take if off. She had already taken a risk removing it before she went into the pub and now even though she hated the thin fabric that she saw as a chain tying her to a faith that she was fast losing hope in, it strangely also made her feel safe.

Reggae music played loudly and stall holders and tourists alike seemed to be having such a happy time but Adeela didn't dare be late home.

She didn't stop to browse at any of the colourful stalls or taste any of the delicious looking food that was on offer; instead she took the underground from Camden Town to Walthamstow Central. The station was heaving with people and she saw the disapproving looks from many of the other travellers. Adeela loved everyone but for many others, as soon as they saw her headwear they gave her a look which made her feel as if she was from another planet. Maybe it was just her own paranoia as there were so many other colours and creeds in London that she really didn't stand out in any way. The thirty minute journey gave her time to reflect on the job offer and she began to panic regarding what her family would say and none more so than her three brothers.

Anwar and Yasmeen Makhdoom had arrived in England from Pakistan thirty years earlier and although their children had all been born here, they still practiced strong Pakistani traditions. In their homeland Anwar and Yasmeen had both come from poor working class castes. Little respect had been shown to them but once Anwar had children of his own, he expected them all to honour and obey him. Three strapping sons had been their fathers pride and joy whenever they visited the local mosque but then Yasmeen had given birth to Adeela and things had started to go wrong. Anwar's health began to decline and all blame was placed firmly on the birth of the girl. Later when he eventually had to resort to an oxygen mask to breath, he would constantly tell his daughter that it was all because she had brought bad luck into the family for not being a boy. The man actually believed that it had nothing to do with the fact that he had smoked forty cigarettes a day for the last thirty years. Yasmeen never stood up for her daughter and as she'd been dominated and brainwashed so much over the years, actually believed every word her husband said. Adeela's only ally came in the form of her aunt Bina, her mother's sister. Bina was far more liberal and had brought shame on her own family by refusing an arranged marriage. Hypocritically, all had been forgiven when she had married a wealthy man, who was, much to the relief of her family, originally from Pakistan. Bina lived in a beautiful house on Richmond Crescent in Islington and never ventured over to Walthamstow. She wasn't ashamed of her family but she hated the hierarchy that saw her niece treated no better than a dog. Once a week Adeela went to visit her aunt and it was Bina who persuaded the family to allow Adeela to continue studying in further education. There was one condition from her father though, there was always a condition, she had to choose a career that would bring in plenty of money for them all once she had qualified. Her brothers, Safeer, Rashid and Akram who were all in their mid to late twenties and who treated their younger sister like a slave, had in the last five years begun to rule the household. Anwar could no longer work and was now totally dependent on his sons financially. He had no option but to allow them to take over, even though it went against the grain in the worst way possible. To Anwar Makhdoom it was the most important thing to be the head of your own household and now he had relinquished that position, he felt worthless. In all honesty he hadn't had much say in the matter and the boys were as disrespectful to their parents as they were to their sister. Adeela and her mother and father didn't know what the boys did for a living but they always had plenty of money, though the household only received the bare minimum and there was never any cash left over for luxuries.

Arriving at the top of Priory Avenue, Adeela stopped and just stared down the road for a moment. Everywhere looked even more run down than it had yesterday and it was a depressing scene. No one seemed to take any pride in their properties and the council were moving in more and more drug addicts, not to mention unmarried mothers and prostitutes. Walking along the road, Adeela surveyed all the rubbish that was littered everywhere and swore it was getting worse by the day. Sighing heavily she opened the gate and headed up the short path to the front door. The house had three bedrooms but it still seemed tiny and cramped with six adults living there.

Thankfully she did have her own small space albeit not much bigger than a box room. The walls were unadorned, the paintwork was scuffed and the furniture was all old. There wasn't a carpet in sight; instead the floors were all bare boards full of cracks and splits in the timber, which Adeela had hurt her feet on many times over the years. Adeela couldn't ever remember her parents buying anything new for the house and even though her mother constantly told her how fortunate they all were to have a place like this, Adeela could never see it. Oh she knew that things would be far worse back in Pakistan but the thought of spending the rest of her life cramped up in this squalor they called a home constantly depressed her. Hanging her bag on a coat hook in the hall, she removed her trainers and pulled on her slippers. Her mother didn't like outdoor shoes to be worn in the house but Adeela couldn't see why not, it wasn't as if there was anything to spoil. When she'd heard her daughter's key in the lock, Yasmeen Makhdoom had marched out of the kitchen and her face was full of thunder. As she spoke she lashed out and slapped Adeela hard across her cheek. Her mother's action wasn't unusual but all the same it was still a surprise. "And just where have you been girl? It's almost five o'clock and the meal isn't prepared yet, your brothers won't be happy when they get here if their food isn't ready. Into the kitchen this instant and be quick about it."

Still holding the side of her stinging check, Adeela did as she was told just as she always did. A mound of vegetables sat on the worktop and removing a knife from the drawer she set about her task with as much enthusiasm as she could muster but in all honesty it was very little. As she chopped and sliced vegetables, she thought of how to tell her family about the job she had secured. It wouldn't be easy and she would have to choose her words carefully, maybe a little reversed psychology might help. Thirty minutes later and by the skin of her teeth, Adeela had prepared two curried vegetable dishes and a large pan of steamed rice. With the food ready and warming on the stove she just had time to make some flat bread. Wiping her brow, she again glanced at the clock and knew that she had to get a move on. Almost running into the front room she began to set out plates on the table. Her father was seated in his chair watching her every move as Adeela went about her tasks but when she smiled at him there was no response. Even with the oxygen mask covering his lower face he could have managed to nod his head but there was nothing. Back in the kitchen and waiting for her brothers to return, she took the opportunity to sit and rest as she knew that at any moment the real hard work would begin. When Adeela heard her eldest brother's voice she immediately began to dish up the food. Safeer was twenty nine and the eldest of the three, he took charge of everything, money,

where the family went and who they saw and no one dared to question him. Five minutes later and Akram and Rashid could be heard in the hallway but as Adeela struggled through with a huge pan of rice, neither brother offered to help her. When the four men of the family were seated at the table and the rest of the food had been brought through, Adeela and her mother retreated to the kitchen to eat their own dinner. It had always been this way and sometimes Adeela felt invisible, even her mother made very little attempt at conversation. When Safeer called out for a glass of water Adeela was instantly on her feet leaving her own food to go cold, no one kept her brother waiting, not if they knew what was good for them. Placing the glass onto the table, Adeela hung her head as she asked if she could speak to him.
"Well spit it out girl, hurry up or my food will spoil."
"My course tutor thinks it will be a good idea if we all get part time jobs and learn what it is like to work in the real world."
She hated lying but there was no alternative, if she'd been honest and said she craved more freedom the answer would have been a swift 'no' followed by a beating. Her brothers were pretty free with their fists whenever the fancy took them and sometimes Rashid would just punch her as she passed by, for no reason other than it amused him.
"So?"

"I have found a job but I don't think you will find it suitable. It's in a pub, only cleaning early mornings and after college. The place won't be open to the public so I won't be mixing with anyone you wouldn't approve of but I wanted to know what you thought and of course get your blessing."
Anwar's hand hit the table and everyone immediately looked at their father. He wasn't happy with what Adeela had just said but within seconds he was ignored and they all began to eat again. Safeer studied his sister as he spoke; she was a good Muslim girl and he knew she wouldn't be led astray. Placing more food into his mouth, Safeer took pleasure in making her wait for an answer. He spoke to Rashid about a new car he was thinking of getting and all the while Adeela stood patiently waiting for his reply. As she watched them all eat she thought of her own food which was probably stone cold by now. Finally he answered and Adeela was really surprised that he agreed but she didn't let her happiness show in any way or he may have changed his mind just to cause her misery.
"I can't see a problem with it but you talk to no one girl and you return home as soon as your work is done. It will make a change for you to pay for your own books and stuff instead of always sponging off of us. Now get back in the kitchen and let me eat in peace."
His words hurt her deeply but she was so happy that she had been given permission to take on the

job and nothing anyone said could spoil her euphoria. The next hour was spent washing and cleaning the kitchen and by eight o'clock Adeela was worn out. Her mother hadn't helped and after finishing her own food, had gone to join her husband in the front room without even putting her plate into the sink. No one had thanked her for the food or told her that it was good and tomorrow would be exactly the same, it always was. Glancing around the kitchen and when she was happy that all was as it should be and there was no reason why her mother would complain, she said goodnight to her parents and made her way upstairs. Her brothers were getting ready to go out and a strong smell of aftershave hung in the air. Some rap tune was blearing out of the Hi-fi and Adeela prayed they would go out soon as even with the door closed the ridiculous noise was driving her mad. The boys were all handsome and they loved the latest designer fashions but she did wonder how they could afford it and where they went to every night, but then maybe it was better if she didn't know as Adeela had a feeling that they were up to no good. Her brothers had a reputation in the area and it wasn't a nice one, they were bullies outside of the house as much as they were in it. The neighbours were all scared of the Makhdoom boys and they ruled the street as if it was their own. Finally there was silence but the excitement of starting her job in the morning stopped Adeela from going to sleep for a long time. She imagined talking to lots of different people and possibly making some new friends, something she didn't have in her life but then in all honesty it probably wouldn't happen as to have any friends, you needed to socialise and her family would never allow that, still it was nice to dream. Eventually she managed to drift off and anyone looking in would have seen that there was just the slightest hint of a smile on her lips as she slept.

CHAPTER TEN

Safeer was the first to leave the house and starting up the engine of his 1985 Mercedes Benz, he waited impatiently for his brothers to join him. The car was Safeer's pride and joy and although it was fourteen years old, it was still in pristine condition. Business had been really good of late and he was now thinking of trading it in but he knew it would still be a wrench to let it go. Safeer had been the first member of his family to own a car and he saw it as a status symbol and not in truth, a vehicle that had been witness to a long list of atrocities. The Makhdoom brothers were soon on their way and driving past the secondary modern school on Woodbury Road, they turned onto Church Hill. The old Burial Gardens were situated at the rear of the school and although it was out of bounds as far as the staff was concerned, it was a place where teenagers, mostly females, would gather in the evenings. Some of the girls were from the area but the ones that the brothers were really interested in, were from the local care home on Brooke Road. A large ten bedroom Victorian house, it catered for youngsters aged from between fourteen to eighteen years of age and the place was always full to capacity. Its residents came from far and wide; Wales, Yorkshire and even Scotland and most had little or no family to bother about them. Brook Road

House was run by Gert and Albert Moore but they had no real interest in the place or where the residents went to each night. The home was a good earner and there was little work to be done, so as long as no trouble was brought back to the Moore's door, all the residents, especially the girls, could do exactly as they liked. On the drive over Safeer had stopped at the corner convenience shop and purchased vodka, sweets and cigarettes, all standard supplies for the line of work that the brothers were in. Parking up, Akram and Rashid headed over to the large granite monument around which stood a gathering of young girls. Lindy Harding had known the brothers for over a year and was well aware of how they made their living but it didn't bother her in the least. In fact she would regularly procure girls for the Makhdoom's. Initially she had fallen head over heels in love with Safeer after he had given her gifts and told her she was his girlfriend. The reality of the situation had hit home like a sledge hammer the night he had driven her over to a flat in Whitechapel and told her she was to have sex with the occupant. Lindy had flatly refused but when Safeer had grabbed her breast and squeezed it so hard that she screamed out in pain, she knew far worse would come if she didn't do as she was told. The place had smelled strongly of cats and the man she was ordered to have sex with was ancient, at least compared to her tender years. Much to Lindy's relief; it was all over in a matter of minutes and after the man handed her an envelope, she ran from the flat and returned to the car where Safeer was waiting. Tearing it open, Safeer Makhdoom counted the contents and then handed Lindy a twenty pound note. She could see that the envelope contained far more but she wasn't in a position to argue. Safeer kissed her tenderly on the lips and told her he loved her. Love was all Lindy Harding had ever wanted but had received very little of in her short life and for several months she actually believed his every word. Now she saw Safeer for exactly the scumbag that he was but she still brought any new girls over to the gardens and would accept payment for the introduction. Her circumstances and experiences in life had made Lindy harden up at an early age and when she heard any of the girls declaring their love for one of the brothers, she would laugh in such a belittling way, it always made the girl in question get angry and there had been many scuffles over the past few months.

Lindy had been short of cash today so she had made sure she was at the burial gardens this evening, she had also brought along a new girl, who at just fourteen, was one of the youngest in the group. Rashid eyed her up and he liked what he saw, he also knew that as the girl looked even younger than her years, they would be able to command a higher fee. The Makhdoom's catered for all tastes and they didn't care what ethnic group they hired the girls out to, so long as they were returned in one piece and not too much damage had been inflicted upon them. Walking over to Lindy, Rashid removed a packet of cigarettes and offered the girls one. Lindy snatched the packet from his hands but Fiona Selby lowered her gaze as she said 'thanks but I don't smoke'. This was a first, as cigarettes had in the past, always been a good ice breaker. Beckoning to Akram he told his brother to join them. Akram really was handsome but in a boyish kind of way and at twenty one, he appealed more to the younger girls.

"Hey Bro, come and say hello to Fiona. Fiona this is my kid brother Akram."

The two nodded to each other and Akram knew exactly how to play his part. Acting as if he was shy, he would glance at the girl every few seconds with a cheeky grin on his face and then lower his eyes to the ground. Fiona Selby had moved to London from Bradford in West Yorkshire two weeks earlier and because she'd been in and out of care and foster homes for most of her life, it had made her timid and withdrawn. Now standing here, she couldn't believe someone like this, someone so good looking, was actually interested in her. Rashid removed the vodka bottle from a bag and offered Lindy a drink. After greedily gulping a mouthful she passed the bottle back to Akram who pretended to take a sip. The bottle was then handed to Fiona who would normally have refused but she

didn't want Akram to think she was a chicken. Every action was so well rehearsed and had been played out a hundred times before on innocent victims that were being groomed for a life of prostitution. Fiona coughed and spluttered until she was red in the face but when Lindy started to laugh, Fiona took another large mouthful. It didn't take long before she was swaying from side to side and the brothers slowly led her back to the car to get her ready for future punters. Rashid shoved a ten pound note into Lindys hand and pushing it into her pocket, she set off for the care home without a second thought for Fiona and all that she knew the girl would be subjected to. Fiona Selby sat on the back seat of the car and Akram had his arm around her, she was starting to feel a bit sick but was also enjoying all the attention. He began to nuzzle her neck and she liked the feeling, leaning in close, Akram whispered into her ear.
"You are so beautiful; my heart began to flutter the moment I saw you. Would you like to be my girlfriend?"
Fiona coyly nodded and when Safeer who was still in the driving seat, looked into the rear view mirror and saw the girl nod, he started up the engine. After driving along the High Street Safeer turned onto St James and then left into South Grove and the public car park that was situated half way along. The car park was never used at night and was always their preferred place to take a new girl.

If there was any screaming, then there was no one about to hear and the twenty four hour toilets that were unattended after six at night, were perfect for either the brothers or the girl to clean herself up afterwards. Pulling up into an unlit corner, Safeer and Rashid got out of the car and lighting up cigarettes, walked across the car park. Akram pulled out the bottle of Vodka and after taking another nonexistent sip, passed it to Fiona who again drank a large mouthful.
"You really like your drink I see?"
Fiona burped and at the same time could taste a small amount of vomit in her mouth. She really didn't feel very well but she also didn't want this night to end and pulling a mint from her pocket, placed it into her mouth in the hope of masking any bad smell.
"Not really, this is the first time I've ever had alcohol."
After a few more minutes of conversation and when Akram had repeated again that she was special and that he was going to treat her like a princess, he moved on to the next stage. Removing a small red velvet box from his pocket, he opened it and lifted out a gold chain. Fiona's eyes opened wide and she squealed with delight. In all honesty it looked far more expensive than it actually was, Safeer picked up the rolled gold chains down the local market at five quid a pop but to Fiona it was the nicest present she had ever received. After clipping the clasp shut

around her neck, Akram gently moved her so that she was now lying across the back seat of the car. Fiona was nervous but also excited at the same time. Even though she had been in one foster home after another and then as she'd gotten older, placed into care homes, she had limited experience of the opposite sex. Many of the other girls she knew had been interfered with by staff in some of the homes, staff that proclaimed to care for these poor abandoned mites and swearing to help them but who in reality were helping themselves to the children's innocence. Fiona saw herself as one of the lucky ones but she had at times in her naivety, wondered if they had left her alone because she wasn't pretty enough. To begin with Akram kissed Fiona tenderly as he slowly unbuttoned her blouse. She happily laid back, subservient to anything he wanted and when he unclipped her bra exposing her firm but underdeveloped breasts, he let out a sigh. Akram took her nipple in his mouth and Fiona groaned in pleasure, he then kissed and sucked hard as he undid his trousers and released his fully erect penis. The tenderness came to an abrupt halt as he lifted her skirt and roughly yanked down her panties. Lying on top of her with his full weight bearing down, he forced himself inside her and she winced in pain. Moving in and out for a few minutes Akram finally came and she held onto him tightly in an effort to somehow relieve the pain which unbeknown to her had only heightened his

pleasure. Getting to his knees, Akram pulled up his trousers as he spoke.
"Good girl, now please my brother he's a nice man."
"What?"
He didn't reply and as quickly as she could Fiona put on her underwear. As Akram left the vehicle the windows had completely steamed up and looking in Safeer's direction he laughed.
"She was good, nice and tight."
Safeer got into the car as Fiona had started to pull her clothes on. The sight of her half naked body made him leer at her with lust. Pushing her down onto the seat he pulled at her panties but this time they were ripped from her body.
"No!"
"Don't tell me no, girl."
Safeer roughly pushed her head back as he quickly unzipped his trousers and entered her but this time it was much harder and more forceful. As she lay there wondering how she'd allowed herself to get into this situation, she looked up at a stain on the lining of the cars roof and concentrated only on that. It didn't help much and she could smell the strong aftershave of the man on top of her as he pleasured himself at her expense. Finally he pulled out and as she licked at the salty tears that ran down her cheeks she was glad that at last it was over. When the door opened and Safeer stepped out, Fiona continued to just lay there. When Rashid's body cast a shadow over her, she started to cry again and

fear was evident in her eyes. Fiona knew that her ordeal was far from over and wondered if this assault would continue all night.
"Please me girl and I will be gentle with you."
With no expression, she nodded her head and waited for the assault to begin as he released his penis and pushed it towards her.
"Put it in your mouth."
Slowly she moved towards him and doing as she'd been told, placed her lips around his shaft.
"Now suck gently."
As he began to thrust in and out, Rashid grabbed the back of her head and held onto her hair tightly. Instantly Fiona began to cough and choke which brought Rashid quickly to a climax as he shouted out in pleasure. Letting go of her, Fiona quickly retreated to the corner pushing herself against the door and covering her body the best she could.
When Rashid got out of the car his two brothers stood grinning.
"Fuck me Rashid, you sounded like a fucking wolf howling."
"Shut the fuck up Akram, now get in there and calm the girl down."
Doing as he was told, Akram smiled and took hold of Fiona's hand as he sat down next to her.
"Good girl, you did very well and to say thank you, I will get you another gift."
The Makhdoom's drove over to the public toilets where Akram told Fiona to go and clean herself up

and because she was still intoxicated, she didn't say a word or try to run. Five minutes later after Fiona had sat on the toilet crying her eyes out and when she was once again presentable, she got back into the car and sat beside Akram. He placed an arm around her shoulder and tenderly kissed her cheek. "You are so beautiful Fiona; I have never met anyone like you before. Say you'll meet me again tomorrow baby?"

Slowly she nodded her head and smiled, he was just so handsome that she couldn't deny him. The thought that she had a boyfriend who would protect her made Fiona's heart swell with pride, even if she didn't like what he had asked her to do. She couldn't wait to get back to the house and tell all the other girls about him and show off her beautiful necklace. Fiona in her ignorance of relationships, thought this was how things were meant to be, of course she would rather that it was just Akram and her but if letting his brothers have their way made him happy, then she kidded herself that she too would be happy. The men dropped her back off at the children's home and when she had disappeared from sight, they all high fived each other. It was another name they could add to their ever growing list of under aged prostitutes and Safeer had an idea that this one was going to be very profitable indeed.

"Well brothers that went well now let's go and get the next two money making little bitches set up.

I think after that we'll get something to eat, I'm fucking starving. I've got a feeling that little Fiona is going to be good, now how much vodka is left?"
Removing the bottle, Akram inspected its contents. "Not much, I think we need to stop off for another. That bitch Lindy drank more than she should have; she's always been a greedy cunt."
"Not just for alcohol, our Lindy likes plenty of cock as well."
The brothers laughed as they set off to do further business. It was just after ten when they pulled up outside the Leisure Centre on Queens Road. Safeer didn't even have time to stop the engine before the back door immediately opened and two young girls got into the car. Dawn and Janice were both now sixteen and had been procured by the brothers a year or so earlier. Their work or want for another word, abuse, had taken its toll and even after such a short space of time, they now looked older than their years. As they were still good at their trade and pulled in punters by the dozen, no comments were ever made. If the day ever came when they stopped being such good earners, then the Makhdoom's would discard them but for now it was onwards and upwards as the money rolled in. Safeer drove over to Kings Cross and pulled up on Euston Road outside the train station. As Janice went to get out Safeer leaned over the back of the driver's seat and grabbed her wrist. There was nothing gentle about his touch and she winced in

pain when he squeezed hard.

"We'll be back at around two and you had both better make it worth my while. Oh and Janice, don't think about pocketing any of my money because you know what happened the last time you tried that little trick."

The girl only nodded her head but the fear in her eyes was enough to tell Safeer that he had got his point across. The first and only time it had happened, resulted in two days of hospitalisation and then also being unable to work for a week. It had not only affected the Makhdoom's living but also her own and as Janice lived from one punter to the next, she had struggled to feed herself let alone pay for her accommodation. For a short while she contemplated going to the Old Bill and reporting the brothers. Late one night she had confided in Dawn but Janice's mind was quickly changed when her friend told her about another girl that used to work for the Makhdoom's. Avril had been a mouthy fifteen years old and when she'd threatened Safeer with the police, he had nailed her tongue to a table. The injury had taken weeks to heal and Avril was left so traumatised that she ended up committing suicide. There was no escaping this nightmare of a life, so linking arms the two girls set off in search of punters. Safeer turned around in his seat.

"Fancy getting something to eat boys?"

Akram and Rashid both answered in unison and

with exactly the same words.
"Good idea I'm fucking starving."
After filling their stomachs at a local KFC, Safeer drove over to Brick Lane and Rashid got out of the car. The brothers had a cousin in the area, Mahmood Bhatti, who also traded in underage prostitutes and once a week he would get together with Rashid to do business. From time to time they would swap girls but mostly the Makhdoom's only wanted to purchase and their cousin was skilful in the art of procurement. Safeer then drove over to Wharf Road in Paddington. Several years ago he had struck up a friendship with Aboka Lawal, a Nigerian who ran the local youth club. Aboka would pick out any girls that had been going through a hard time or whose family life was less than desirable. When the youth club closed, a meeting would take place back at Aboka's flat and it was then decided which girls should be targeted and terms agreed. Yesterday Safeer had received a call from the man advising him that there were some new members and he could provide fresh meat, at a cost of course. This was Akram's territory and after being given instructions from his older brother, he went inside. Safeer returned to the cross and parked up in Balfe Street. Situated at the rear of the station, it was an ideal spot to wait. Setting the alarm on his mobile for two am, he got comfortable while he waited to pick up the girls and then go on to collect his brothers. The scenario was the same

night after night but he never tired of it, especially as the girls always came back with a good wedge of cash.

CHAPTER ELEVEN

Safeer, Rashid and Akram arrived home at six am. Normally they would bang about and make so much noise that it would wake Adeela, it usually bothered her and she would curse them under her breath but today she was glad of the interruption to her sleep. Hearing her brothers climb the stairs, she waited until she was confident that they were all in bed and then she ventured into the bathroom to have a wash. Putting on her hijab, she grabbed her bag and without a sound left the house and headed towards Walthamstow central underground. It was still relatively quiet at this time of day and apart from a couple of underground cleaners who were going from one station to another, she had the carriage all to herself. Adeela was excited at the prospect of starting a new job and meeting other people. University was alright but she hadn't managed to make many friends due to her shyness. Now she would be working with everyday people, normal people and Adeela made a promise to herself to try and be more approachable. Leaving the station she walked along Chalk Farm road and when Rosie's pub came into sight she could feel the onset of anxiety but with the sun shining and the warmth on her face, she also felt more alive than she had in months. Already she knew she would have so much more to tell her aunt Bina on her regular

Saturday morning visit. Tapping on the glass she waited to be let inside and when a bleary eyed Frankie opened up, she looked at him properly for the first time. She couldn't be off noticing the expression on his face and she closed her eyes for a second when she remembered that she was still wearing her hijab. Adeela had meant to take it off when she reached Camden but it had completely slipped her mind. Still there was nothing she could do about it now and as the man opened the door a little wider, she stepped inside. The smell of stale beer hung in the air and much to Frankie's amusement he smiled when she wrinkled up her nose.

"You'll get used to it sweetheart. Now follow me and I'll show you where everything is, oh and sorry about my appearance but I overslept this morning." Adeela didn't reply and followed the man through into the back office. After Frankie had given her a list of things to do, he disappeared upstairs to get ready. Adeela Makhdoom scanned the paper and smiled; she did more work than this in an hour at home. By the time Frankie came down from the flat, the bar and floors had been washed, empty glasses had been collected and rinsed and Adeela was in the process of wiping down the last of the tables.

"Bloody hell girl you're a fast worker, I wish all my staff were as efficient as you. Take a seat and I'll fetch us both a coffee."

She wasn't being asked but told, so Adeela felt she couldn't refuse and besides it would be nice to rest for a while. Frankie asked her how she took her coffee and he grimaced when she said 'no sugar or milk and as strong as you can make it please'. A couple of minutes later and he had taken a seat opposite her. Adeela studied her new boss and saw how handsome he was; he also seemed like a kind man which was something she hadn't experienced before. In Adeela Makhdoom's world men were king and they could treat a woman exactly as they liked and more often than not it was as a second class citizen.

"So Adeela, tell me a little bit about yourself, only we didn't have much time to talk yesterday."

It was difficult to begin with but he was so relaxed that after a while the conversation started to flow. She told him about her family, though not how she was treated, her time at university and all that she hoped to achieve, she even mentioned Aunt Bina and how liberal the woman was.

"You seem to have a very full life sweetheart; I expect it's nice to be part of a large family. I aint never had that myself but I suppose eventually you stop longing for it. The old saying 'you don't miss what you aint had' isn't true but I can't complain. I mean there aint many people under the age of thirty that run a pub, especially in London and there's nowhere else I'd rather be than in good old Camden."

Adeela could sense sadness in the man and she felt sorry for him. She also felt something else and it was alien to her, butterflies were beginning to dance in the pit of her stomach every time she looked at him. Frankie waited for her to speak but when nothing was said he couldn't help but stare long and hard into her beautiful brown eyes. Adeela blushed and turned her gaze away from him which embarrassed Frankie. Desperate to get the conversation going again he spoke.

"So do you go down to the lock much?"

"No, usually when I finish Uni I have to go straight home and help my mother but when I passed it the other day it looked amazing."

In truth, she passed through the lock area often but had never had the time or courage to look around.

"It's just the best; I go down there whenever I have some spare time. The only problem is time seems to stand still and if you're not careful you can end up being down there for hours. I love the music and the people, it's like you never see the same person twice, that aint true but it feels like it none the less. The food, well the food is out of this world. Next time I go I'll get you some to try."

"Thank you that would be very nice but I wouldn't want you to go to any trouble on my behalf."

"It's no trouble I can assure you and it would give me an excuse to pop down there."

Adeela smiled, drank the last of her coffee and stood up.

"Will there be anything for me to do later, only I wouldn't want you to give me work for the sake of it Mr West."

"Don't you worry about that, with a place this size there's always something to do but leave it until about four o'clock and please, no more of the Mr West it's just plain old Frankie."

Adeela then gathered up her bag and made her way to the university. For Frankie, the rest of the day passed quickly. There were plenty of punters and when he finally locked the doors again at three pm he felt ready to drop but today there would be no time for a quick nap, today he wanted to give his newest employee a surprise. Frankie tried to kid himself that he was just being kind but deep down he knew it was more than that. Adeela made him feel like he'd never felt before and he liked it. He also knew that she came from a Muslim background and that could be a real problem but for the time being he put it to the back of his mind. At ten past three he headed down to the lock. As usual music was playing and people were laughing and having fun. Walking over to the food area he ordered Chinese, Mexican and Argentinean food to take away. When the containers had all been packed he took a slow stroll back to the pub. Laying out plates, he went into the back kitchen and placed the food into the oven to warm. Something told him that Adeela wouldn't be late; in fact he knew she would be dead on time which would give them an

hour before opening to enjoy the food. With the table set, Frankie sat down to wait. There was only ten minutes to go and for some strange reason he was starting to feel nervous. When the knock came at the door, he jumped up and ran to let her in. Not once in his whole life had he ever felt or acted this way, Frankie West felt like a teenager on a first date and he liked it. The only trouble was he didn't know if she could look upon him in a romantic way and that thought worried him. Unbeknown to Frankie, Adeela could think of nothing or anyone else all day and her course tutor had actually commented that she was not her usual diligent self. For the whole of her life she had accepted the fact that she would have an arranged marriage but now, well now she knew what it was like to be attracted to a man of her own choosing. This time she wasn't wearing her hijab and her beautiful black hair was neatly tied back in a ponytail. As soon as she walked in and saw that the table was set for two her heart skipped a beat but then she inwardly laughed to herself, the man probably had a girlfriend and this was all for someone else.
"So where would you like me to start Mr West?"
"I told you before to call me Frankie and I would like you to start by taking a seat over there."
Frankie disappeared into the kitchen and when he came back with a tray full of food, Adeela smiled. The butterflies were back in her stomach and she was sure that she wouldn't be able to eat a thing.

"Right I've got Chinese, Mexican and a bit of Argentinean so take your pick. I tell you what, I'll just put it on the table and we can have a try of everything."
"What's all this for Frankie?"
"Well you said you never went to the lock so I've brought some of the lock to you; now dig in before it gets cold."
The couple ate in silence but every so often Adeela would glance up and catch Frankie looking at her. She hadn't eaten all day and the food was delicious but for a moment she did wonder if he was expecting more from her and the worry of that thought suddenly made her lose her appetite.
"What's the matter, don't you like it?"
"It's absolutely delicious but it's the first time I've ever eaten anything foreign and besides I will have to eat again when I get home."
Frankie wanted to laugh at her reply regarding eating foreign food as he was sure that what she had at home definitely wasn't roast beef and veg. Not wanting to offend her he kept his amusement to himself.
"So would you like me to come again tomorrow?"
"Of course, you're the best cleaner this place has ever had."
"Well I really should be on my way now."
Standing up Adeela thanked him again for the food and then made her way towards the door. Time was getting on and not only did Frankie have to

open up the pub soon but Adeela was frightened of being late home and feeling the wrath of her family. At least the job meant that she wouldn't have to prepare the evening meal anymore and she was grateful for that. As she put her hand onto the highly polished door handle she felt him behind her and when he placed his own hand on hers, she didn't pull away. This was so wrong and went against everything she had ever been taught but she just couldn't help herself. Just the feel of his breath made the hairs on the back of her neck tingle and stand on end. Frankie leaned towards her and slowly kissed her cheek, it was tender and not overly sexual as he didn't want to scare her off but it felt so good and so right. Adeela could feel her face begin to flush and she pulled open the door and quickly went outside. Frankie closed up with a smile on his face, this was all happening so quickly but he wouldn't have changed this afternoon for anything.

Once again Adeela stopped at the stable toilets to apply her headwear before getting on the tube to Walthamstow.

Harry West had pulled up outside just as Adeela had left and the sight didn't make him happy. Marching into the bar his face was like thunder and his words came out in an aggressive manner.

"Why the fuck was she here again?"

"She's the new cleaner and her name is Adeela."

Harry glanced around and saw the plates and

takeaway containers on the table.

"Since when did you start wining and dining the fucking staff? Are you trying to get into her knickers boy?"

Frankie ignored the question and began to clear the table. He'd had such a nice time but as usual, Harry had to spoil everything, well not this time.

"Did you hear what I said?"

"Of course I did! Look Uncle Harry, she's a bloody good worker and I just wanted to do something nice for her alright?"

Harry walked behind the bar and offered up a glass to the whisky optic. Looking in the mirror he studied Frankie's face, trying to see if he was hiding anything. Always good at sniffing out a lie, he was certain that Frankie was scheming. Harry took a large gulp of his drink and sighing heavily, turned around to face him.

"Look it aint that I'm racist but I just don't want her sort working in my pub. They all fucking stink of curry and once you let one in they'll start trying to get work for their fucking relatives."

"Don't talk rubbish Harry."

"Have you ever seen a corner shop that's run by one of her sort and who hire whites? No I didn't think so."

Frankie couldn't believe what he was hearing; his Uncle was the most racist person he knew. Now he was standing here trying to deny it and at the same time being racist with his very own words.

Just then the door opened and two of the girls that worked in the hairdressers across the road walked in.
"Hi Frankie!"
Glancing at Harry, Frankie saw him give the thumbs up and nod his head as if to say 'now these are the sorts you want to get in with'. Totally ignoring his uncle, Frankie went behind the bar to serve.

As Adeela placed her key in the lock she could hear the clattering of pots and pans in the kitchen. It wasn't the usual sounds as Yasmeen was slamming the cookware down onto the work surface. It was five forty five and for once her mother had been forced to cook, a task she hadn't carried out in a long time and one she hated. As Adeela walked into the kitchen, one look at her mother's face told her that the woman wasn't best pleased with the new arrangement.
"Oh so you've finally decided to come home, well don't just stand there like a spare part girl, give me a hand. The men will be here soon and I'm very behind. I don't know if I am going to be able to cope, maybe I should have a word with Safeer and see if he will force you to give up this stupid idea of going out to work."
Adeela was nervous at the thought but she didn't let it show, instead she knuckled down and started to peel the mound of vegetables just as she always did. When her brothers had at last come home and been

served their food, she began to tidy the kitchen. Knowing that her mother was in the front room talking to her brothers and trying her hardest to make them change their minds regarding Adeela's job, she was on tenterhooks and was finding it difficult to concentrate on her chores. When she heard Safeer call her she immediately stopped what she was doing and went to see what decision he had made.

"So sister, how did your first day at work go?" Adeela knew she had to play things down and not let anyone know that she had enjoyed it more than anything ever before.

"It was ok brother but very hard work. I am happy to stay here and help mummy if that's what you want. Joining the working population isn't as easy as I thought it would be so I will do just as you command."

Hanging her head low, she waited for the outcome but her hands were behind her back and all of her fingers were crossed. Silently she prayed to Allah that her wish would be granted.

"So now you know what hard work is all about! I'm sorry Mum but she has to learn the hard way and the extra income will be worth it. Adeela can still do all the cleaning when she gets home but for now you will have to cook for your family without any complaint."

Yasmeen's face was a picture of pure rage as she stormed out of the room but she knew better than to argue any further. There was no one to fight her corner and even her own husband would always side with his sons. The use of her own personal slave had been taken away and she would make the girl suffer for that but for now she would just have to get on with things. The life of a Pakistani woman wasn't easy, she never expected that it would be but when she'd given birth to a daughter, Yasmeen had at least hoped to pass over a lot of the household duties and work load. Now Safeer was making his mother work even harder and Yasmeen was as mad as hell.

CHAPTER TWELVE

After several drinks, the high tension between Harry and Frankie had finally subsided. Harry had started drinking with the hairdressers almost as soon as they had walked in and now a bit worse for wear, he was focusing his attentions on Linda, a leggy peroxide blond who wearing a skimpy outfit, was showing more than her fair share of flesh. He loved Bella dearly but it had never stopped him flirting and on occasion, having a bit on the side as he liked to put it. Bella wasn't stupid and had known for years exactly what went on but as long as she felt secure in her marriage and Harry didn't bring any trouble home with him, she was content to turn a blind eye. By seven o'clock the hairdressers, Simone and Linda, who had only popped in for one on their way home, were happily on a path to becoming bladdered. Deciding to make a night of it, they accepted every drink that Harry offered and Linda in particular had taken a real shine to the man. Frankie knew how this was going to pan out; it was something he'd been witness to on numerous occasions over the years. After all this time it still bothered him and when he thought about poor Bella waiting patiently at home it made him angry. He never bothered to voice his opinion though, firstly no one ever dared question Harry West and secondly the man wouldn't ever change

so there was little point in wasting his breath. As the place filled up with more and more people, Frankie noticed that Uncle Harry was missing and when he saw that Simone was now standing alone, he knew the score. The door to the office was firmly closed and as Karen, one of the barmaids, tried to open it the door wouldn't budge. Frankie tapped her on the shoulder.
"Give it a minute love."
Karen James rolled her eyes upwards; she found Harry West's action disgusting. Most of his conquests were young enough to be his daughters and wouldn't have given him the time of day if he wasn't a known face. Karen also adored Bella; she found her to be sweet and kind and for the life of her couldn't see what the woman saw in her boss. When the door at last opened Harry casually strolled out and Linda followed behind tucking in her blouse and straightening her hair as she walked. After making sure the women had another round of drinks, Harry winked in Frankie's direction.
"About time I was off Frankie so I'll catch you tomorrow.
Jimmy Fingers was sitting patiently waiting outside to take his boss home and seeing Harry stagger a little; he grabbed hold of the man's arm and guided him into the back of the car. It was just before seven when Harry West walked through the front door and when Bella emerged from the kitchen to greet him; he noticed how tired she looked.

"Is everything ok darling?"
Bella tenderly kissed her husband on the cheek and for a moment thought she could smell a strange perfume on his collar. Too tired to start a row, she smiled and made her way back into the kitchen. Pouring her husband his nightly scotch, a practice she'd carried out since the day they were married, Bella waited for him to join her.
"You didn't answer my question honey, are you alright?"
Bella perched herself on one of the leather breakfast bar stools and leaning on the surface, placed her other hand onto her forehead.
"It's Helena that's all. Harry have you been drinking?"
"Just a couple after work, anyway what's she done? She aint hurt is she?"
"To answer your question, no, the little cow isn't hurt, but for your information, my nerves are in shreds. I had hoped as she got older she would calm down but her behaviour is getting worse not better. I really think she needs to see someone or I'm going to end up in the bleeding nut house."
Harry had never seen his wife so upset and when he noticed the tears begin to form in her eyes, knew that something had to be done.
"I've got a lot of work to do tonight but I promise I will make time and have a chat to her. Now I'm going to my study so when she comes down send her through."

Bella nodded her head and watched her husband as he left the room. Talking to Helena would do no good at all, she was totally spoilt and turning into a complete brat. Bella couldn't help but think back to when it was just Harry, Frankie and her, god she missed the boy so much. Suddenly her thoughts came crashing down to earth when her daughter entered the room.
"What's for dinner?"
"I've made a nice shepherd's pie."
Helena West turned up her nose at what was on offer and as she spoke to her mother, tilted her head back just a fraction, as if she was looking down her nose at Bella.
"Shepherd's pie! I'm not eating that shit; it's what poor people have. Now Lydia Coleman at school, she eats nothing but French cuisine. Why can't we have food like that instead of the rubbish that you always dish up?"
Bella was still seated at the breakfast bar and she could feel her nails dig into her palm as she clenched her hands in frustration.
"Why are you such a nasty child Helena? On second thoughts don't answer that. Your father is in the study and he wants to talk to you."
Helena West flounced towards the door and Bella knew that nothing was going to change, the girl could twist her father around her little finger and Bella would be the one made to look bad. Helena didn't knock on the study door and instead burst in

like a tornado.

"Daddy, daddy! I've missed you so much."

Pushing his chair away from the desk he patted his knee and Helena ran over and sat down. Wrapping her arms around his neck she covered his cheek in kisses and just as Bella had anticipated; all ideas of Harry chastising the child went right out of the window. He did feel honour bound to say just a few words but he might as well have saved his breath.

"Your Mum says you've been playing up princess, is that true?"

Helena's bottom lip began to quiver and she forced a tear to fall. Instantly Harry was putty in her hands and he couldn't bear the thought that he'd upset his little princess.

"I promise I haven't daddy, it's her not me. I really think that she's jealous because I speak so nicely and mix with such fabulous people. I can't help it if you want me to have a good education and make something of my life now can I?"

Harry hugged his daughter tightly to him as he rocked back and forth.

"No of course you can't princess, leave it with me and I'll have a word. Now off you go as I have a lot of work to do tonight. Why don't you go and give mum a hand in the kitchen?"

Helena stood up and smiled sweetly but when she reached the hall, curled her lip in a look of distaste. Her mother could take a run and jump, at only nine years old, Helena West saw herself as far to superior to do menial tasks. Harry was still smiling to himself as he removed a vast amount of paperwork from his case.

For the last two years he had been setting up a long firm. It hadn't been done in London for quite some time, well at least not on the scale that Harry was planning and he intended to make a massive amount of money if everything went to plan. A warehouse had been rented in the east end at the rear of Old Billingsgate Market. Harry had purchased a dormant limited company and had set up under the name of British Electrical Wholesale Trading Co limited. Employing a team of grafters to act as managers and reps, Harry had set about making the company into a respectable business. There was only ever one person at the warehouse, Frieda Parker, an ex con and a woman who was also very knowledgeable in the world of fraud. Frieda had been successful for many years and the only prison sentence she had ever received was a five stretch in Holloway several years ago. It hadn't deterred the woman and after serving half of her sentence, she happily joined the general population with three hundred thousand pounds that the legal system had never been able to recover. Frieda Parker handled the ordering side of the company and acted as secretary whenever a supplier called. Small orders were placed each month and invoices were paid promptly. The grafters were used as and

when needed and would call on businesses to discuss placing further orders and to gradually begin to mention that they would in the future, be in a position to secure a very large order for a prestigious company. In the late nineties, internet sales were still in their infancy and although companies were starting to use this way of selling, it was slow and relatively small. Nothing compared to the good old face to face method and the grafters when asked, carried out their roles expertly.
At eleven that night Harry was still holed up in his study reading sales charts and lists of companies that he intended to hit. Bella had called him numerous times to come and get something to eat but eventually she had given up asking and had gone to bed. Nothing could have pulled Harry away from the paperwork, not when he realised just how much money was involved. From the outset he had imagined that it would be several hundred thousand pounds but in reality it was more likely to be a couple of million. He wasn't apprehensive in the least; in fact he was the complete opposite and couldn't wait to get started. Picking up the phone, he dialled Frieda Parker's number. Harry didn't care what the time was, when he wanted to speak to someone they listened no matter what time of day or night it was. Frieda had been in bed for an hour and was now in a comfortable sleep, reaching over she snatched up the phone and shouted into the receiver.

"Yes?"

"Hello darling, its Harry."

As soon as she heard his voice her tone changed. There were three reasons why Frieda didn't tell him to fuck off, firstly Harry was the boss and you always made time for him, secondly there was also a big payout coming her way if this was successful and last but not least, she absolutely adored the man but in all the time that they had been setting up the long firm he never once even gave her a glimmer of hope that he was interested, in fact he'd never even looked at her in that way but she still lived in hope.

"Hi Boss, what's wrong?"

"Nothing's wrong it's just that I've been going over all the sales invoices and I think we should strike while the iron is hot so to speak. Freddie Grange has done a cracking job in the rep department and I think the twats are ready to be taken down."

"I couldn't agree more Harry."

"Good, I'll come over to the warehouse tomorrow and we'll start planning. If this all goes to plan I reckon we can finalise everything within the next month but we're going to need several trusted bodies to help carry it out."

"Leave it with me Harry, I know a lot of people who..."

Harry didn't let the woman continue, he liked to stay in control and it was one thing letting Frieda run the day to day business but now he had to up

his game and let them all know who was in charge.
"That's alright sweetheart, I have my own blokes to help out. Now you have a good night's kip and I'll see you bright and early in the morning."
Harry had hung up before Frieda got a chance to say goodnight but she would still sleep well after having heard his voice.

At eight thirty the following morning and by the time Bella got up, Harry had been gone for over thirty minutes. He had driven himself to Camden as he wanted to talk to Frankie but as he walked into the pub had found the boy, he always thought of Frankie as a boy, laughing and giggling with the Asian bird from yesterday. The sight instantly put him in a bad mood and when Frankie saw the look on his face he mentally said to himself 'fuck me, here we go'.
"Hi Uncle Harry, you're up with the larks today aint you?"
"And a fucking good job I am boy, looks like you took no notice of what I said yesterday. Anyway, if you can drag yourself away from the paki for a minute I need to talk to you in the office."
Adeela didn't flinch at his words as it was nothing she hadn't heard before but Frankie was mortified and as he looked at her he furrowed his brow and moved his head from side to side. As always he did as he was told and when the two were in the office and the door was firmly closed her turned on Harry.

"What the fuck did you say that for? All that bullshit yesterday about you aint a racist and you insult the poor girl to her face."

"Leave it out you twat or are you going to tell me she's born and bred and from the Home Counties."

Frankie momentarily closed his eyes, this was all he needed. He knew he should just ignore the comment but at the same time, something deep inside made him feel as if he had to defend Adeela.

"Well for your information and as it happens, she was born and bred in Walthamstow not that it will make a shits worth of difference and to be honest, I really can't fucking be bothered arguing with you today. Now what did you want to talk to me about?"

Harry had already taken a seat behind the desk and Frankie's last sentence had been totally ignored. He didn't like the girl working here but if the boy wanted a bit of Asian pussy, why should he be concerned with that.

"You know I said I thought you should get more involved in the other side of my businesses, well the time has come."

Harry explained all that had been happening for the last two years and as he did so Frankie's face went white. He didn't want any part of it but then how did you tell a man like Harry West 'no'. Frankie decided that for now he would go along with his uncle, at least until he could figure out a way to get out of this mess and that's exactly what it would be, a complete and utter mess that he wasn't prepared to risk his liberty for.

CHAPTER THIRTEEN

Two weeks had now passed since their first meeting and Adeela was head over heels in love. It hadn't been long but she still felt as though she had known Frankie West for all of her life. Her afternoon shift of cleaning had gone out of the window since the first day and the couple, even though they only had a few hours to spend together, crammed in as much as they could. Frankie West was the perfect gentleman and even though he was always kissing her passionately, things hadn't gone any further. His loins ached for her but what he didn't realise was the fact that she was feeling exactly the same way to. On Friday afternoon the couple both knew that they wouldn't set eyes on each other again for two whole days and the thought of it was causing anxiety for them both. In the middle of a chat over coffee, Adeela suddenly stood up and taking hold of his hand, led Frankie upstairs and into his room. Not one word was spoken between them, there was no need as they were both aware of what was about to happen. Holding hands they entered the room and as Adeela passionately flung her arms around his neck they fell against the door. As it slammed shut Adeela couldn't help giggling at the noise but they both felt as if the world had been shut out and it was all that mattered. The love and wanting that they felt consumed them and as Adeela slowly

unbuttoned Frankie's shirt, he knew he wouldn't be able to resist her. He wanted her so badly and holding her tiny waist he pushed his body hard against hers as he kissed her face, cheeks and neck. She kissed him back, lingering for a second and then concentrating on the task in hand pulled his shirt from his trousers. Running her fingers through the soft hair on Frankie's strong muscular chest, she seductively nibbled at his skin. Frankie was so turned on by her actions that he started to remove Adeela's clothes. He tried to be gentle but at the same time he couldn't hold back and knew he was rushing. Adeela stopped him in his haste.
"Be patient Frankie, let me do it."
She held her hand to his chest as she slowly released her zip allowing her jeans to drop to the floor. Raising her arms above her head she swiftly removed her top revealing her bare breasts. Stripping for her man as he watched her delicate but perfectly formed body come into view was a real turn on. Stepping forward Adeela's hands went to Frankie's waistband and as she unbuttoned his trousers they to fell to the floor. He was already hard as she reached forward and took his penis in her hand. Adeela had always imagined that her first time would be with someone like Frankie and now she was certain that it would be romantic and tender. He was tall, strong and handsome; he also had a lovely nature, in fact to Adeela he was nothing short of perfect.

As they swiftly progressed, some of the tenderness went out of the window and what was about to happen would be raunchy and hot. Leading him over to the bed, Adeela gently pushed Frankie down and then straddled him. As they kissed it felt like they had become one and neither could wait a second longer. Slowly she eased him into her warm moist body.
"Aghhhh that's so good."
Adeela started to move up and down on Frankie's mid section as he lay back mesmerized at what was happening. This girl had come from nowhere and in a matter of days they were totally in love with each other.
"Ohhhh Frankie something's happening to me."
For the first time in her life Adeela was experiencing a very powerful orgasm. She began to move faster and more forcefully and she dug her nails into his waist. Frankie groaned in pleasure, he was near to climaxing himself and sharing this together was the best experience in both of their lives. Leaning forward Adeela's body went tense and so did Frankie's as they shuddered and climaxed together. There had been no pain as she was so relaxed and now as she kissed him again passionately her long ebony hair fell loosely onto his cheeks.
Oh my god, that was fantastic Adeela, I love you so much."
She blushed and her beautiful tanned skin had a pink hue as happiness flooded her whole body.

"Me to Frankie."
"I want you again and again."
"Me too!"
"Is that all you can say 'me to'."
They both laughed but at the same time couldn't keep their hands off of each other. Frankie kissed her breasts and her stomach and when he reached the soft downy area at the top of her legs, Adeela experienced an even greater orgasm which she didn't think was possible. Frankie couldn't get enough of her and his enthusiasm showed as he engrossed himself in every part of her. Twice more and both times in different positions, they climaxed together but finally they lay back on the bed exhausted.

"That was fantastic! Don't ever leave me Adeela stay in my life forever."

"I'm so happy Frankie and I promise there will never be anyone for me but you."

Lying in each other's arms the time had flown by and when the sound of banging could be heard on the front door, Frankie shot up and looked at the bedside clock. It was almost five thirty and the regulars outside were frustrated at not having their after work drink. Quickly pulling on his trousers and top he gently touched Adeela's shoulder. She had drifted off into a blissful sleep but now as she opened her eyes they were full of fear. By the time she got home it would be past six and her family would be on the war path. When she explained to

Frankie and he saw the fear in her eyes he ignored the din from downstairs and sat back down on the bed. Taking her in his arms he pulled her close. "Don't worry babe, I'll hail you a cab it'll be a lot quicker. Now hurry up and get dressed darling, you need to be on your way and I've got a hoard or irate punters trying to break down the door."
Within twenty minutes the black hackney had whizzed through the traffic and was dropping Adeela off at the top of her road. Unbeknown to her, Frankie had paid the driver double to get her home as quickly as he could. She was still late though, and as she placed her key into the lock, could visibly see her hand shaking. Walking into the kitchen she spied her mother eating alone, the men must have already been fed and she knew that any moment she would be summoned through to the front room. Her mother's face was set like stone and as Adeela sat down and put food into a dish, she looked up and into her mother's eyes.
"You really are a silly girl but then your misfortune is my gain I suppose, there's no way Safeer will allow you to keep working now."
Adeela didn't reply and her mother studied her face in depth. The girl's cheeks were flushed and even though Yasmeen couldn't put her finger on exactly what it was, her daughter was definitely different. Before Adeela had a chance to put any food into her mouth, Safeer's voice boomed out from the front room demanding that she came in and explained

her lateness. Slowly walking through, she hung her head as she entered and reaching the table didn't speak until she was given permission.

"And where the fuck have you been girl?"

"I'm sorry I'm late brother but the place was very messy today. It took me a lot longer to clean up and then the underground was packed and I missed two trains and........"

"Shut up! Maybe you should work harder or maybe even pack the job in? I've been thinking about this and I'm having my doubts that it was such a good idea in the first place."

Adeela knew this would happen and removing the five crisp twenty pound notes that Frankie had given her, she placed them onto the table and prayed the money would change his mind. Safeer was a greedy man and as soon as he saw the cash he backtracked on the words he had said a few moments ago. Snatching up the notes he quickly placed them into his pocket. Anwar silently watched his son and he didn't like what he was hearing, as much as he disliked his daughter, her place was here in the family home at least until her marriage.

"Well I suppose the money will come in handy but you had better be behaving yourself girl. If you ever bring shame on this family and act like the white slag's do around here, you will pay the price. Do you understand me?"

"Yes brother."

"Good, now go and eat. You need to keep your strength up."

Adeela did as her brother ordered but as happy as she was with Safeer allowing her to carry on working, she was also in a state of shock. In the whole of her life he had never said a kind word to her and now he had just told her to eat to keep her strength up. Passing her mother in the hall, Adeela knew that Yasmeen had been listening at the door and had heard everything. Her mother would be angry now and Adeela would end up paying the price but if it meant being able to be with her Frankie, then it would all be worth it. Tomorrow was aunt Bina's annual big party and Adeela couldn't wait to take her only ally to one side and reveal all that had happened.

The Makhdoom brothers set out at just after eight. Friday night was always a good earner and they didn't want to risk losing even a single punter. Business had been a little on the slow side for the last couple of days and tonight Safeer planned to have as many of his girls out working as possible. On the drive over to the old Burial Gardens the brothers discussed their plans, in reality it was Safeer doing the talking and the other two just listened.

"Akram I'm going to drop you off and I want you to wait with Lindy and Fiona. Tell Lindy she has to work tonight and no arguments. I've got a special client for the younger girl so keep her sweet; tell her you're desperate for money of something. Me and Rashid will pick Dawn and Janice up and drop them at Kings Cross as usual."

Rashid and Akram didn't argue with their brother and after picking up Vodka and cigarettes, they pulled up at the long forgotten rundown gardens. As soon as Akram got out of the car Safeer drove off in the direction of the Leisure Centre. Dawn Spicer and Janice McDonald were already waiting but tonight they had someone else with them. Safeer stared out of the car window and let out a groan, the woman was older and even though his own girls were starting to show signs of wear, this one had well and truly been around the block a few times. Safeer opened the window and Janice leaned forward to speak to him.

"I've brought you a fresh girl Safeer."

"Fucking fresh! She looks fucking rotten to me and you know I don't want anyone over twenty Janice. What the fuck were you thinking girl?"

Janice grinned at his words, sometimes Safeer could be so funny and that was probably one of the reasons she'd fallen for him in the first place.

"I know babe but she's good at her trade. Her pimp up in Glasgow got shot last week and she needed to make a hasty departure, that's why she's here. Give her a chance Safeer; I know you won't be disappointed."

Safeer nodded for the girls to get in and as Janice opened the door he quietly said under his breath,

'You'd better be right girl.' Mary Matson was all of thirty five and had been on the game since she was fifteen. She'd seen men like Safeer before and they were no good, now poor old Gordon, her last pimp, had been totally different. He was or had been a fair man and had always shared her earnings fifty fifty but Mary knew Safeer Makhdoom would take far more. The trouble was, until she got to know people and where the best locations were, Mary needed to stay safe. She decided that she would give it a week and then move on but she didn't mention her plans to Dawn or Janice. She didn't know if she could trust them to keep their mouths shut and pimps had a habit of turning nasty if they didn't like what they were hearing. The women were dropped off at Kings Cross and were all given a stern warning from Safeer.

"I need you all to work your arses off tonight. I'm short of reddies at the minute so you need to work harder, it aint as if you don't owe me now is it?" Mary Matson was about to say she owned him nothing but one steely glare from Janice told her to keep her trap shut.

"I'll be back at two to collect you, usual place, now get moving, you're wasting valuable time."

With that Dawn slammed the door and the car sped off. It was now time to do the most important business of the night and Safeer knew that he was about to earn some serious money. Just as he'd been told, Akram had stayed at the Burial Gardens with Lindy and Fiona. Fiona Selby had her arms draped all over him as Lindy leaned against the monument. Her face was set in a deep scowl at what she knew she was going to have to do later. She could have just walked away but that wasn't really an option as no one walked away from Safeer Makhdoom, well at least not without permission and if they did there was always a massive consequence to face. When Akram saw the car he breathed out a sigh of relief. The girls had argued nonstop since he'd got here and he was scared that they would end up scraping and mark each other's faces. Taking Fiona's hand he led her to the car with Lindy following on behind them. It was a bit of a squash in the back with the three of them and Akram made sure he sat in the middle to stop any further squabbles. Safeer drove over to south London to the Tyers Estate situated close to Guys hospital. The older girl had been here before and she knew what was expected of her. Lindy hated these special nights and thanked god that she was only asked to do them now and again. The flat was in a rundown building and there would be three or four men in residence all with their cameras set up on tripods. It would start with her slowly taking off her clothes while they all snapped away but would end up as a glorified gangbang and she hoped that this time Safeer would pay her far more than he did last time. At least when it was over, George Sewell who ran the so called club, would always drop her

back off at the care home so it was some small consolation. Unlike Lindy, Fiona didn't know what she had to do tonight but Akram was overly loving and attentive towards her. Had already given her a bracelet that she couldn't stop admiring and right at this moment, Fiona felt like the luckiest girl in the world. After dropping Lindy off, Safeer made his way over to Soho and for the entire journey the cars passengers were silent. This was a new expansion for the Makhdoom's, Safeer was nervous and when Safeer was nervous, no one spoke for fear of making him angry. He had recently made a contact with Barry Carter who managed a sex booth shop on Dean Street. Punters paid a score a time to sit in a booth and ogle a naked woman playing with herself and more often than not, the men would masturbate as they watched but now he had telephoned Safeer and said he needed something a little different for a client of his. Barry was street wise and he always weighed up a punter before committing. Once he was happy, he would telephone one of his contacts and Safeer happened to be the newest on his list. Fiona was the chosen girl to do the business and was to be driven to a small bed and breakfast on Greek Street. The place hired out it's rooms by the hour and no questions were asked as Barry paid the owner handsomely for the privilege. Pulling up outside, Safeer and Rashid got out of the car and left Akram alone to talk to the girl.
"Baby I need your help."

Fiona couldn't stop fingering her new bracelet but at the same time she was taking in all that he was saying to her. Fiona Selby adored the man beside her and right at this moment would have gladly done anything for him.

"What's wrong?"

"Look I'm in trouble and Safeer has sorted out someone who can help me out of this mess but only if you are willing to go along with it?"

Fiona looked into his big brown eyes; he had bought her a bracelet so how could she refuse him.

"I'll help you in any way I can, what do you want me to do?"

"Go into the B & B and have sex with a man. I promise it will be over quickly but it will sort out all of my problems and then we can be together."

Fiona looked longingly into his eyes and knew deep in her heart, that he was telling the truth.

"Ok baby, if it means that much to you I'll do it."

"Good girl, now go inside and up to room twelve, the man will be waiting for you."

Fiona got out of the car and doing as she was instructed, ignored the reception area and walked straight up the stairs. The place was run down and with each step she could hear the floor boards beneath her feet creek. Knocking timidly on the door marked twelve, she waited to be invited inside. Trevor Long, a deviant sexual predator who had never before had the balls to carry out any of his fantasies, answered the door within a few seconds. As he opened up, he licked his lips when he saw what was on offer. Barry Carter had really come up trumps and Trevor would be forever in his debt. Inviting Fiona inside, he offered her a drink which she declined. The man was about sixty years old and his appearance was dirty not to mention the fact that he smelled. When he smiled at her in a leering way, Fiona could see that all of his teeth were rotten and suddenly she felt that this wasn't such a good idea but then again she had promised Akram, so gritting her teeth she took a seat on the bed. After showing her a hard core porn movie and when the girl still wasn't in anyway interested, he decided that he'd paid his money and he wanted value for it. Pushing her down, he roughly lifted up her skirt and removed her underwear. Fiona fought him all the way but her actions only fuelled his desire and physically she was no match for him. The rape was over almost as soon as he entered her but unbeknown to Fiona, her torture had only just begun. An hour later and Safeer, Rashid and Akram were still seated in the car outside. It shouldn't have taken this long and Safeer was beginning to panic. His concern wasn't for Fiona; only for his loss of earnings should anything have gone wrong.

"Akram go inside and see what's happening and tell that dirty old cunt that if he's much longer then he'll have to pay double."

Doing as he was told Akram climbed the steps of

the B & B and went inside. There was no one on reception so he made his way up to room twelve and tapped on the door. When there wasn't any answer he turned the handle and what greeted him on the other side caused him to run into the bathroom and vomit. Trevor Long had disappeared and Fiona's lifeless body lay on the bed, her throat had been cut and even without looking to closely, Akram could see that her breasts and vagina had been mutilated. There was blood everywhere from the frenzied attack in which Trevor Long had stabbed Fiona over and over again. Using the cuff of his jacket to wipe the door handle clean, Akram made a hasty exit out of the rear fire door, in all probability it was the same door that Trevor had used. Walking around the outside of the building, he threw up twice more before he reached the car.
"Fuck me you took your time, what's going on?"
Safeer suddenly stopped talking, as even in the dim light of the car's interior he could see that his brother's normally handsome face was ashen.
"Are you alright Akram? What's happened and where's the girl?"
"Just Drive Safeer, get us out of here now"
Safeer Makhdoom didn't need to be told twice, whatever had happened had scared the life out of his brother and he knew that it must be bad. Starting the engine he pulled away as quickly as he could without drawing any suspicions from anyone passing by. As the car moved in the direction of

Soho none of the brothers said a word but their silence spoke volumes, they were worried. Safeer parked the car on Balfe Street where he had arranged to pick up Dawn, Janice and the new woman. Switching off the engine, he turned in his seat to face Akram.
"So how bad is it?"
"About as bad as it can get, she's dead."
Safeer turned back in his seat and placing his elbows on the steering wheel put his head in his hands. Tomorrow he would go and see Barry Carter to find out what the fuck had happened. Safeer then whacked the steering wheel with the palms of his hands over and over again as frustration began to build. Rashid and Akram remained silent, they had seen this action from their brother before and when Safeer was angry you kept your head down if you knew what was good for you. An hour later and Janice opened the car door, Dawn and Mary stood on the pavement as they could see there wouldn't be enough room in the car and were now wondering how they would get back to Walthamstow. Janice handed over a large wad of notes, the girls had worked extra hard tonight and she hoped Safeer would be pleased. He didn't count it, he had too much on his mind and instead he peeled off two twenty pound notes and slapped them into her palm.
"Get a taxi back."
"Oh alright Safeer, same time tomorrow?"

Starting up the engine, he didn't reply but his silent rebuff went unnoticed and as he pulled the car away from the kerb, Janice had to quickly jump back or he would have ran over her feet. Safeer had decided that things couldn't wait until later and with a bit of luck Barry would still be at the booth. Luck was on his side and as the brothers walked along Dean Street, Barry was in the process of pulling the shutters down. Swiftly ducking underneath, Safeer came face to face with Barry Carter. The man was short, no more than five feet four in his stocking feet, and must have weighed close to twenty stone. He'd been in the sex industry for a long time and there wasn't anyone or anything that he didn't know about porn and the sale of sex. As far as Safeer saw it, Barry Carter was a very good contact to know, or at least he had been until a few hours ago.

"Hello mate, bit late for you to be out and about aint it?"

"Bit fucking late! That fucking nonce you set my girl up with has only gone and slit her throat, what the fuck were you doing putting me onto a cunt like that?"

Barry Carter blew his cheeks out in shock; this was all way out of his depth.

"No! I knew he could cut up rough sometimes, that's why he paid as much as he did but kill the kid? Fucking hell, I don't believe it!"

"Believe it my friend, there's blood everywhere!

What a fucking mess this has turned out to be."
"Fuck me, what can I say?"
"There's nothing you can say."
"Fuck fuck fuck!"
"So, now what do we do? The Old Bill will be all over the place before daylight?"
Barry rubbed furiously at his balding head as he thought and after what seemed like an age, he finally spoke.
"Leave it with me and I'll get someone to do a cleanup. Debbie who runs the place knows the score and as long as we leave it spotless she'll keep her trap shut. Stay away until I contact you and for fucks sake don't talk to anyone about this or we'll all be well and truly fucked."
Doing as he'd been told, Safeer and his brothers drove home in silence. Safeer was contemplating the worst case scenario of what could happen, Rashid didn't really give a toss about any of it and was looking forward to his bed but Akram, Akram was beginning to blame himself for the tragedy and it would play heavily on his mind.

CHAPTER FOURTEEN

When Adeela woke she could feel the warmth of the sun on her face through the open curtains. Normally she hated the weekend and that hatred had only increased since she'd met Frankie as she now wouldn't see him for two whole days but today was different. Today was aunt Bina's annual garden party and Adeela couldn't wait. Stretching out her arms she yawned and then giggled to herself, she couldn't remember ever being this happy and it was becoming more and more difficult to keep that happiness to herself. By the time they were all ready to leave it was midday, lunch was being served at one pm so there would be plenty of time for light refreshments and Adeela hoped there would also be time to get her aunt alone. Frankie had given Adeela a mobile but she kept it on silent so that her family wouldn't find out. It was the first mobile phone that Adeela Makhdoom had ever owned but it hadn't taken her long to master and within a few days messages had been flowing back and forth between the pair. With one last adjustment to her hijab, she sent him a voice mail saying how much she missed him; at the end she paused for a second and then said 'I love you'. Frankie hardly ever answered his telephone, so it at least saved her any embarrassment at actually having to speak to him. Adeela adored Frankie and she knew he liked her but she wasn't sure how deep his feelings really were, he'd told her that he loved her but she was so insecure and afraid of losing him that it was constantly on her mind. She wanted him to tell her over and again, no it was more than that, she needed him to but at the same she was scared that she might be rushing things and it would put him off. This was all so new to her and she prayed that he wouldn't let her down.

Arriving at aunt Bina's large three storey Georgian house, Adeela made her way up to the bathroom to check her phone but there was nothing. With a disappointed heart she put it into her handbag and went downstairs. The kitchen was a hive of activity, several family members had gathered, some she hadn't seen for years and some she had never met before. Yasmeen grabbed her daughters hand and began to introduce her but as always Adeela just stood with her head down as she meekly said 'hello' to each of them. Uncle Danish and Aunty Javeria were there with their son Parvez, who Adeela hadn't seen since she was a little girl. There were also people from the Pakistani community who were high caste and not the types of people Adeela would normally get to mix with. She had been ordered by her parents to be on her best behaviour and not cause them any embarrassment but there was no need as she was always as quiet as a mouse anyway. As soon as she had entered the room, uncle Danish could visibly be

seen pushing his son forward. Parvez had always been a shy boy and even though he was now an adult, he hadn't changed. At twenty three years old he had yet to find a bride and his thick black glasses and slightly bucked teeth did nothing to endear him to the opposite sex. His parents were desperate for grandchildren, so desperate in fact, that they had lowered their standards and allowed Bina to be a matchmaker. Yasmeen now pushed her daughter forwards and the pair just stood staring at each other in awkward silence. After a poke in the back by his father, Parvez finally asked Adeela if she would like to take a walk in the garden and Adeela, desperate to escape the sideshow, nodded her head. Outside Safeer, Rashid and Akram were standing at the bottom of the garden. Deep in conversation, they didn't see Adeela and Parvez walk outside but even if they had it would have made little difference. Safeer was trying to justify to his youngest brother all that had happened the previous night but he wasn't having much success. Spying her brothers, Adeela stopped, she didn't want to go anywhere near them and Parvez sensed that something was wrong.
"Are you alright?"
"Yes I'm fine thank you Parvez but you know what my brothers are like and I really would like to stay out of their way."
"I'm sorry about this."
"Sorry about what?"

"Our parents pushing us together, you do know aunt Bina is trying to match us?"
Adeela's face flushed with embarrassment but she was also angry. She loved her aunt dearly and would never have imagined in her wildest dreams that the woman would do something like this, at least not without speaking to her first.
"No, I didn't."
"That's typical of the family, so how do you feel about it?"
"Feel about it? Parvez you've just told me that they are all hoping we will marry and you want my thoughts on it? Well without having much time to consider it, I don't like it one little bit."
Parvez grabbed her hand and for a moment Adeela was taken aback.
"Praise be to Allah, I'm so glad you said that. I don't mean to cause offence in anyway but, well if I'm truthful, I don't want to get married either."
"You don't? I thought that's what every man of your age wanted."
Parvez hung his head, he wanted to explain but he didn't really know how. Adeela was a very pretty girl and if he didn't choose his words right she may get offended. On the other hand he couldn't allow this silly setup to continue but what he was about to reveal needed a great deal of trust on her part and Parvez wasn't sure he could trust her. Still there was no point in lying, so taking the bull by the horns, he spoke.

"Can I tell you something in confidence?"
"Of course you can cousin Parvez."
Parvez squeezed Adeela's hand, not so much that it hurt but just enough to let her know that what he was about to say was deadly serious.
"Truly Parvez, whatever you say will go no further I promise."
"I'm gay Adeela but if my parents found out they would disown me, come to that the whole family would disown me."
Adeela began to laugh and when he thought that she was mocking him, Parvez instantly let go of her hand. Adeela could see that she had upset her cousin and that definitely wasn't her intention so tenderly she picked up his hand and caressed it.
"I wasn't laughing at you cousin, only the fact that I to have a secret. I already have a boyfriend who I'm madly in love with but he's white and my family would also never approve. I think that as ridiculous this charade is, something good could come out of it."
"How do you mean?"
"Well what if we went along with it, tell them that we agree? Tell them that we might and I do mean might, be a good match. It would end up being the longest engagement in history but at least we would both be free to be with the people that we really want to be with."
When she saw the grin on Parvez's face, her heart went out to him. Raising her hand, he gently kissed

the back and then mouthed the words 'thank you'.
"Don't worry; your secret is safe with me as I trust mine is with you. Now I need to speak to aunt Bina about something but we're in agreement, that as far as everyone is concerned we are a couple?"
"Yes and I thank you cousin, I thank you from the bottom of my heart."
As Adeela entered the house, she knew that the arrangement wasn't perfect and that it couldn't last forever but it would at least buy her some precious time with her Frankie. En route to the bathroom to check if she'd received any messages on her phone, she was stopped when aunt Bina touched her arm.
"Well?"
"Aunty I need to go to the toilet and then can we have a word in private?"
"Of course we can, go on up and I'll be with you in a couple of minutes."
Desperate to check her phone, Adeela didn't need to be told twice and almost ran up the stairs. When she heard Frankie's message her heart skipped a beat, he was saying the words 'I love you to', over and over again. A knock on the door brought her back to reality and after quickly slipping her mobile into her handbag, she opened the door. Aunt Bina, as far as Adeela was concerned, was a fabulous woman and a true confidant so she had no fears about what she was about to reveal.
"So darling, what did you think of him?"
Adeela sat on the edge of the bath and tapped the

side for her aunt to join her.

"Parvez is a lovely man aunty but he's not for me."

"Why? I thought you two would be a perfect match, so did the rest of the family."

For a moment Adeela had second thoughts about telling her aunt that she already had a boyfriend. It was the biggest secret she had ever kept and one that could ruin her whole life if her family ever found out but she had to confide in someone or she'd go insane.

"I have a boyfriend aunty and I'm head over heels in love with him but there's just one problem."

Bina furrowed her brow as she waited to hear the rest. Deep down she already knew what her niece was about to reveal and it would at the very least, bring nothing but heartache.

"He's not a Muslim, just an ordinary white man who totally adores me. Oh aunty what am I going to do?"

Bina placed her arm tenderly around Adeela's shoulders and pulled her in close. Years ago when she had refused her own arranged marriage her family had made her an outcast. She was in no doubt that if she hadn't have married Omar Raja, who had made a fortune in the steel industry, then she would still be an outcast today.

"My darling you are going against everything we believe in. You know my story but I was very lucky and besides uncle Omar was a Muslim and from a Pakistani family. There is no way this man would

ever be accepted, you must know this?"
Adeela's reply came out in a sharp tone, one that she had never used before and it shocked her aunt.
"Of course I do! But how can I stop loving him and how could I ever marry another man when I'm in love with someone else, it would be a disaster."
Bina stood up and turned to face her niece. She was about to ask a question that Adeela wouldn't like but all the same, it had to be asked.
"Are you sleeping with this man?"
Adeela hung her head, she wasn't ashamed just embarrassed that her aunt would even ask such a thing. Not answering the question was enough for Bina to know that her niece was no longer a virgin.
"Oh Adeela how could you! Falling in love with someone is one thing but giving your body to a man outside of marriage is so wrong my darling. What if you get pregnant?"
Adeela hadn't even thought about that possibility but now that she did, well maybe it would be the answer to all her problems. She was sure Frankie would stand by her and she could go and live with him at the pub. The smallest hint of a smile crossed her lips and aunt Bina took it as read that Adeela was already pregnant.
"Oh no girl, whatever have you done?"
Adeela stood up and taking Bina's hand began to laugh at her aunt's reaction.
"Of course I'm not pregnant."
"Thank god for that, you nearly gave me a heart

attack! I think I need to meet this man and have a chat with him, when you visit next Saturday bring him along but don't let anyone see you or you know what will happen. Now what about poor Parvez, what will you tell him?"

"It's already been sorted out and for now we will both go along with the engagement. Aunt Bina I can't explain why because I made a promise, but for his own reasons Parvez doesn't want this match either. At least if we play along with things then it will give us both some breathing space."

Bina shook her head, she had never heard anything like it before but at the same time she loved her niece dearly and wouldn't betray her. She only hoped that this man, whoever he was, would see sense after Bina had explained exactly what it would mean to her niece if he continued this relationship.

"We should get back to the others now and please Adeela, try and show more interest in Parvez. Your mother and father were really hopeful about this match and I'm only glad that I won't be the one that has to tell them what's really going on. I actually think if your father found out it would finish him off."

"Would that be so bad?"

"Adeela! How could you say such a thing?"

"Oh come on aunty, you know how they all treat me, your two dogs have a better life than I do. The only reason they are trying to set me up with Parvez is because his family have money, other than that I would remain a slave in that house for the rest of my life."

Bina hugged Adeela tightly. She couldn't condemn the girl because every word she had just said was the truth and it hurt Bina to think how Adeela had suffered for the whole of her life.

The party was in full swing when they went down stairs and when Adeela told her parents that she liked the young man; they smiled at her for the first time in years. Glancing across the room she grinned when her eyes settled on Parvez and when he winked at her, Adeela knew that at least for a while their secrets would be safe.

CHAPTER FIFTEEN

On Sunday Frankie was enjoying his one and only lay in of the week as unlike on a weekday, the pub didn't open until twelve. Picking up his telephone from the bedside chest he dialled Adeela's number but wasn't disappointed when it went straight to voicemail.

"Hi babe, just wanted to say morning and tell you that I love you so much. I hope the party went well yesterday at your aunts and that you had a chance to speak to her about us. I can't wait to see you tomorrow Adeela, I'm crazy about you."

Suddenly he could hear someone on the stairs. "Sorry I've got to go, I'll call you tomorrow." Frankie quickly pressed the end call button and placed the telephone back down. When his bedroom door opened and Harry West walked in Frankie was surprised to say the least. His uncle never paid social calls let alone come up to his bedroom and Frankie could feel a dark cloud begin to loom over his head.

"Get your arse out of that bed; you've got work to do."

"No I aint, we don't open until noon."

"I don't mean this place, I want you to come over to the warehouse with me and get up to speed with what's going on."

"I told you last week, if you don't mind I'd rather

not get involved."

"Well I do fucking mind, so move your arse!"

Frankie knew it was best not to argue any further and hauling himself from the bed, got dressed. Uncle Harry was determined that he would be part of the family business so to speak but Frankie West had hated the idea as soon as it was mentioned. He had already decided to have a word with Bella on the side in the hope that she could convince her husband to keep their so called son out of things. For now he would do as ordered and after quickly washing and cleaning his teeth he joined the man downstairs. Harry was standing in the bar area and already had a glass of brandy in his hand, which wasn't a good sign.

"Fuck me you took your time. Well come on then, we need to get a move on if you're to be back here ready for opening."

Downing his drink in one, the two men walked outside and Frankie was surprised to see that Harry was driving himself. Normally he didn't go anywhere without Jimmy Fingers in the front seat. Getting into the passenger side he eyed Harry with suspicion but he didn't ask any questions, preferring to wait until he was more informed. The journey took just under twenty minutes and there was not a hint of a conversation for the whole of that time. Pulling up on Lower Thames Street the men got out of the car and as Harry marched off in the direction of the old Market, Frankie reluctantly followed. The building was smaller than he'd expected and as Harry opened up the door inserted into the roller shutter, Frankie let out a gasp. "Impressive aint it? There will be double this amount next week, that's why I want you to be a part of it; I need people I can trust."

Frankie surveyed the racks and racks of computers, televisions, Hi-fi's, washing machines, fridges, freezers and all manner of the latest electrical items and gadgets you could name. For a second he wondered if Harry really wanted someone he could trust, or if it was just a case that anyone who knew about what was going on and was involved in the operation, wouldn't then be able to grass him up.

"So what is it you want me to do and why can't you get more of the blokes from the club to help out?"

"When I'm finally finished in a couple of week's time, the total value should be around two million. Do you honestly think I want just anyone helping when we come to shifting it all?"

"Look Uncle Harry, it's not that I'm ungrateful but things are really going good for me at the moment. I know you don't like Adeela, though I'll never understand why but I do and if I end up getting banged up for this, then my relationship will be over before its even got started."

Harry stepped inside the warehouse office and Frankie followed. Flicking on the light switch he took a seat on one of the chairs and beckoned for Frankie to join him.

"No one's going to get banged up; look let me tell you how it works. I've had this place for a couple of years. In that time I set up a limited company and ran everything by the book, now I've placed really big orders but when it comes time to pay and they start chasing this company for payment, we will be long gone. Although the company's been trading for a decent amount of time and the merchandise has been regularly updated, we've only just been keeping the place afloat. I've been selling on to other retail shops and stores at a slightly discounted price. I've made sure that we always file our returns on time and everything appears above board. I'm going to be offering massive discounts to the retailers, as long as they make payment upfront of course. It will seem so appealing that they won't be able to say no, an opportunity to get rich quick if you like. We have a fantastic credit rating so no one's going to say no and when the delivery comes in and I sell it on to the retailers and, well contacts that are a bit below the law and only deal in cash. They shift the stuff out of the back of vans all around the country, they make money, I make money and everybody's happy. Well apart from the legitimate companies that I've ordered from but it will be a couple of months before they start chasing hard and by then we will be long gone without leaving a trace. What with the upfront payments from the outlets, I'll be fucking quid's in." Frankie's brow was furrowed in confusion.

"I know I might come across as a bit thick at times but won't it be easy for them to find you?"
Harry laughed and leaning over ruffled Frankie's hair.
"Well it would be if we were stupid enough to use our own identities, you really are a naive twat sometimes. Look, the company address is registered here and all of the directors have been dead for ages. Actually I thought that was a stroke of genius on my part, I trawled the London registers for details on deceased people. I managed to get their national insurance numbers, addresses, in fact you name it I got it and they all appear to be upstanding members of the community and very much alive. Fuck me it's going to be funny when the law starts chasing after dead men."
Frankie stood up and walking from the office, inspected all the racks of merchandise. Everything he saw was bang up to date and would fetch a good price. For a second he almost relented at the thought of how much he could stash away for his future life, a life that he hoped would include Adeela but just the thought of her name was enough to make him realise that this was all too risky.
"Can I think about it?"
Harry turned and Frankie could see by the look on his face, a look that he'd seen many times over the years that said Uncle Harry was far from happy.
"No you fucking cant. Now either you're in on this

or you aint but let me give you a word of warning before you decide. If you choose to walk away, then you walk away from everything and that includes the pub. How I see it Frankie, is if you aint prepared to help me then I can no longer help you. I wonder just how long your little Asian tart will hang around for when you aint got a pot to piss in, let alone a roof over your head."

Frankie could feel his blood begin to boil; he also knew that Harry meant every word he was saying. Trying to keep his calm, he stared at his uncle and decided that just for now he would go along with it. Bella would help him, he was certain of that but until he could get to see her, he had to agree.

"Ok ok but its fucking blackmail. All this don't sit well with me Uncle Harry but you've forced me into a corner, so alright I'll do it."

"Good lad I knew you'd see sense. Let's get back to the pub as you aint got long before opening."

As he drove along Harry was full of himself as he elaborated further on all that it had taken to set the long firm up. Frankie smiled and nodded from time to time whenever Harry glanced in his direction but in all honesty he wasn't the least bit interested. He had a sick feeling in the pit of his stomach that something would go wrong and he knew that whatever happened, he had to see Bella the next day.

More by luck than judgement the pub had opened on time and it was unusually hectic for a Sunday.

When the last punter had left at three pm and when the doors were finally locked, Frankie flopped down onto one of the chairs. For the whole shift he had been running over in his mind all that Harry had said, well actually threatened him with and it hadn't gone unnoticed by the regulars. Several had commented that he was away with the fairies today but even their words couldn't raise a smile on Frankie West's face. Now he had the onset of a headache and it was the last thing he needed. Grabbing his keys and phone he let himself out of the pub and began to walk. Initially he had intended to go down to the lock but something had made him enter the station and before he knew it Frankie was on a tube and heading for Walthamstow. Excitement was building even though he wouldn't get to be with Adeela but just to be on the street where she lived was enough. As he exited the station and made his way to Priory Avenue, Frankie pulled up the hood of his coat. He could see from the shops and people walking about, that the area was just as run down as Adeela had described. Crossing the road he walked along until he was level with her house and staring up at the window, wondered if it was his girl's room. Just then the front door opened and Safeer, Rashid and Akram came out. Safeer looked across the road and when he saw Frankie, he stopped. Frankie immediately began to walk on but it was too late he'd been seen and with Safeer being so paranoid about the Old Bill since the incident the other night, he waited to see where Frankie was heading to. Akram was still suffering mentally and had shouted at his older brother several times when he'd kept referring to Fiona's death as an accident. The tension in the house had been so high today that Safeer had decided to start work early in the hope that a change of scenery would lift his brother's spirits. As they got into the car and when Safeer was about to start the engine, Frankie came walking back in the opposite direction. He kept his head down but it was too late as Akram had now spotted him.

"Look Safeer, aint that the bloke who just walked down the road. You don't reckon he's fucking Old Bill do you?"

"I don't know but I'm going to fucking find out!" Safeer got out of the car and ran across the road. When Frankie clocked him out of the corner of his eye, he immediately quickened his pace but he wasn't quick enough. Safeer Makhdoom grabbed his arm and Frankie spun round to face him. For a split second no words were forthcoming as Frankie stared into eyes that were cold and hard and right then he could only imagine how this man must treat his sister.

"I saw you walking up and down, you were looking at my house, who are you?"

Frankie had to think on his feet and said the first thing that came to mind.

"Look mate, I don't want any trouble, I'm just trying to find someone."

Safeer eyed Frankie suspiciously. He looked a bit gormless but then half the people around here looked gormless so that didn't tell him anything. "So who are you looking for then?"

As Frankie explained himself he never once took his eyes off the man. He didn't want to appear shifty and hoped that his lie would be believed. This had been such a bad idea and he wished he was back at the lock with the people he felt most comfortable with. This area was so close to his home and yet it felt alien and slightly intimidating.

"My aunt, she used to live here years ago, number ten I think but no one seems to have heard of her. It was just a stab in the dark really and it's turned out to be like looking for a needle in a haystack. You aint ever hear of her have you, her name was Agnes Grange?"

Safeer, who was still holding onto Frankie's arm suddenly let go. He had no reason to disbelieve the stranger and accepting that the man wasn't Old Bill, Safeer was now in a better mood.

"Sorry mate can't help you."

Frankie nodded his thanks and then turned and walked away, he could feel perspiration running down his back but at least he'd gotten away with it. He only hoped that Adeela hadn't been watching from the window. Safeer got back into the car and both of his brothers were desperate to know what had passed between the two men.

"Well?"

"There's nothing to worry about. It was just some tosser looking for his family. Right boys, we need to get back to work. It's been a while and we aint heard anything so I think it's ok to continue building up our little empire."

Akram sighed he really was fed up with living like this and since Fiona had been murdered, he was beginning to feel guilty regarding what they were doing. Akram now needed some assurance that it wouldn't happen again.

"We're not doing business with that Barry Carter again are we?"

Safeer smiled to himself when he heard the nervousness in his younger brother's voice.

"Akram don't look so worried; we'll give Barry a wide berth, for a while at least."

Safeer and Rashid both laughed but Akram couldn't see anything funny in what his brother had just said. Still he knew that for a few days at least it would be back to their usual business and not the depravity that Safeer wanted to start dealing in. Sitting back in his seat, Akram relaxed a little as they once again drove over to the old Burial Gardens.

CHAPTER SIXTEEN

Adeela was up bright and early and had slipped out of the house an hour before she needed to. Everyone else in her family was still sleeping and even though she knew it was a risk, thought her chances of being caught out were low. Exiting the station she ran as fast as her legs would carry her, desperate not to waste a minute that could be spent with Frankie. Banging on the door he instantly opened up and had in fact been waiting in the bar long before Adeela had even got out of bed. All thoughts of cleaning went out of the window when he saw her and even though he knew that Karen would be fuming when she arrived to find the place unclean, he didn't care. They would all have to muck in and work a little harder but for now all he wanted was to take Adeela in his arms. Minutes later and the couple were upstairs naked. Their love making was tender but also electric and as their bodies entwined Frankie never wanted this feeling to end. Previously they had reserved the afternoons for intimacy but they just couldn't help themselves. After fulfilling each other totally, Adeela laid her head on his chest. There was still an hour to go before she needed to leave for university and it would be nice to spend some time just talking.
"So how did the party go?"
"It could have been better. I didn't realise they

would all be trying to set me up in an arranged marriage."

"What!"

Frankie sat bolt upright in the bed and Adeela giggled as she tenderly stroked his back.

"Don't worry it isn't going to happen but me and my supposed fiancé have hatched a little plan. Dear sweet Parvez is gay but no one knows it, so for the time being we have decided to go along with the farce to allow us both to live the lives we want."

Frankie lay back down and turning to face her, kissed Adeela tenderly.

"You had me worried there for a minute, I thought you'd gone off me and found someone else already."

Adeela playfully poked him in the ribs.

"Never!"

"So did you get a chance to speak to your aunt?"

Suddenly Adeela stopped playing around and became deadly serious. Frankie noticed the look on her face and knew that he probably wasn't going to like what he was about to hear.

"I did but she wasn't happy. She won't betray my confidence but she said we had to end it, she also asked if I would take you to visit her when I go next Saturday."

"Of course I'll come with you but does she really want to meet me or will she just try and get me to finish with you?"

Adeela propped herself up on one elbow and stared deep into his eyes as she spoke.

"All I can tell you is it won't be a good visit. My aunt Bina is a wonderful woman but I've realised there's no way she will ever support us in this. Still I suppose we need to do as she asks, even if it's only for the sake of keeping our secret."

Frankie wrapped his arms around her and pulled Adeela close.

"I promise you darling, nothing will ever keep us apart."

When Adeela left the pub and headed off to her studies, Frankie started to clean like never before. Thoughts whirled around in his head about the conversation he'd had with the woman he loved and no matter how hard he tried, he couldn't see a solution to their problems. By the time Karen Jones arrived for her shift at ten o'clock, the place had been tidied but the floors were still yet to be cleaned. Even though he'd done his best, as Karen scanned the room she didn't look to happy.

"I thought you'd hired a cleaner?"

"I did."

"Well it doesn't look as if she's much good. Now I'm going to have to wash the floors as well as get the bar ready, it's not on Frankie really it isn't."

As Karen disappeared out the back, Frankie sighed heavily, this was all getting to much for him to cope with. When Karen appeared again with a mop and bucket, Frankie already had his coat on.

"And where are you off to?"

"Look I need to go out, if Harry comes in asking

where I am, just say I've popped to the cash and carry."
"But we only stocked up on Friday, there's nothing we really need."
Frankie raised one of his eyebrows in a show that silently said 'that's not where I'm really going'.
"Oh I see mum's the word then. Will you be back before opening?"
"I'll try my hardest and thanks for this Karen, I really mean that."
Hailing a taxi, Frankie asked the driver to take him over to Belsize Park. When the cab pulled up outside the house on Primrose Gardens and after Frankie had paid the fare, he got out and stood staring up at the place he had once called home. The large stucco house was magnificent and the two vast columns that flanked the entrance appeared decadent but also elegant at the same time. It seemed such a distant memory now, all the laughter and fun he'd experienced not to mention the love. Now he was angry, why should he have to come cap in hand and ask for help from someone, who as far as he was concerned had abandoned him. Marching up to the door he rapped heavily on the highly polished brass knocker. When Bella opened up she was shocked to see him but instantly a broad smile covered her face. Stepping forward she hugged her son tightly and Frankie could feel nothing but pure love from the woman. This show of emotion only confused him but her embrace and

the soft touch of her motherly arms, made his anger subside.

"Oh darling, you don't know what this means to me. Come on in sweetheart."

Entering the hallway he saw that nothing had changed. The fine antiques and contemporary paintings still filled the walls. Even the French aubusson rug that had cost Harry over two grand at auction, was as bright and as clean as it had been a decade ago. Frankie remained silent, even after they had gone into the kitchen and had taken seats at the table. Bella had made a pot of tea and after pouring two cups she waited for him to begin but it was as if Frankie had been struck dumb. He was struggling to think of a way to start the conversation and it didn't go unnoticed by his mother.

"I take it you're in some sort of trouble? I mean it's been getting on for ten years since the last time you were here."

"Nine actually."

"Don't split hairs Frankie. Now what's the matter?"

"I know this won't go down well, especially with him."

"Who? What are you talking about because I can't make any sense of what you're saying."

"Uncle Harry."

"You mean your father, why are you calling him uncle?"

"Because that's what he insists I call him, anyway he came to see me yesterday and wants to involve me in something that I'd rather not get mixed up in. I've met someone mum and I'm head over heels in love but Harry said that if I didn't help him out, then I've got to leave the pub and it's the only home I've got."

"Whatever are you talking about? Your home is here but you chose to leave, though to my dying day I will never understand why you wanted to go."

Finally Frankie understood, understood that his mother had never known what had gone on between him and Harry and just like he'd felt abandoned, she must have felt exactly the same. Leaning on the table, Frankie placed his head in his hands and as Bella gently stroked his cheek she could feel the wetness of tears.

"I bet you think I'm a right fucking twat, coming round here and blubbering like a baby?"

"I think nothing of the kind love but I do think it's about time you told me exactly what's gone on and promise me Frankie that you won't leave anything out."

Frankie realised that he was opening up a whole can of worms but at the same time he thought that maybe Bella deserved the truth, after all as much as he'd been denied a mother , hadn't she also suffered, hadn't she been denied the love of a son and all because of Harry. No matter how much trouble it would bring, Frankie knew that it was time for some home truths, regardless of how hurtful those truths might be.

"You really want to know, because I tell you it aint pretty and by the time I've finished you may end up not liking the man you've spent the best part of your life with."

"My darling trust me, I need to know. I've waited a long time to see you back here and whatever you say, I'm certain it will be the truth."

Frankie looked deep into the eyes of the woman he had loved since as far back as he could remember. Bella West was a perfect example of what a parent should be and he'd missed her terribly. That said he wasn't out to feather his own nest and needed what he was about to say to be as honest a recount as he could remember.

"God this is going to be hard, I never came here to cause you any pain and that's exactly what I'm about to do."

Bella remained silent and Frankie knew that she would stay that way until she had heard everything.

"Ok, here goes. Just before Helena's first birthday Harry called me into the study. He said I had to leave school and this house, said you wasn't my mother and that my real mum was a drug addicted prostitute. Harry said I probably had a bit of black in me, I think that's the real reason he wanted me out of here. He also said I was to tell you that it was all my idea and from then on I had to call him uncle instead of dad. My world was completely ripped apart mum, I mean you are the only mother I've ever known and it's been so hard all these years.

You can't begin to imagine the pain and rejection I was feeling but I don't want to dwell on that, today I am here to ask for your help."

Bella West was instantly out of her seat and embracing the son she thought she'd lost. As she hugged Frankie to her breast he could feel her tears as they dropped onto his neck. They must have remained in that position for several minutes, neither wanting to ever let go. Finally when Bella had wiped her eyes, she gently lifted Frankie's chin so that he was looking directly into her eyes.

"You always were and always will be my son. As for Harry, you leave him to me but you can take it as read that you will not be forced into his scam no matter what he says. You also have a home here or at the pub whichever you prefer for as long as you want and once again Harry will have no say in it. As for how he looks upon you, my darling that is out of my hands but you will never be short of love from me and that I promise from the bottom of my heart. It kills me to think of all the years that have been wasted and all because your so called father is a complete and utter arsehole!"

"I feel like I'm running to you telling tales but nothing could be further from the truth."

"I know that sweetheart and believe you me, from now on things are going to change."

Frankie stood up and after embracing her one more time, left the house and set off for the pub. As soon as the front door was closed Bella went back into

the kitchen and snatching up the wall phone, called her husband at the club. It was unusual for her to ring him during working hours and when he heard her voice he immediately went into panic mode.
"What's happened? Is Helena hurt, are you alright?"
"We are both fine but I would like you to come home Harry. We need to talk and I would rather it happens while our daughter is still at school."
With that she hung up and Harry was left staring into the receiver. This wasn't like Bella, she never phoned him at the club, well not unless it was an emergency. Now all sorts of images were invading his mind and he called out to Jimmy Fingers to fetch the car. He arrived at Primrose Gardens in record time and as he opened the front door called out to his wife but there was no reply. Walking into the kitchen he was surprised to see her sitting at the table with a cold hard expression on her face.
"Fuck me girl! You nearly gave me a heart attack when you didn't answer, now what's all this about?"
"I had a visitor today."
"Did you now and who might that have been?"
"Our son!"
"Don't fucking raise your voice to me Bella, I aint having it do you hear. Now whatever that soppy twat said to you, you should take it with a pinch of salt."
"How do you know he said anything?"
Harry slapped his hand down onto the table in a show of frustration but his wife knew him better

than anyone and Harry wasn't frustrated, he was worried.

"Don't play silly buggers, I aint got time for it. Now you've dragged me back here for what exactly?"

Bella West stood up and walked up to her husband. Unlike many others, she wasn't scared of Harry and if he knew what was good for him, then he should be the one who was scared.

"To tell you what you are going to do and before you start screaming and shouting that no one tells you what to do, you'll hear me out. Frankie is our son and what you made him do was downright bleeding cruel. For years I've been wondering what I did wrong, only to find out it was all down to you. After all these years, I feel as if I don't know you at all. You took my son from me, yes Harry my son and I will never forgive you for that. From now on you will leave him alone to run the pub. You will not force him to help in your criminal activities, nor will you mention any of this to him, do you hear me?"

Harry laughed sarcastically.

"Or what?"

"Or, you will come home one day and Helena and I will be long gone. That is not a threat Harry West, it's a promise. I am so angry and hurt about all of this that I don't think I will ever be able to look at you the same way again. Now what's it to be?"

Harry knew he was between a rock and a hard place. If he called her bluff then he was certain she would leave him, on the other hand to accept all that she had said would make him feel like a henpecked fool. Deciding to agree for the time being, he took her into his arms.

"Ok, whatever you want. Bella you know I wouldn't hurt you for the world and Frankie shouldn't have spoken to you about all of this, especially about my business dealings."

Bella pulled away from the man she had loved for the last thirty years and it was like she was seeing him in a new light and it was a light she didn't like.

"My son can tell me whatever he likes and neither you nor anyone else will ever stop that, do you hear?"

"But he aint your son Bella, not really now is he?"

Instantly she raised her hand and for the first time in all of their married life, she struck him hard across the face.

"Being a mother aint about giving birth to a child Harry, it's about loving and caring for them and that I have done with all of my heart, well until you made him leave. Now go back to work, because right at this moment I can't bear to bleeding look at you."

Harry stormed out of the house and as he got back into the car his face was red with rage. Jimmy didn't know whether to speak or not but going against his better judgement, he opened his mouth anyway.

"You alright Boss?"

"No I fucking aint, just drive the bastard car will you."

No more was said on the matter but as the vehicle weaved its way through the traffic, Harry West was silently cursing the day that he'd ever taken Frankie into his home, he also swore to himself that one way or another he would have his revenge.

CHAPTER SEVENTEEN

Several days had now passed since Frankie had been to see Bella and even though he was pleased to be close to her again, the meeting hadn't gone as well as he'd wanted. As yet he hadn't heard anything more from Harry regarding the long firm, so at least that was some consolation. That said, he was more astute regarding his father or uncle as Harry liked to be called and Frankie knew that sooner or later the man would tackle him about what had been said, he just hoped that Bella's influence would lighten the blow. Harry West could be as mean as hell and without his mother by his side; he knew that he was on a hiding to nothing where Harry was concerned. Frankie had never enjoyed life so much as he was at the moment, he was in love and things couldn't have been better, so he didn't want anyone to spoil things. Every morning his girl would turn up for her shift, but no work was carried out as they would always end up in bed, still it set Frankie up for the day and he would carry out her duties in record time. Karen had stopped complaining, she knew what it was like to be in love and there was no way that she would ever burst his bubble. They hadn't openly flaunted their relationship but on the odd times she had seen them together, it was obvious what was going on. Trade was still good and Harry had nothing to complain about, he didn't come in daily to check the books as he usually did but it didn't bother Frankie in the least. A Couple of times in the last week Bella had turned up and taken him to lunch and those times were special. It felt as though their old bond was returning and he couldn't have wished for more. One thing that did bother Frankie was the amount of complaining his mother did regarding Helena. The girl appeared to be turning into a real handful but as his mother repeatedly told him, Harry wouldn't have a word said against her. Adeela was arriving earlier and earlier for work, not that Frankie minded and when Saturday arrived he was happy that for a change he would be seeing her at the weekend. Adeela's aunt Bina had invited them over and he made sure that he was up early. Putting on his smartest clothes, he popped down to the lock and purchased a bouquet of flowers. They were contemporary in the way that they had been wrapped and were tied with raffia which Frankie thought she might appreciate. Agreeing to meet Adeela outside Islington tube station, he took a seat in the bar to gather his thoughts and wait until it was time to leave. He didn't know where this was all going but he prayed the outcome would be good. After swearing to himself years ago that he would ever allow anyone into his heart, he had gone and done just that but Adeela was different and he wanted to spend the rest of his life with her. Glancing at the wall clock just as the hand hit nine

am; he knew he should be on his way. Islington was always awash with tourists at the weekend and the underground was no different, so picking up the flowers he walked out of the pub. Jimmy Fingers was just pulling the car into the kerb and Harry stared out of the window. He didn't acknowledge Frankie and Frankie could only imagine that Bella must have given him hell, still if it meant he was left alone Frankie knew it had all been worthwhile. Just as he'd expected the tube was heaving and as he was jostled from all sides, he tried desperately not to squash the flowers. Emerging for the Angel station he glanced at his gift and saw that he had accomplished his aim, the bouquet looked just as beautiful as it had when he'd collected it. Adeela was standing waiting and when he saw her in her hijab his heart went out to her. Frankie knew how much she hated wearing the headwear but that she felt she had no other choice. When she saw him she smiled.
"Oh Frankie they're beautiful."
"Sorry babe but they aint for you."
She playfully punched him on the shoulder.
"I know that silly. Frankie would you mind either walking ahead or behind me, it's just that if anyone sees us together then the object of this visit will have all been for nothing."
Frankie didn't answer but marched off ahead which made her laugh. He had only got a few hundred yards when he stopped and began to speak, it

looked as though he was talking to himself and again Adeela laughed.

"Would you mind taking the lead only I aint got the foggiest idea of where we're going to."

Adeela continued to walk and she was soon well ahead. When she turned into Richmond Crescent, Frankie could instantly see that Aunt Bina had money. The houses were all painted in a brilliant white and the black high gloss doors were all topped off with the obligatory potted bays that stood on either side. Adeela climbed the front steps and as she knocked, Frankie held back. A small petite smartly dressed woman answered the door but she wasn't wearing a hijab like her niece. As Adeela entered, Frankie saw that the front door had been left open and he could only assume that it was open for him. Climbing the steps he walked in and after closing the door behind him, the woman he loved was instantly in his arms.

"I'm sorry about that but you really have no idea what my family are like. Now come through and meet my aunt."

Bina Raja was already seated at the table and unexpectedly, she smiled warmly at Frankie as he walked in.

"It's nice to meet you Mr West, as you can imagine my niece has told me so much about you. Please take a seat and Adeela will make us some tea."

Doing as he'd been asked, Frankie thanked Bina for inviting him to her home and then handed her the bouquet.

"Please call me Frankie Mrs Raja, Mr West sounds so formal."

"As you wish Frankie and you must call me Bina. These are lovely, thank you. Adeela dear would you put them in some water for me."

Adeela took the flowers and as she stood at the sink filling the kettle, smiled when she heard the beginning of the conversation. Walking over to the tea caddy she saw that it was empty and turning towards her aunt, tipped it upside down.

"Aunty where is the tea?"

"Oh, I asked my cleaner to get some more and the silly girl has forgotten. Adeela dear would you mind just popping to the shop for me?"

"No of course not, it will give you both some time to get acquainted while I'm gone."

It had all been planned and within seconds of Adeela disappearing into the hall, Bina didn't waste a moment to begin talking. Frankie wasn't naive and had read the sighs but if Bina thought that ending the relationship was a foregone conclusion, she had another think coming.

"I'm hoping that you know why I've invited you here today Frankie?"

"Well no not really, I thought that when you saw how happy we are together and how much I loved Adeela, then perhaps you would have a word on our behalf. From what Adeela has told me, if anyone has any influence with her parents then that person is you."

Bina could only shake her head, this man really had no idea what he was dealing with, well if the soft approach wasn't working then she had no alternative but to tell him how it really was.

"You seem like a nice man Frankie and I don't doubt that you have feelings for my niece but what you are getting mixed up in, well you really have no idea. Pakistani girls do not marry outside of their own kind, well not if they want to remain part of their family. There is no way on earth that my sister and brother-in-law would ever accept you no matter how well you treat Adeela. Then there are my three nephews and I expect you've been told how Adeela is treated. They would all rather take matters in their own hands than lose their sister. Believe me, their actions would not be out of any love for her but purely for their family and the family's standing in the community. In our world Pakistani women have no life of their own and must do as they are told. It is the way we live and believe me, it will never change."

As Bina spoke Frankie could only politely nod his head. When she had finally finished, Bina really thought she had gotten through to him, so his next sentence came as a shock.

"I don't mean to be rude Mrs Raja but you don't seem to be under anyone's control and from what Adeela has told me, you are a free spirit who does exactly as she wants."

Bina sighed heavily; she had a bad feeling about how this was all going to turn out. Even if it wasn't necessary, her sister would wind her boys up until they took action and Bina knew how they would react with or without their mother's interference. "My circumstances were and still are entirely different. Even though I refused my arranged marriage I did end up marrying a Pakistani. The fact that he is very rich helped to soften the blow but I know without any shadow of a doubt that had I have wanted to marry a westerner, then the outcome would have been very different indeed. All I want is for my niece to be happy but a relationship with you, will in the long term, only bring her misery. I beg you Frankie, if you really love her like you say you do, you will end this now!"

Just then they both heard the front door close and when Adeela appeared they acted as if only polite conversation had passed between them.

"Here we are, at last we can have some tea. What have you two been talking about while I've been gone, only my ears have been burning for the entire time I was out of this house."

At the same time both Frankie and Bina looked at her and smiled.

"Just this and that sweetheart, I've been telling your aunt how much I love you that's all."

Adeela bent and placed a kiss on his forehead.

"Ahhh, isn't he just the sweetest person you've ever

met aunt Bina?"
Bina smiled and nodded. When the three had finished their tea, Frankie got up to leave and saying his goodbyes he walked to the front door. Adeela was behind him in a second and the pair kissed passionately.
"I have to stay here babe as I always spend the entire morning with aunty."
"That's fine honey, I'll see you bright and early on Monday morning."
Frankie didn't know how he'd returned to Chalk farm Road, the journey was taken on auto pilot and the rest of the weekend wasn't much better. Every hour seemed to pass in a haze as he couldn't concentrate on anything other than what Bina had said to him.

Up with the larks, Frankie paced up and down the bar as he waited for her knock at the door. They had to do some serious talking and he wasn't looking forward to it.
After Frankie had left, aunt Bina hadn't spoken about him again which Adeela had thought strange but she wanted to let things settle and not push the matter to hard. Now as she walked along Chalk Farm road she was full of hope and couldn't wait to see the man she had fallen deeply in love with. When he opened up the door, Frankie bent and kissed her on the cheek but he wasn't smiling as he usually did and Adeela could feel her heart drop. Maybe he'd gone off of her, maybe now that she'd

had sex with him he wanted to move on and the thought unnerved her. His next words shocked her to the core, was this the beginning of the end of their relationship?
"We need to talk."
Oh no, this was it, this was how he was going to finish things. Taking a seat at the table she waited for him to continue.
"Did your aunt say anything after I left on Saturday?"
"No not really why?"
"Adeela I love you more than anything but Bina laid it on the line, she told me you would become an outcast from your family if they ever found out about us. She even said that your brothers would definitely take exception and would at best, make our lives a misery. Now I don't know about you baby but I can't live like that. I want to spend the rest of my life with you but that's a big ask and knowing how important family is to you, I don't think I can put that kind of pressure on you."
Suddenly her tears began to fall and there was nothing she could do to stop them. Frankie guessed that he wasn't explaining himself very well and taking her hand, began to cover it with kisses. Adeela was so confused, if he was ending things then why was he now being so intimate and loving.
"Frankie I don't understand any of this."
"It's simple, I can't imagine my life without you but your family will never accept us."

"I don't care about them, honestly I don't. All I want is to be with you."

"In that case, I think that for a while at least you should move in here with me. I have some money saved up and once I've got a bit more together, we can leave London and get married if that's what you'd like to do?"

Instantly Adeela was out of her seat and had flung her arms around him. A few seconds ago she had thought he was about to dump her but now he was asking her to marry him.

"Oh Frankie, yes that's exactly what I want. My family have treated me as nothing more than a slave for the whole of my life, so will I miss them? Definitely not! It will take a week or so but if I bring a few of my things here each day, by the weekend we could be together."

The loved up couple who naively thought that their dreams were about to come true, hugged and kissed and planned their future together until it was time for Adeela to leave for university. For the rest of the morning Frankie was on cloud nine and when Karen came in, the cleaning had been carried out in record time, much to her amazement. The hours would pass slowly until Adeela's return but for once Frankie West didn't mind for once he couldn't stop visualising being with her all day every day.

CHAPTER EIGHTEEN

The next day when Adeela arrived for her morning shift, Frankie wore a grin that had spread from one side of his face to the other. The couple couldn't stop hugging and giggling and it was a race to see who could make it to the bedroom first. Their lovemaking was to become a lot more passionate as Adeela Makhdoom felt totally at one with herself. Just making a decision on her future life made her feel more in control. Frankie couldn't believe how she was acting but he wasn't about to complain. To date their intimacy had been very good, from day one Adeela was always willing to please him but today there was something different, today she seemed totally free and was in fact pleasing herself. She was blowing his mind; there wasn't anything Adeela wasn't up for. Normally shyness would eventually overcome her and force her to cover her body but today she willingly showed him just what she wanted, today she climbed on top and rode Frankie West in a way she'd never done before. God she was beautiful and if this was just a taste of what was to come, he couldn't wait to marry her. Lying in each other's arms Frankie told her that he had twenty thousand pounds saved up.
"I know it's not a king's ransom but at least it's enough to get us started. Have you ever thought about going abroad Adeela, have you even got a

passport?"

"I have but it will be impossible to get my hands on it. A few years ago we all returned to Pakistan for my grandfather's funeral, so I know I have one but my mum keeps things like that under lock and key and I know it's because she thinks I might run away."

They both laughed at the absurdity of Yasmeen Makhdoom's actions.

"So your old lady thinks that would stop you? I think she's in for a bit of a surprise don't you? There's no need to worry about it, we can soon say that you've lost it and get another. I've always fancied starting up a little bar somewhere, what do you think?"

"Oh Frankie that would be great, Mr and Mrs West licensees, it sounds good don't you think?"

About to answer, Frankie stopped when he heard the stairs creak and putting his finger to his lips, silently told Adeela to stop talking. The handle turned and suddenly the door swept open to reveal Harry West standing there.

"What the fuck, why are you ..."

Harry cut Frankie off mid sentence and Frankie could tell by the look on the man's face that he was spoiling for a fight.

"Get down those fucking stairs now! You might go running to Bella when you want something but it doesn't wash with me. This is still my pub and whether you like it or not, I'm still your fucking boss!"

With that Harry turned and stomped back down the stairs. Frankie smirked to Adeela, shrugged his shoulders and then whispered in her ear.

"The sooner we're out of this place the better. You get dressed and then come down, I'm sure he'll be gone in a few minutes."

Frankie pulled on his dressing gown and wearily descended the stairs.

"So what's all this about Harry? I thought it was all sorted?"

"Fucking sorted, you cunt?"

Harry lunged forward and in a second had Frankie pinned up against the wall by his throat. Frankie had seen the man angry before and was well aware just what he was capable of but he never thought that violence would be used on him. It seemed Bella hadn't got her way after all, and now Frankie didn't know what was going to happen.

"Never, I repeat never, come to my home and speak to my family, do you hear? As far as involving you in my plan, I have to back off or risk losing my wife but believe you me sunshine, this aint over by a long way. When the dust settles I'm going to make your life a fucking misery and when you've finally had enough and moved on, I'm going to hang the fucking flags out."

Just as Harry released Frankie, Adeela came down the stairs and when Harry saw her he snarled back his lip as he spoke.

"Been shagging the little darky have we?"
With that he turned and walked out of the pub and Adeela ran into Frankie's arms.
"I'm so sorry about that, he's nothing but a fucking racist pig and I'm ashamed that you had to witness his behaviour darling."
"I'm used to it Frankie, it's something I've had to deal with for the whole of my life but he did scare me a bit."
"Don't worry babe, his barks worse than his bite and anyway, we'll be out of here soon."
As he hugged her to him, Frankie tried to believe his own words but something deep inside wouldn't let him. He now knew that Harry would be coming after him with all guns blazing and it wasn't a case of if they would be leaving London but when and how quickly they could do it.
Harry sat behind his desk at the club and was seething at the situation and the fact that he felt as though his hands were tied. When Jimmy came into the office, he took one look at his boss and turned around. About to walk back out again, he stopped when Harry began to speak.
"Jimmy get your skinny arse back in here! I've got a job for you."
Jimmy Fingers rolled his eyes upwards, any job Harry gave to a person when he was angry would always turn out bad and it was just the luck of the draw that he'd been the first person to clock in today.

"What's up Boss?"
"That little wanker in the pub has been shagging an Asian bird; he's also pissed me off big time so I think it's about time for some payback. I've checked the payroll and her names Adeela Makhdoom, what a fucking mouthful that is, anyway here's the address. I want you to find out as much as you can without anyone knowing. If you get stuck, because I know them fuckers close ranks, Keith Harman who runs the Bell in Walthamstow might be able to shed some light. Well go on then what are you fucking waiting for! Oh and catch the tube or bus, I might need the motor."
A disgruntled Jimmy Fingers walked down the stairs to the foyer and passed Kelly Graham as he did so.
"Where are you off to?"
"An errand for the boss but I'll warn you Kelly he's in a real shitty mood."
"What's new? At least you get out of here for a bit you lucky cunt."
Jimmy slapped Kelly on the shoulder and laughed as he went out of the main entrance. He'd already decided to take his time and enjoy a day out, Harry would never know and the job had to have some perks. Jimmy had caught the bus to Walthamstow and getting off on the high street, he was forced to dodge the hoards of shoppers, mostly women who were heading for the local market. He didn't really know where to start looking, so after a quick

inspection of Adeela's house and unlike Frankie he made sure he wasn't seen, he headed onto Hoe Street. The Bell was situated on Forest road and even though it was a straight route, it was a much longer walk than he'd expected. The pub was an old school establishment, built in the eighteen hundreds it's four storeys sat proudly on the corner of the road. Pushing open one of the large double front doors, Jimmy entered the newly refurbished bar. It was certainly different from the outside and had a warm homely feel. Ordering a pint from the young barmaid named Sue; he had a friendly conversation with her about the place and the area.
"You lived her long sweetheart?"
"All my life and it's a fucking shithole I can tell you. When I was a kid it was a really nice place to grow up in but now with all of the, well you know what I mean."
"It's the same all over London love, like an alien invasion."
His words made her laugh and also relaxed the conversation to a point where Jimmy felt able to enquire after the landlord.
"Sorry love but he's away for a few days, a bit of a bus mans holiday so to speak. He's left me in charge, so can I help in any way?"
Jimmy scratched his head in a show of should he ask or shouldn't he. It wasn't what he was really thinking but he wanted the girl to feel she was important and past experience had taught him that

it always seemed to do the trick.

"Well you might be able to, I'm trying to find out something regarding a local family, their surname is Makhdoom."

"Fuck me you don't mean Safeer and his brothers? Them lot are a right bad bunch."

"How do you mean, a bad bunch?"

"Well, the rumour round these parts is that they're into child prostitution, though I don't know how true it is. If you want some real information on them you need to go and talk to Andy Stone down at the Queens Arms, I've heard he's had a couple of run-ins with them. I don't know why but by all accounts he's banned them, so he's the one to tell you more. There are a lot of racists around these parts and that's on both sides, this country has made some big mistakes."

"Thanks for that sweetheart, maybe I'll go and have a chat with him."

Finishing up his pint Jimmy said goodbye and Sue was still moaning as he walked out of the door. Heading for the Queens Arms, he was glad to be away from the woman but it showed just how high tensions were running in the area. Walking back down Hoe road, Jimmy passed the tube station and turned left, his legs had started to ache but he knew better than to return to Harry with no information, well none that he could use. This pub was a lot smaller than the last and similar to the ones in Camden. Again it was situated on a corner plot and pushing open the doors, Jimmy ventured inside. It was obvious from the second he entered that the landlord was behind the bar. Andy Stone was as wide as he was tall and the large beer belly told anyone that cared to look, he loved his ale and probably drank half of the profits that the place took. Jimmy walked up to the bar and ordered his second pint of the day. He smiled and tried to appear friendly as he spoke but his actions didn't come naturally to Jimmy Fingers.

"Nice day for it landlord."

Andy looked at the stranger with suspicion but smiled and nodded all the same. Passing Jimmy's pint over, he held out his hand for the money but also eyed Jimmy up at the same time.

"You aint from round these parts are you?"

Jimmy laughed; no matter where you came from in London, everyone always seemed to know if you were from somewhere else in the smoke. It was almost as if you were a foreigner but it wasn't any different in Camden so he didn't dwell on the matter.

"No I'm from Camden; I'm here on a bit of business that you might be able to help me with."

Suddenly the landlords guard went up. He stared at the customer for a few seconds longer than normal and Jimmy instantly knew that the man was checking him out and trying to work out if Jimmy was Old Bill.

"Yeah, what's that then?"

"I aint Old Bill if that's what you're thinking, quite the opposite actually. My Boss is a well known face and he needs some information on some people. I've just been to The Bell and they told me to come here and have a word with you. Now I don't want to start naming names as this is all a bit hush hush but my Boss is a real hard bastard and it wouldn't do you any harm to help him out. Sue at the Bell said you know more about the people I'm interested in than she does."

"And who might that be?"

"The Makhdoom's?"

Jimmy didn't need to ask more because as soon as the man heard the name he went off on one.

"Those dirty cunts want skinning alive. I'll tell you this for nothing Son; if the likes of them were removed from the streets of London then it would be a far better place. There are three of them and they prey on young women and I don't mean girls who have reached the age of consent either. Those three target under age kids and I've got it on good authority that most of them come from the local care home. They came in here a couple of times and they always had some waif in tow. Anyway, the first time I didn't take any notice but the second time I overheard them trying to sell the girl to one of my regulars. I don't mind telling you that I hit the fucking roof. Seems they meet the girls over at the old burial gardens each night and drive them off to punters, anyway they scarpered pretty quick and they aint been back since. That must have been about six months ago now but if I had to hazard a guess, I'd put a large punt on it that they are still up to no good, the dirty rotten bastards. Since I blew me top, I've heard from a few of the locals that they're a right nasty bunch so I suppose I was lucky that night, by all accounts they run their home in a traditional manner but when it comes down to white girls, they look upon them as scum. The poor little fuckers don't stand a chance, not after those cunts get their hands on them. I tell you, I don't know what this fucking country is coming to! The Old Bill ain't interested and the locals are well pissed off. A word of warning son, stay well clear because sooner or later, their sort always gets their comeuppance and you wouldn't want to be associated with them when they do."

Jimmy had intended to enjoy his day out and take full advantage but after what he'd just been told, thought it best to return straight to Camden. When he knocked on the office door, Harry was a little surprised to see him back so early.

"Fuck me Jimmy that was quick. I thought you'd be gone for hours?"

Jimmy Fingers realised that he could have got away with having the rest of the day off. For once pulling the wool over his boss's eyes would have been easy and he now regretted returning so early. Still he was so excited regarding what he was about to reveal that he hadn't been able to stop himself from racing back to the club.

"I know Boss but it didn't take much to find out about the girls family and what a nasty load of bastards they are. The landlord of the Queens Arms couldn't wait to spill his guts, I don't think there's a lot of love lost there. Actually he hates the cunts with a vengeance and told me all I, well you, needed to know?"

"How do you mean?"

Jimmy began to walk around the office as if he was trying to draw things out, get Harry chomping at the bit so to speak.

"For fuck's sake Jimmy spit the fucker out, you aint fucking Poirot you know, now what was said?"

"Well Boss, it seems that her brothers are real shits, the lowest of the low."

"How do you mean?"

"Well they procure young girls, mostly underage kids and force them into prostitution. They seem to like getting them from the care home, no comeback I suppose. From what I've heard, they are a proper Pakistani family when it comes to home life, but once they're out on the street its different matter altogether."

For a moment Harry didn't say anything as he thought about his own beautiful Helena and what people like that were prepared to do to someone of her tender age, still she would never be a factor in any of this as Harry kept a close guard on her at all times. Life was a bitch and there was nothing he

could do about it but one thing he was certain of, from what he'd just learned, this Adeela birds behaviour wouldn't sit well with her family.
"Thanks Jimmy you did a good job."
Jimmy nodded and as he walked out of the office he met Kelly coming up the stairs.
"How did it go?"
Jimmy raised his hand in the air and Kelly slapped it in a high five.
"I think I've just scored a few brownie points, when he heard what I had to say he had a grin on his face wider than the fucking Thames."
Back in the office Harry was mulling over his options, he could do nothing and keep Bella happy or he could crucify the little tosser who he had once called son. Harry wouldn't hurt his wife for the world but his need for revenge far outweighed his loyalty. Nobody got one over on Harry West, well not without paying the consequences. Sitting back in his chair Harry smiled to himself, tomorrow was another day and it was one he was going to relish.

CHAPTER NINETEEN

The following morning Harry rose early, he was nervous about what he was about to do but only in case Bella found out. Entering the kitchen he saw Helena sitting at the table eating breakfast. In Harry's eyes she really was the most beautiful thing he had ever seen.
"Morning baby, sleep well?"
"I did daddy thank you and did you?"
"I always do babe, my old mum used to say I could sleep on a linen line."
Helena hated her father talking about his roots; as far as she was concerned it lowered the tone and was embarrassing. They were people with money now and she would rather her friends didn't know anything about her parents humble beginnings. Harry poured himself a coffee and when he sat down and opened up his paper, Helena knew it was the right time to strike. Getting up from her chair she walked around the table until she was standing behind her father. Draping her arms lovingly around his neck, she kissed his cheek and at the same time whispered in his ear.
"Daddy?"
"Yes sweetheart."
"I need some money and mummy won't give it to me."
"What's it for and how much?"

"Well Octavia Holmes has a new pair of trainers and she mocked me yesterday because mine are not the latest fashion, she said we couldn't afford any better. When I told mummy, she said that my trainers were only two months and were perfectly adequate for the time being, but in all honesty they are virtually antique Daddy."

Harry laughed at his daughter's choice of words.

"So how much is it going to cost me?"

"One hundred."

Harry West didn't flinch at the amount and pulling a bundle of notes from his pocket, reeled off one hundred and twenty in twenty pound notes.

"Here's a little extra for some sweets and stuff but for god's sake don't tell your mother."

Helena snatched up the money and then skipped out of the room. Harry watched her until she disappeared up the stairs; there was no doubting that she was his. The girl had a knack of getting whatever she wanted and she could twist him around her little finger. God help the man she ended up marrying was all that he could think.

At nine o'clock Jimmy Fingers knocked on the door and just as Harry was about to leave, Bella came down the stairs. Things were still tense between the pair but Harry knew she would soften eventually.

"Morning darling!"

"Morning."

Bella's hair was a mess and she wore no makeup but to Harry she was beautiful and would only ever be

the woman for him. His dalliances meant nothing, as far as Harry was concerned it was just a man thing but Bella, now Bella was the love of his life.
"I'm going to be a bit late home tonight love, It'll probably be around nine before I get finished so don't wait for me. You and Helena eat and I'll get myself something while I'm out."
"Where are you going?"
"Oh nowhere special, just a bit of business I need to take care of."
In all the years they'd been married Harry never answered her properly when she asked what he was up to and it always annoyed Bella but there was no changing him so she didn't dwell on the matter. Making her way into the kitchen she thought no more of it, if anything she was grateful for her time alone and it was just a pity that Helena wasn't on a sleep over or a school trip tonight.

    At the club it was business as usual and Harry had given Jimmy and Kelly a couple of hours off as they would be working late tonight. Staring out of the office window he watched the traffic and looked up and down the road, he loved Camden it was so alive. Just then he saw Adeela exit the pub and his mood instantly changed, picking up his camera, Harry snapped away as Frankie appeared at the door and passionately kissed his girlfriend goodbye. Speaking to himself, his words were venomous.
"I hope you enjoyed yourself you little tart, because

after today things are going to be very different for you."

Harry began to laugh out loud, revenge was so sweet and today he would have his. Oblivious to his father's actions, Frankie closed the front door wearing a soppy loved up expression on his face. In another couple of days they would be together forever and the thought sent exciting shivers down his spine.

The day passed quickly for Harry West, he had several business meetings lined up and then there was the long firm to finalise. They were moving the remaining stock out of the warehouse in a couple of days in readiness for the large deliveries the following week and then the real profit making could begin. By five that evening Jimmy and Kelly were sitting outside the office waiting to go and Jimmy was bored out of his brains. Earlier Harry had sent him to get some pictures developed but that felt like ages ago and he was desperate to be given something to do. It was alright for Kelly, as Harry's minder he was used to waiting around for hours but Jimmy Fingers always liked to be on the move. When the office door at last opened at seven pm they were on their feet in seconds and as Harry threw the car keys up in the air, Jimmy Fingers grabbed them before Kelly had a chance.

"Right lads let's get going, Jimmy you can drive."

Making their way along Walthamstow High Street, the place looked even drearier at night. To Harry it

seemed that every lowlife in the area only came out after the sun started to go down. Staring out of the window, Harry West was just glad that he didn't live here.
"So where's this place we're going to?"
"It's called the old Burial Gardens Boss. I had a bit of a scout about when I was here yesterday so I know where to go, though I bet it's going to be a case of sods law and them fuckers don't turn up tonight."
"Maybe they won't but we'll give it a while and if not we'll just have to come back tomorrow, in fact every fucking night if we have to."
Jimmy pulled into the secondary school on Woodbury road and parked behind the sports hall so that they wouldn't be seen.
"Kelly, go for a walk about and see if anyone's about."
After instructions from Jimmy about where the Makhdoom's usually congregated, Kelly set off on foot. He was gone for a good twenty minutes and Jimmy was getting worried, if the landlord had fed him false information he wouldn't be happy but he needn't have worried as a few minutes later Kelly opened the door and got back into the car.
"Fuck me I'm knackered."
"Just get on with it will you?"
"Well to begin with there wasn't anyone around but then these girls turned up. They went over to a big granite statue type thing and were just hanging

around. I walked past but they didn't take much notice of me. Then I hid in the bushes for a few minutes and this old Merc pulls up and three blokes got out. I'm sure they're the geezers you're looking for Boss."

"Jimmy, pull the car a little closer will you."

As the car came to a standstill, Harry turned to his minder.

"Kelly you go over to them first and I'll wait here in the motor. Get the oldest to come over, tell him I'd like a word, you know the score."

Kelly and Jimmy still sat in the car waiting for further instructions and the sight of his gormless employees pissed off Harry big time.

"Well what the fuck are you waiting for, get going!"

As Kelly approached, the men were deep in conversation with the girls. Lindy and Katie Watson were chatting away and a new face, Tina Malone, a girl that the brothers hadn't seen before but who they were more than interested in, stood silently beside her new friends. Katie Watson was the second newest resident at the care home and as soon as Lindy had set eyes on her, she had gone in for the kill. It hadn't taken long for Lindy to explain to the girl how wonderful the Makhdoom brothers were and she was promising Katie all sorts of presents, the sort of gifts that a young girl could only dream off. Tina Malone had arrived at the home that very morning and Katie had shared everything she'd been told by Lindy with her.

The poor girl was so lonely and so desperate to fit in that she'd begged them to take her along tonight. Akram was now in the middle of working his magic when Safeer turned and saw Kelly out of the corner of his eye.
"Go and stand over near my car girls, it looks like there's going to be a bit of trouble."
Doing as they were told, Lindy, Katie and Tina headed in the direction of the Merc. Katie was scared but she was soon reassured by Lindy who told her it wasn't anything Safeer couldn't handle. All three Makhdoom brothers now faced the unwanted visitor.
"Hello mate, my guv'nor would like a word."
"And?"
"Well he's over there in the motor and like I said, he'd like a word."
"I won't be able to hear him from here."
Safeer looked at his brothers and they all burst out laughing but being mocked didn't go down well with Kelly.
"Besides, I'm not about to go over there with a strange man now am I? Didn't your mother ever warn you about talking to strangers?"
Again all three Makhdoom brothers began to laugh and Kelly was really starting to get pissed off.
"I wouldn't take the piss if you know what's good for you pal."
Safeer took a step forward and as he straightened his stance his lips curled back in anger as he spoke.

"I aint your pal so fuck you and fuck your boss! If he wants a word with me, tell him to get off his fucking arse and come over here. Tell him I aint no fucking messenger boy!"

Kelly turned and walked back in the direction of the car but before he could reach it, Harry had stepped out.

"Got an attitude has he?"

"You could say that boss."

"Ok boys, come on then let's get this show on the road. I want you two close behind in case things take a turn for the worse. If that should happen, we'll be evenly numbered. I don't expect the bastards will have much about them, not if they only trade in young girls for a living, the dirty cunts!"

The grass was wet and as Harry looked down at his handmade brogues he wasn't happy. By the time he reached the monument he was ready for a row if that's what it would take to get respect from the Makhdoom's.

"You looking for someone in particular or just trouble?"

As Safeer had been the first to speak, Harry took it that he was the oldest or at least the one in charge.

"Neither Sunshine, I just thought you might be interested in a little bit of information I've got. I take it you're the Makhdoom brothers?"

Safeer studied the man but he still wasn't sure what was going on. Placing his hand in his pocket, he was a little more at ease when it rested on his flick knife.

"What's it to you?"

"Don't get all fucking hostile with me pal. Like I told you, I have some information that you might be interested in."

Kelly and Jimmy had now closed in but Harry wasn't worried in the least. He assumed the brothers had some kind of weapons on them but they wouldn't be anything to match the pistol he carried in his pocket. Taking a step towards Safeer, Harry asked if they could talk in private. Rashid and Akram stared at Jimmy and Kelly but in all honesty they wouldn't have been any match for Harry's men. Walking for several yards, Harry finally stopped and Safeer waited for him to speak.

"You have a sister right? Adeela?"

"So, what about her?"

"She works for me at the pub."

"So? What you've come to tell me that she's a lazy cow like she is at home?"

Safeer laughed out loud at his own statement but it was in a mocking way and only done to show Harry that he had no fear.

"No sunshine, what I've got to tell you is bad, at least as far as your lot are concerned. I have a bar manager called Frankie and it seems that your sister has struck up a rather close friendship with him."

Safeer didn't like where this was leading but at the same time he was desperate to hear what the man

had to say. He tried not to sound overly bothered as he spoke but the attempt made no impression on Harry.
"So?"
"Well, yesterday I called into the pub and found them in bed together, naked as the day they were born."
"Fuck off you white cunt! My sister would never do such a thing, I don't know why you're coming here and trying to stir up trouble for my family but it aint going to work."
Harry had expected that this would happen, that's why he'd had the sense to take the photographs. Reaching into his inside pocket he removed a manila envelope and pulled out two pictures. Handing them to Safeer, he was certain he wouldn't have to add anything else as the snaps spoke for themselves. Harry watched the man closely and when he noticed Safeer's eyes narrow, he got a warm feeling inside. This was all going exactly to plan, all he had to do now was sit back and watch the fireworks and as far as Bella was concerned, she would never know he'd been involved.
"Can I keep these?"
"Of course you can sunshine. Now your sister seems a nice enough girl but I know how you lot get if anyone messes with one of your girls. My barman aint a bad lad but I would rather he concentrated on his work than on your sister's cunt all the time."

Harry knew his words would infuriate Safeer; in fact he had banked on it. The more irate the man became, the more severe the punishment would be. Safeer pulled the knife from his pocket and flicked the blade open.

"How about I stick you right now you racist cunt!" Safeer took a step forward and held the knife low but as he did so Harry removed the gun from his pocket and pointed it directly at Safeer Makhdoom. "That may impress your little girl's Sunshine but it don't impress me. Now if you don't like the truth then you should take it up with the two in the photo and not try and shoot the messenger so to speak, or should I say stab. Jimmy, Kelly, time to go."

Safeer was fuming inside and Harry knew it. Waking a few paces on, Harry looked back over his shoulder and could see that Safeer was once again staring at the pictures. It instantly brought a grin to his face but he really didn't have a clue what a can of worms he had just opened up. Akram ran over to his elder brother but Safeer quickly stuffed the pictures back into the envelope. He didn't want anyone else knowing about this until he'd decided what to do.

"Whatever was all that about and who was he?"
"Just a business opportunity but I aint made up my mind if it's worth getting involved in. Now let's get a move on, we've wasted enough time already. The three brothers walked over to the car and Lindy, Katie, Tina, Safeer and Rashid got in. Akram was

being allowed to take the evening off or so he thought but Safeer had also asked him to call in at the local arcade and check for any new blood. Inside the car Lindy tried to speak to Safeer and protest that she didn't want to do this anymore but it was as if she was invisible as he totally ignored her. Safeer drove to his punters flat, the same place that held the monthly camera club and Lindy was told to get out and do her job. Safeer then drove to the car park on South Grove where Tina and Katie's initiation would begin just as poor Fiona's had only a short while ago. Unlike Fiona, Katie wasn't such an easy lay and she screamed and scratched as hard as she could. Safeer had been the first one to break her in and as she caught the side of his cheek with her nails, he lashed out and slapped her hard across the face. After what he'd just been informed of, there was no way he was in the mood for the softly softly approach. When Safeer sat upright in his seat, an indication that he was finished, Rashid got back into the car. He could clearly see that Katie was bleeding and that her bottom lip was split, still he knew better than to question his brother. By the way Safeer was acting, whatever the stranger had said to his brother, it couldn't have been good. Tina had stood and witnessed her friends attack and knew that if she didn't surrender willingly, she would experience the same violence. Katie was dragged from the car and Tina, without being asked, climbed inside. Luckily she only had to endure an assault by Rashid as Safeer was to wound up to perform again. After it was over she pulled her dress down, stepped from the car and smiled weakly at her friend. Driving back to the burial gardens, Safeer stopped and told Rashid to take the girls over to the monument. Alone in the car he switched on the interior light and removing the photographs, surveyed them again. There was no question it was Adeela but what he was going to do about it was another matter. If he went in all guns blazing when he got home, things could go drastically wrong. Deciding to sleep on it, he would inform his parents in the morning and together they would all decide what to do. Whatever the outcome, Safeer knew that Adeela would pay dearly for the shame she had brought on her family. No decent Pakistani man would ever want her now, so for all intent and purpose she was damaged goods and a complete waste of space. When his brothers returned to the car they could both see that Safeer wasn't any happier. The three drove home in silence and Rashid and Akram just hoped that tomorrow would be different because in this mood, Safeer was a nightmare to work with.

CHAPTER TWENTY

By six thirty the next morning Adeela was on her way to Chalk Farm road. She struggled with the two large black bags she was carrying but Adeela would have happily walked over hot coals if it meant getting to Frankie. Her only concern was if her mother went snooping in her room and noticed that the majority of her clothes were missing, still that was a risk she was prepared to take. Banging on the door she didn't have to wait more than a few seconds and as he opened up her heart skipped a beat.
"Here let me take those for you."
Frankie grabbed the bags but as soon as they were inside he dropped them and scooped her up into his arms.
"Adeela Makhdoom, I love you with all my heart."
"Ditto baby. I think tonight will be my last night at home, there are only a few more things I need to get and then we'll be together forever. Oh Frankie I'm so excited, when do you think we can get married? Once I have a ring on my finger I will be truly free of them all and the Makhdoom name."
"How does next week suit you?"
Adeela squealed in delight, this was like a fairy tale, a fairy tale that she never wanted to end. The couple carried the bags upstairs and then immediately jumped into bed.

Two hours later over in Walthamstow, Yasmeen was in the middle of preparing breakfast when her eldest son walked into the kitchen. She was surprised to see him this early as he never normally got up until well after eleven.
"Are you alright son?"
"Why do you ask that woman? You are always trying to poke your nose into my business. Get on with your work and keep your mouth shut!"
Safeer grabbed a piece of toast from the table but his action was just a bit too quick and his mother flinched away. He didn't strike her but if he had, it wouldn't have been the first time that Yasmeen Makhdoom had been assaulted by one of her sons.
"Make some tea and bring it through and for once I want you to join us as what I have to say concerns us all."
His tone was ratty but Yasmeen knew her place and nodding her head didn't question him further. Before coming downstairs, Safeer had woken his brothers and told them he wanted a meeting and to be at the table in five minutes. Rashid and Akram hauled themselves up; they didn't dare do anything else and were now in the front room waiting to see what all the fuss was about. Safeer came in followed by his mother and after they had taken a seat, Safeer began to speak.
"I met with a man last night and what he had to tell me about our sister was devastating."
Safeer looked to his father but there was no sign or

any expression. Recently Anwar seemed to be permanently hooked up to his oxygen mask and there was little response or none that anyone could see.

"It seems that her job is not the only thing she's been enjoying. This man, who I have no reason to disbelieve, told me that my sister the whore, has been sleeping with the bar manager at the pub where she works."

To Yasmeen, his words made her feel as if she'd failed in her job as a mother and she couldn't help but plead her daughter's innocence. It wasn't out of any fear for Adeela's safety but purely down to wanting to hide her own shortcomings, or at least that's how she saw it.

"Never! I have brought your sister up to know better. I'm sorry for speaking out Safeer but I'm sure even your father will agree with me on this?"

Safeer looked in Anwar's direction and the man slowly nodded his head. He didn't feel that he owed any loyalty to his wife but even he couldn't deny that since the day she'd been able to walk, his daughter did everything she had been told and would be a good match for someone in the future. Safeer had anticipated this reaction and pulling out the photographs, he placed them onto the table.

"If you don't believe me, see for yourselves."

Rashid and Akram leaned over the table and their faces wore the look of complete shock at the images. Rashid held back but Akram couldn't contain

himself and was the first to speak.
"The dirty little whore!"
When there were no protests at his brothers words, Rashid now felt free to speak.
"She has dishonoured her family, disgraced herself and betrayed her faith, so what are we going to do about it?"
Yasmeen took her time and as she studied the images, images that showed her pure daughter flaunting herself over a white man, it broke her heart. It wasn't a case of love or disappointment but just the fact that the girl had brought shame upon them all and she didn't know what to do about it. When news of this reached their community they would be a laughing stock and looked down upon just as they had been all those years ago back in Pakistan.
"As I see it we don't have much of a choice. When this gets out and I am in no doubt that it will, as a family we have to show that just punishment has been administered."
Safeer got up from the table, walked over to his father and held the photographs up in front of the old man's face.
"Dad, what would they have done to her back in Pakistan?"
Anwar removed his mask and beckoned for his son to come closer. His voice was weak and almost inaudible but as everyone stretched their necks to hear, his words couldn't be mistaken.

"Kill her."
No one in the room appeared shocked; it was something they had all been thinking. Honour among the family was the only thing that mattered and Adeela had shamed each and every one of them. A plan was then talked about and one which they were all in agreement with but it would have to wait until this afternoon when Adeela returned from her job. For now Safeer would fill his day by making preparations.

Just after lunch Yasmeen slipped out of the house on the pretence of going to the supermarket. Catching the number thirty eight bus to Islington, she prayed her sister would be at home. Yasmeen wasn't having any second thoughts about what the family had planned but she always liked to get Bina's opinion on important matters. If the truth was told, she just wanted a change of scenery and not be forced to wait around until her daughter got home. Knocking on the door she anxiously awaited and when it opened up, Bina Raja was a little surprised to see her sister standing on the step.

"Yasmeen! What a lovely surprise, come on in." Bina knew that something had happened as her sister never just turned up, at least not without phoning first. Convinced that this visit had something to do with Adeela, Bina would play her cards close to her chest. She didn't want Yasmeen to know that she already knew what the girl had been up to because it would appear like a betrayal to the family by her not informing them straight away. After making tea, the two women sat at the table and chatted about this and that, anything rather than discuss why Yasmeen was really there. When Bina thought that her sister might actually go home without spilling the beans, she couldn't hold back any longer.

"So Yasmeen, what's on your mind?"

"Whatever do you mean?"

"Come on now, you never come to my home unless I invite you. Not that I'm saying you are not welcome but I know you and something is bothering you?"

With that the flood gates opened and Yasmeen Makhdoom began to cry. Through sobs she told her sister what Adeela had been up to and when she had finished, looked to Bina for comfort but there was none.

"So what did the boys say?"

"Say! They are so angry with her and when she returns tonight they plan to administer a just punishment."

Suddenly Bina felt scared, she knew all about Pakistani punishment and it was never treated lightly. Hopefully her niece would get off with a good beating but she knew her nephews well and they were all cruel and nasty men.

"What have they got planned?"

"Only what the dirty little whore deserves! Put it like this, come tomorrow it will be as if Adeela

Makhdoom never existed."
Bina put her hand to her mouth in shock and disgust.
"Oh Yasmeen no! Anything but that please!"
"Look sister, I am not the mistress of my own home as you well know. The men in my family have always ruled with an iron rod, it has always been that way and will continue to be so. You on the other hand have tasted freedom and maybe that is why my daughter has done this terrible thing, maybe she wanted to be like you!"
Bina couldn't believe what she was hearing, she was getting the blame for something she had known nothing about, well at least not until her niece had told her. Standing up from the table, she was hurt at her sister's words but also angry.
"How dare you blame me? Yasmeen I would like you to leave my house now."
Doing as she was asked, Yasmeen Makhdoom walked out on her sister without a goodbye. She didn't feel bad about what she'd said as she actually believed every word and besides, she had always been jealous of Bina and it felt good to cause the woman some pain even if it was only emotional.

    Just as she'd done for the last two weeks, Adeela left university and made her way to the pub. With no idea what was happening at home, her head was filled with planning her final move tomorrow. Walking along, she imagined herself in a long flowing gown and as she mentally said her vows, the vision made her feel all warm and tingly inside. Pushing open the pubs front door, her face beamed when she saw that Frankie had laid one of the tables and a candle was softly burning in the centre. Frankie came from the back room carrying two plates of food and they smelled delicious, putting them down on the table, he pulled out a chair.

"Take a seat princess. I thought that as this was our last day of having to sneak around, we should celebrate it with a nice meal together."

The couple enjoyed the food and then cuddled up together on one of the sofas in the bar area, happy just to sit and chat about all they were going to do. Two hours later and Frankie and Adeela had just finished clearing away the dishes when Karen arrived for her shift.

"Here we go, the love birds are at it again."

Adeela giggled and smiled, she had gradually got to know Karen and she liked her. The girl had kept their secret without being asked and for that Adeela would be eternally grateful. When the front door again opened and a few of the early doors regulars came in, she knew it was time to be on her way.

"I think I should get off now Frankie. I'm a little late as it is but I'll just use the excuse of being extra busy again; it seemed to work last time."

Frankie hugged her to him and in full view of his regulars, tenderly kissed her on her check, much to the applause of everyone in the bar. For once

Adeela didn't mind, for once knowing that in a few hours she would be free, filled her with joy. Twenty minutes later as Frankie was collecting glasses, he saw the piece of material laying over the back of the chair, it was at the same time as Adeela emerged from the station and realised that she wasn't wearing her hijab. Filled with panic, she prayed for luck to be on her side, if it was then she would be able to slip upstairs without being seen and replace it. Opening the front door, she couldn't hear a sound. There was no clinking of pots in the kitchen and the television that her father usually had up so loud that you had to shout to be heard, was silent. Closing the door, she was just about to place her foot on the first stair tread when her mother appeared in the hallway.
"Can you come in here Adeela, your brother needs to speak to you?"
Yasmeen's tone sounded calm, to calm and Adeela began to get a sinking feeling in the pit of her stomach. She knew better than to ignore the request, so with her head bowed she walked into the front room to find all of her brothers seated at the table. On seeing her Safeer stood up.
"Sit here."
Still with her head bowed, she did as she was told.
"What have you been up to girl?"
Adeela had all her fingers and toes crossed and hoped with her entire being, that whatever trouble she was in it had nothing to do with her and

Frankie.

"I don't know what you mean brother?"

Safeer's voice seemed overly deep as he spoke and his words sounded menacing.

"You have betrayed this family and brought shame upon us all. You have given your body to a man who is an outsider. No decent man will look at you as you're no longer pure. You are nothing but a dirty little whore and you will be punished for bringing shame and dishonour on our good family name!"

For once Adeela broke the house rule; for once she tried to defend herself.

"No Safeer you've got it wrong, I'm a good girl and would never do anything to hurt my family."

Safeer Makhdoom slammed the pictures down in front of her and her gasp was audible to all. No one waited for the conversation to begin again and immediately Rashid and Akram were standing beside their elder brother. Safeer punched Adeela on the side of her face with as much force as he could muster. The strike instantly knocked her to the floor and she laid there not daring to get up. Praying that this was her only punishment, she soon realised that it would not be the case when Rashid's foot made contact with her stomach. The contents of her earlier meal, the meal that Frankie had so lovingly prepared, now erupted in front of her and onto the carpet. Akram picked up a large metal ornament of a fish that had been a wedding present to his parents and threw it at his sister's head. Adeela heard the bone in her cheek crack as the ornament made contact but her torture had only just begun. Blow after blow rained down on her and Adeela gasped for breath as blood oozed from her mouth and nostrils. Her left eye was completely closed now but as she looked in her father's direction for pity, she could see enough to notice that he wore a cruel grin on his face. Safeer began to rant and rave, he called her all the sluts and whores under the sun and as Adeela began to lose consciousness, she prayed that one way or another this beating would soon end.

CHAPTER TWENTY ONE

Ever since her sister had left, Bina Raja had been pacing up and down in the front hallway. Aware of what was about to happen, her loyalties were divided. She could say nothing and carry so much guilt that it would probably end up destroying her, or she could go to Frankie West and warn him but then if she did that and was ever found out, she would be shunned by her community. It had only ever happened to her once and it had only been for a short time until she married her husband, but just those few months were bad enough and the feelings she'd experienced were still etched firmly on her mind. As the hours passed she still hadn't come to a decision but suddenly she stopped thinking about herself as an image of Adeela entered her mind. Poor sweet Adeela who had always loved and adored her aunt, shouldn't she put the girl first. Bina felt as if she was going out of her mind and heading in the direction of the kitchen, poured herself a large glass of brandy. It was something she had never done before but desperate times called for desperate measures and maybe a little Dutch courage would help her make up her mind regarding what she should do.

In Walthamstow things were at boiling point. Adeela was still lying on the front room floor not daring to move and every time she looked up; her father was staring at her. Safeer, Rashid and Akram had disappeared and for that she was grateful. Her mother could be heard busying herself in the kitchen and Adeela couldn't understand why the only other female in the house, didn't come to her rescue or at least offer her comfort and a drink of water. The taste of congealed blood in her mouth was rancid and she was so desperately tired. Every time she looked in Anwar's direction he just glared at her and she tried to remember a time in her life when she must have disappointed him to such a degree, that he could hate her so much now. There was nothing, she had always been a good daughter, had always been desperate for his love and approval but as he stared at her, even wearing his oxygen mask, she could see nothing but hatred in his eyes. A few minutes later and Adeela Makhdoom thankfully passed out.

By now Bina had consumed two more glasses of brandy and as the saying goes, 'drunks speak the truth', she had made up her mind what she had to do. To hell with her community, and to hell with her family, a human life was far more important and if that life happened to be the one of her beautiful innocent niece, then it was doubly important. Picking up the telephone she dialled a mini cab and within ten minutes she was on her way to Rosie's pub on the chalk Farm road. The thought of what she was about to do had slightly sobered her up which she was glad of. Not once in

her entire life had Bina Raja set foot in a public house and as she stepped from the taxi, she didn't know what to expect. Nerves began to set in as she tentatively pushed on the door and the smell of beer instantly filled her nostrils. Music was blearing out and the sound of laughter and chatting was somehow comforting, that was until she thought of why she was here. Long before the ban, smoke hung heavy in the air but it didn't offend her, in fact her late husband had been a twenty a day man and even though she had nagged him for years to stop, she now realised that she missed the aroma,.
Walking towards the densely populated bar, Karen was in front of her in seconds.
"What can I get you love?"
"A large brandy please."
"Any preference love?"
"Whatever you've got, it's only to give me a bit of Dutch courage."
Karen studied the woman and could tell by the diamond rings on her fingers that she had money, so rather than the house special, she opted for a vintage cognac and pushed up on the optic twice. Bina took a sip and then scanned the place looking for Frankie but he was nowhere to be seen. As Karen went to collect some empties from the top of the bar, Bina placed her hand on top of the barmaids.
"Is Frankie here?"
"Somewhere about but he's probably busy love."

"Please, I really need to speak to him."
There was something in the woman's eyes, almost as if they were pleading and the look made Karen stop what she was doing and go straight into the back office. She didn't knock like she usually did and marching up to the desk, her tone sounded strange as she began to speak which made Frankie look up.
"There's a middle aged woman in the bar asking for you and I really think you need to see her. I think she's Indian or something like that."
Karen's last sentence made Frankie really take notice and she saw how his eyes seemed to open wide.
"I'll show her in then?"
Frankie could only nod and less than a minute later Bina entered. She was still holding the glass and Frankie raised his eyebrows and smiled.
"I thought your lot didn't drink?"
Normally she would have found his words amusing and would probably have even laughed but the situation was so grave that she had no time for niceties. Taking a seat opposite she began to speak and with each word Frankie's heart sunk further and further into his chest.
"My sister and her family are aware of what's been going on between the two of you and I might add, it didn't come from me. Frankie I'm here because something bad is going to happen to Adeela and I didn't know who else to turn to."

"Where is she?"

"Honestly I don't know. All I do know is that my sister came to see me today and said they would be administering punishment. That can come in many different forms but because of what she's done, Adeela will receive the harshest punishment there is."

"What do you mean?"

Bina stopped herself from going any further for fear of incriminating herself. Standing up she placed the glass onto the desk and then walked towards the door.

"I can't go into any more detail but I just wanted you to know, what you choose to do about it is down to you."

With that Bina Raja walked from the office and out of the pub. Frankie just sat there, he didn't know whether to believe her, go and look for himself or just wait it out. Making his way into the bar, he served a few regulars in the hope of taking his mind of things but it didn't help. His thoughts went into overdrive and when he couldn't stand it any longer, he came to the conclusion that he had to at least try and find out what was going on. Grabbing his jacket, Frankie told Karen to take care of things and then hailing a cab, instructed the driver to take him to Walthamstow as quickly as possible.

On Priory Avenue Adeela was starting to come round, her father was still seated in his armchair staring at her but apart from that nothing

had changed. Every inch of her body was racked with pain and as hard as she tried, she wasn't able to lift herself up. Adeela's head was hurting, especially her right side which had taken a direct hit from the heavy ornament and Rashid's boot but she was still able to hear the front door as it slammed shut. She tried to focus but it was difficult and when she saw three sets of feet come into the room, knew that her brothers were back for the next round of abuse.
"Akram secure her legs, Rashid do her arms."
Rashid Makhdoom roughly pushed his sister so that she was flat on the floor and as he shoved her hard in the back, Adeela let out a low groan.
"Shut the fuck up you dirty whore!"
As he yanked both her hands behind her back and secured them with duct tape the pain was excruciating and this time she screamed.
"I said shut up!"
Punching Adeela hard in the back of the head, he ripped off another piece of tape and roughly placed it across her mouth. Akram was slightly less violent in his actions as he bound her legs but it made little difference, Adeela didn't know what was going to happen but she was now frightened beyond belief.
"Right, get her to her feet."
Rashid and Akram did as they were told and as they carried her towards the hall, Adeela gave one last pleading look in her father's direction but all he did was remove his oxygen mask and give her a

sickly grin. Just as they reached the front door, Safeer threw a coat over her in case any of the neighbours were looking out of their windows. Bundling their sister onto the back seat of the Merc, Akram climbed in beside her but not once did he look in her direction. With Rashid and Safeer in the front, the brothers set off for the car park on South Grove. The dark corner that they usually parked in to initiate the girls would be perfect but it would mean having to find somewhere new as after tonight there would probably be a heavy police presence.

Frankie was like a man on a mission and as the cab came to a stop outside Adeela's house, he quickly paid the fare and then marched up to the door. Using his fist he banged as hard as he could and was prepared to take his chances if one of her brothers answered but it was Yasmeen who opened up.

Yes, can I help you?"

"I've come for Adeela and neither you nor anyone else will stop us being together."

Yasmeen began to laugh and at the same time Frankie could feel a shiver as it ran down the whole length of his body.

"You're too late and if my son's were here, I have no doubt that you would be joining the dirty little whore."

Yasmeen slammed the door shut in Frankie's face but he didn't give up and continued to hammer away for quite a while. When he finally accepted that no one was going to answer he stopped and for a moment just stood there not knowing what to do. If he went to the police he had no proof that anything bad had happened so they wouldn't be interested. He couldn't go looking for her as he didn't have the foggiest idea of where to start and as anxiety began to build he felt totally helpless. Slowly he turned and walked away and at the same time his mind was filled with all sorts of images of his beautiful girl and what she might be suffering. Frankie tried to push the images from his head and decided to just wait it out until morning; hopefully Adeela would arrive at the pub just as she always did. If her brothers had beaten her it would be horrendous but at the same time it wasn't something that she couldn't get over in time. No, Frankie was now confident that it wouldn't be anything worse than that and once again hailing a cab, he made his way back to the pub. The place was still busy with customers and Frankie forced himself onto auto pilot, that or he knew he'd go crazy waiting to hear something, anything that would tell him his girl was safe. In the car park, Safeer turned off the cars head lights and told his brothers to remove Adeela and take her a few hundred yards further along onto the grass perimeter. As they threw her down onto the grass she tried to focus her eyes and see if she recognised the place but she didn't. Rashid and Akram just

stood staring at her as they waited for Safeer to tell them what to do next. Finally he came over and in his hand he was carrying a petrol can, opening the lid her poured the entire contents over Adeela's body and when she smelled the fumes and knew what was about to happen, she desperately tried to scream but the tape was still securely stuck over her mouth. Safeer ordered his brothers back to the car and told Rashid to start the engine in readiness for a quick getaway. They did as they were told but as he walked away, Akram couldn't help but keep looking back over his shoulder. He saw Safeer strike a match, throw it down and then swiftly walk away. As the flame made contact with the fumes, a small boom and whooshing sound was heard. Instantly the flames shot up into the air but they soon calmed down and as they wrapped themselves around Adeela's body, licking every inch of her flesh, her face contorted as she writhed in agony. Now totally engulfed by fire, the sight was horrendous. As Akram looked back, he saw Adeela's once beautiful face appear to melt and distort like plastic. A slight breeze was blowing in their direction and Akram could also now smell the pungent sickening stench of Adeela's burning flesh. The stench and the thought of his actions finally hit home and bending over double, he wretched and vomited onto the ground. Rashid placed the palm of his hand onto the centre of Akram's back.
"Come on Bro, we need to keep moving. This place

could be swarming with coppers in a few minutes and we don't want to be here when that happens." Standing up Akram breathed in deep as he tried to compose himself and with the help of his brother, they managed to make it back to the car. Getting in, Rashid had only just turned on the ignition when the passenger side door opened and they were joined by Safeer.

"Right, now that's been taken care of we need to go home and change our clothes. After that, it's business as usual my brothers, time is money and all that!"

Akram couldn't believe how casual his brother was being. Even though he'd had little feeling for Adeela, they had still just murdered their sister but Safeer didn't seem bothered and it scared Akram. No matter how big or hard his elder brother was, they were not above the law and if they ever got caught for this, well Akram didn't even want to dwell on that but they definitely wouldn't see the light of day for many years to come.

Reaching home, Safeer placed his key in the lock and was met by his mother. Yasmeen was wringing her hands and she had a worried look on her face.

"What's the matter woman?"

"A man has been here asking about your sister, I think he's the one she, you know what I mean."

"I no longer have a sister and you'd do well to remember that. From now on you will never mention her name or speak of her in any way, do you hear? As far as this man is concerned, he can't prove anything and if the police start asking questions, we will all just say that she was a bad girl and ran away. Rashid, Akram, upstairs. I want you both to shower and change your clothes. Mum, wash them two or three times so that there is not a trace of evidence, come on then, what are you all waiting for."

Safeer walked into the front room and when his father saw him he lowered his oxygen mask.

"Is it done?"

"Yes."

"Good."

Anwar nodded his head several times in approval and then replaced the mask. As far as he was concerned there was no more to say on the matter, Adeela had made her choice and she had suffered the consequences of her actions.

CHAPTER TWENTY TWO

Frankie hadn't been able to sleep a wink all night. Thoughts of Adeela filled his mind and he was desperate to hear from her. Throughout the night he had sent countless voice mails, all pleading with her to get in touch but by the morning there was still no word. The pub was spotless as he'd tried to use his time by keeping busy and at six am the place was ready to open, the bar had been restocked and the lunchtime sandwiches prepared. Making a coffee he sat down to wait and with each passing hour, he became more and more convinced that she wasn't going to show. He must have nodded off as he sat bolt upright and was slightly disorientated when Karen Jones walked through the door.
"Bloody hell, someone's been busy?"
Karen laughed but was immediately stopped when she saw the state of her boss.
"Whatever's the matter Frankie? You look terrible love."
He was about to speak when the barmaid put up her hand to stop him.
"Wait a minute, don't answer that until I've got us both a coffee, you look like you could do with one."
Karen walked behind the bar and was pleased to see that the cappuccino machine had been filled up. Pouring out two large cups, she went back to the table and placed them down.

"Right, tell me what's been going on and don't say 'nothing' because by the look of you I know that's not the truth."

Frankie studied the girl as if seeing her for the first time. She was bright and funny, knew how to keep a secret, but more than that she was caring and right at this moment Frankie needed a friend like never before.

"Adeela's gone missing."

"What? Are you sure, how do you know?"

"We've kept our relationship a secret for weeks and she was planning to move in with me today. You remember that woman who came in here looking for me yesterday?"

"What about her?"

"That was Adeela's aunt Bina and what she really wanted was to warn me."

"Warn you about what, oh Frankie whatever's going on love?"

"They don't live like us Karen and it was intended that Adeela would marry one of her own so to speak. Her family are oppressive and it seems that someone let the cat out of the bag and they found out about us. Her aunt Bina came to tell me that the family were going to punish her."

Karen took a sip of her coffee and wiped away the frothy moustache from her top lip.

"Is that all? Goodness me, you had me going there for a bit."

Frankie shook his head and was starting to wish he

hadn't begun to explain. No one would ever understand, least of all his barmaid but he had to keep talking, had to try and unburden himself.
"When I say punishment Karen, I don't mean a fucking slap on the wrists. These people are fanatical about honour and will go to any lengths to retain it. You must have seen this sort of thing on the telly and in the papers?"
"Well yes but surely it doesn't happen that often and not round here, well at least I've never heard of anything like that."
"God you're naive, it happens a lot more than you think. Most of the girls don't get reported as missing, so no one ever knows what's happened to them. Anyway, I couldn't stand it any longer so last night I went to her house. I was so fired up and I was ready to take on the whole family if it meant I could bring her back home with me. Her mother or at least I think it was her mother, answered the door. The old cow laughed at me Karen; she stood on the doorstep and actually laughed in my face and said I was too late."
"Too late, what did she mean?"
"I don't know, she slammed the door shut and no matter how hard I hammered, she wouldn't open up again. I came back here to wait; I didn't know what else to do. I aint a godly bloke Karen but I prayed all night that she would turn up as usual but now, now I've got a sinking feeling that I aint ever going to see her again."

"Oh you poor love. Frankie you really shouldn't think like that, you have to stay positive."

Karen Jones stood up and walked around the table to where Frankie sat. Placing her arm over his shoulder, she pulled him to her. There was nothing more than offering pure comfort in her gesture, just one friend trying to console another. They must have sat like that for some time because when Karen looked up at the wall clock, it was close to eleven am. Gently lifting her arm she moved away slowly.

"Frankie it's almost time to open up. Why don't you go upstairs and try and get some sleep. Markey Taylor will be here within the hour to do the glasses and I'm sure together we can manage to get through the lunchtime rush."

Frankie tried to put on a smile but at best it was weak.

"It's good of you but I know I couldn't sleep, I will go through to the back though if you don't mind. Give me a shout if you need me."

Standing up he kissed her on the cheek.

"Thanks for being a friend Karen."

With that he walked to the rear of the bar and into the back office. When Karen had put her coat and bag away and tied her waist high apron into position, she poured another coffee. Switching on the television she took a seat on one of the high bar stools. It would be at least another fifteen minutes before anyone came in so she decided to see what had been going on in London overnight. The image that appeared on the screen was a cordoned off grass area in Walthamstow but she didn't recognise it. Police officers could be seen scouring the land and as Karen turned up the volume, her jaw dropped when she heard the reporter's words.

'The burnt remains of a body have been discovered early this morning by a member of the public out walking their dog. Police reports confirm that the body is female but as yet they are the only details being released. Local speculation is spreading that this may have been an honour killing but the police refuse to comment further. We will bring you updates as more information comes to light. This is Gerald Stewart reporting for city news.'

Karen put her hand up to her face and as she looked in the mirror behind the bar, could actually see the colour drain from her cheeks. Karen was in turmoil, should she go and tell Frankie or would that cause him even more pain for no reason when she didn't even know if it was Adeela. Deciding that she had to, because if he walked in during opening hours and saw the news, she didn't know what would happen or how he would react. Slipping off the stool she slowly walked towards the office and tapped gently on the door. Even though she didn't know anything for sure, Karen really wasn't looking forward to this but taking a deep breath, she turned the handle and went in. Frankie was sitting behind the desk with his head in his hands and for a second she thought that he might be asleep, but when he lifted his head and smiled, she walked over to the desk.

"Is there a problem love?"

"No Frankie, there's not anyone in yet. I've just..." Karen paused and as she did so Frankie's brow furrowed.

"What is it? What's up?"

"I just switched on the telly to watch the news."

"And?"

"Oh Frankie I don't know if it has anything to do with Adeela but something terrible has happened and..."

Frankie West didn't give her time to continue, in a second he was on his feet and running though to the bar. Picking up the remote, he switched on the television and turned to the news on another channel, where a similar bulletin to the one that Karen had seen was being shown. Karen had followed him into the bar but she didn't speak and stood beside him waiting for the report to finish. Slowly Frankie turned to face her.

"It's Adeela."

"Now you don't know that Frankie, nothings been confirmed."

"It doesn't need to be. I know it's her Karen, I just know it."

Frankie hung his head and she knew that nothing she said could convince him otherwise. All Karen could do was to hug him close to her, in a vain attempt to offer some kind of comfort. Leading him back into the office, she quickly returned and placed the bolt on the front doors and put the closed sign in the window. Harry wouldn't like it when he found out but for now Frankie had to be her main priority. Pouring a black coffee, she added a liberal measure of brandy and then returned to the office.

"Here drink this; it will help calm you down?"

"Oh Karen, I don't know how I'm going to live without her."

"Are you going to contact the Old Bill?"

Frankie could only shrug his shoulders, in less than twenty four hours his world had been taken from him and right at this moment all he wanted was to be left alone to think.

"I don't know, I need to think but I'll be alright Karen. I just need some time to get my head around all of this. Open up as usual, as long as you can cope?"

"Of course I can, now if you need anything you just call, ok?"

Frankie nodded his head and she could see the pool of tears that he was so desperately trying to hold back. In the office and when the door was firmly closed, Frankie once again placed his head in his hands and this time he allowed the tears to escape. He must have sat there just staring into space for over an hour. He could hear the punters in the bar all laughing and joking but the sound seemed distant and so far away. His mind was racing and every thought seemed to mingle with another until nothing made sense. Frankie's head began to ache and he knew he had to do something, knew he had to find out the truth. Opening the drawer he flicked through the numerous phone books that they had amassed over the years and pulling out the one for north London, he began to scan the pages.

Bina Raja stood at the kitchen sink with tears streaming down her cheeks. She too had seen the news report and without being told, was convinced the body was that of her niece. When the telephone burst into life it startled her and for a second she could only stare at it. After the fifth ring she found a tissue and wiping her face, picked up the receiver. To begin with there wasn't a sound so after sniffing loudly, she spoke.

"Hello?"

"Bina its Frankie, I know what's happened and I want to know who did it, was it those scumbag brothers of hers?"

Bina slowly shook her head, she hadn't given Frankie a thought but now that he was on the other end of the line she knew trouble was brewing.

"My darling nothings been confirmed yet and I haven't heard anything from my sister. I plan on making a visit this morning and then I will know more. Give me a couple of hours and then call back ok?"

Frankie was reluctant at first but finally he agreed, after all what was time to him now. Bina wasn't trying to put him off in any way, she was broken hearted as well but she was also angry and wanted some answers. Fifteen minutes later the cab collected her and by the time it pulled up on Priory Avenue, her face was set in stone. The Makhdoom's front door was opened after just one knock and when Akram saw his aunt he knew that things were about to kick off.

"Hello aunty, how are you?"

"How am I? Get out of my way you sorry excuse for a human being!"

Bina pushed past and walked along the hall into the front room. Everyone was seated at the table but it was Yasmeen that Bina's words were directed towards.

"Is it true?"

Safeer interrupted and tried to speak on his mother's behalf but Bina soon put him in his place.

"Was I talking to you Boy? Yasmeen, I will only ask you one more time, is it true?"

Yasmeen nodded her head and then lowered it just as Adeela had always done. She didn't feel remorse or shame, just embarrassment that her sister had felt the need to barge into her home and speak to Safeer this way. Bina turned to the brothers and looked from one to the other.

"You think you are so high and mighty don't you, well allow me to let you into a little secret, this is not over not by a long way. Frankie West loved your sister..."

"We no longer have a sister."
Bina's hand was swift as it made contact with Safeer's cheek, his face showed rage at being struck by a woman but he knew better than to do anything about it. His aunt was rich and well respected, and this was one time where violence wouldn't be accepted by anyone in the community if he retaliated.
"As I was saying, Frankie West loved you sister with all of his heart and he's already been on the telephone to me this morning wanting to know what's going on. If you think for one moment that he will leave the matter alone you have another think coming."
Akram said the words that everyone else wanted to but didn't dare.
"You've been discussing family business with a stranger and a white man at that?"
Bina could only shake her head. Her family were living in the dark ages and things were never going to change. Family loyalty now meant nothing to her and there and then she decided to help Frankie in any way that she could.
"Family, what family? As far as I'm concerned you are no longer my family. What you did to poor sweet Adeela, well I'm shocked to the core but not really surprised. You are all pathetic, people like you tar us all with the same brush. You don't help matters in the least with you archaic values and hypocritical views. All three of you are murderers,

come to that all five of you are."
Bina stared hard in her sister's direction.
"There is no excuse or reason for your disgusting despicable behaviour. From now on you are all on your own and when Frankie West comes after you, may god help him and not you!"
Bina walked from the house and slammed the door as she left. The place now gave her a terrible feeling as she imagined all that her niece may have gone through in the very room she'd just been standing in.
Back inside, nobody spoke for a while as they were all trying to digest exactly what Bina had said. Yasmeen was upset when she thought about the regular cash handouts she would loose from her sister, not to mention all the highly thought of people that she was always introduced to at the family parties. As usual, Rashid wasn't really bothered about anything but it was a different case for Safeer. He was worried in case all of this would affect his business and whether or not the girls would be frightened off if they ever found out. Anwar studied his family from behind his oxygen mask and the one thing he did notice was Akram. Akram looked scared and he had every right to feel that way. None of them knew Frankie West or what he was cable of but it wouldn't take long for them to find out.

CHAPTER TWENTY THREE

As soon as Bina arrived home she was on the telephone, she couldn't wait for Frankie to call her later. Anger raged through her and she was well aware that she was about to stir up a hornet's nest but Adeela deserved some kind of justice for what they had done to her. Sitting in the office, Frankie jumped when the telephone rang and for a minute considered not answering. He really couldn't face talking to reps and suppliers today but then work was all he had at the moment and if word got back to Harry that he wasn't doing his job properly, well he didn't need any more aggravation.
"Hello?"
"Frankie its Bina, I'm sorry but I couldn't wait for you to call back, I've just got back from my sisters."
"What happened?"
"Those animals that I reluctantly call nephews did just what I thought. I'm sorry Frankie but Adeela is dead."
For a moment there was only silence and Bina wondered if she'd done the right thing contacting him. In reality she knew that there would be no justice but she had to speak to someone and Frankie West was the only person who understood how she was feeling.
"Frankie, are you there?"
"Yes, yes I'm here Bina, it's just that I was still

hoping and......"
"I know and to be honest with you so was I but it wasn't to be. What do you plan on doing now?"
She could hear him sigh on the other end of the telephone and Bina's heart went out to him.
"I haven't got a clue Bina; can you tell me their names?"
"Why? You're not planning on going to the police are you?"
"I won't lie, I have thought about it but in all honesty I don't think the Old Bill are an option. I don't want to offend you but I mean let's face it, most of the time these crimes go unpunished. The Met are more worried about being politically correct regarding certain ethnic minorities, than getting any justice for the victim."
"I understand where you are coming from my dear but even if the police did get involved, it wouldn't be as simple as that. The boys will have made plans for such an event, I'm sure of that."
Frankie had already decided that going to the police wasn't an option. The idea that there was even the slightest chance of them getting off with murder didn't bare thinking about. He was certain that they would all close ranks and deny any knowledge of Frankie and Adeela's relationship. Her murder would count for nothing and the culprits would go unpunished.
"So they just get away with it scot free?"
"It is our way Frankie and I know you don't agree

with it but you will never change tradition. What do you want to see happen?"
"I'd like the bastards to go through exactly the same as Adeela did.""
"Now Frankie, you're not about to do something silly are you. Darling I am as heartbroken as you are but if anything happened to my nephews or if the police do become involved, well blood is thicker than water after all and as much as it would pain me, I would have to come down on their side. Now promise me you aren't going to do anything rash?" There was a lot more behind Bina's words, she no longer cared about her family but she did care about the disgrace and trouble it would cause to her community. Frankie didn't like lying but then again, he wasn't lying because as yet he didn't know what he was going to do. The hypocrisy of it all galled him, they always seemed to defend their own regardless of the crime or who got hurt. Frankie wanted to scream down the telephone and tell Bina that she was as bad as the rest of them for not seeking justice but he knew it wouldn't do any good.
"No of course not but I would still like to know the names of the murdering bastards who took my girls life. Does that sound insane, that I need to know what they are called?"
"No sweetheart it doesn't. Well there's Safeer, he's the oldest, then there's Rashid and Akram the youngest. Frankie I have to go now as there is

someone at the door but please tell me you'll keep in touch?"

"Of course I will and thank you Bina, thank you for all that you've done."

"Frankie I didn't do enough and maybe if I had acted sooner Adeela would still be alive and that's something I will have to carry with me for the rest of my life."

The line went dead and he knew that the woman was full of guilt but maybe she was right, maybe she could have done more, maybe they both could have. It would soon be time to close up but Frankie still went into the bar and did his best to muster a smile for the regulars but it was difficult. The last thing he wanted was to listen to some old drunks reminisce about their lost loves and then having to come across all sympathetic, but that's exactly what he did. When they finally shut up for the afternoon and when Karen had left, Frankie went upstairs and lay down on his bed. Caressing the sheets, he thought back to the last time Adeela had been beside him and the tears came thick and fast. Getting through the evening shift was even more difficult and he was so glad when the last punter had left and he was able to bolt the door. Pouring a large brandy, Frankie hoped that it would help him relax but it wasn't to be and sleep would evade him for most of the night. By four am he decided to stop tossing and turning and get up. Sitting alone in the office he finally came to the conclusion that he had two options, one, sit and wallow for as long as it took to come to terms with his loss or two, seek revenge for Adeela. Frankie already knew which it would be and an hour later he had hatched a plan. Papers now filled the desk as he scrawled out the different scenarios and what the outcome could be. By all accounts the brothers might be a handful but then the way he was feeling at the moment, he didn't care if he lived or died and anyone with that mentality could be a very dangerous person in deed.

Karen had made an effort to come in early for her shift. She wanted to see how her boss was holding up and offer further support if it was needed. What greeted her in the bar shocked her to the core but in a good way. She had been expecting to find Frankie a broken man sobbing into his drink but nothing was further from the truth. Washed and dressed in dark jeans and a black leather jacket, he was ready to go out. A small rucksack sat neatly on his back but Karen didn't have a clue what it contained.

"Well I must say you look a lot brighter today." Frankie smiled and walking over to her handed Karen an envelope.

"I need you to run this place for a few days as I won't be around much, well not in a work sense at least. I also need to borrow your scooter if that's alright? There's three hundred in there to cover any taxi fares and your trouble."

Karen Jones stared at the envelope; she didn't mind lending him her wheels and the extra money would certainly come in handy.
"That's fine but what are you up to?"
"Sorry babe but the less you know, the better it will be for all of us. If Harry comes in make some excuse but if he presses you, oh fuck it, if he presses you tell him I said to go fuck himself."
Frankie took the keys from her hand and with that he walked out of the front door. Karen could only sigh with a heavy heart, she had a bad feeling but there was nothing she could do about it. She had a habit of putting two and two together and coming up with ten, so to stop herself from worrying unnecessarily Karen decided to keep busy by doing a stock take. Frankie rode over to Walthamstow, parked up the scooter and walked down Priory Avenue but this time he was on his guard and took extra care not to be seen. Removing a notepad from the rucksack he wrote down the registration of Safeer's car. He then headed over to the car park where Adeela's body had been found. The area was still taped off but as there was no one around, he laid a small bunch of flowers that he purchased from one of the local shops, down onto the ground. Instead of the tears that he expected to fall, he was suddenly filled with rage. A rage that was so fierce, he knew whatever happened the Makhdoom brothers were going to suffer a horrendous end. Frankie hung around the area for most of the day

but surprisingly the time went quickly and when it finally started to get dark he went back to Priory Avenue. Frankie was just in time to see the brothers exit the house and starting up the scooter he pulled out onto the road. He had already made plans in advance and borrowing a copy of the blue book from a friend was the first. The blue book was carried by everyone learning the knowledge to become a London cabbie and if the Makhdoom's became suspicious; they would soon relax when they saw him with the book clipped to the front of his scooter. It was a common sight on the streets and roads of London and nothing out of the ordinary. Pulling on Karen's black crash helmet, Frankie followed the old Mercedes at a safe enough distance not to be seen but close enough that he wouldn't lose them. When the car drove into the old burial gardens, he stopped and parked up on the main road. Frankie has specifically chosen his clothes so that at night he had less chance of being seen and slowly walking along he tried to stay as close to the bushes as he could. As usual it was the same routine that the brothers always followed and the girls were already waiting for Akram to join them. When Safeer and Rashid, along with one of the girls headed towards the car, Frankie ran as fast as he could back to the scooter. Starting it up, he again followed and watched as Rashid got out at the flats and led Lindy by the arm to another appointment. When he returned, the two brothers continued on to the leisure centre and Frankie watched as Dawn and Janice got into the car. After dropping the girls off in Kings Cross, Safeer then parked up on Balfe Street to wait. Frankie wasn't certain what was going on but he had a pretty good idea and it only fuelled his anger more. The hypocrisy of these people was unbelievable and as much as they might have carried out Adeela's murder as a warning to other Pakistani girls, his warning was going to be far worse.

By the time he returned to the pub it was the early hours of the morning and the place was in darkness. Pushing the scooter into the rear yard, Frankie then climbed the stairs and still fully clothed, flopped down onto the bed and immediately fell asleep.

Waking up the next morning he had a strange feeling, oh he was missing Adeela like mad but this anger that now filled his whole being had taken over and had given him strength and purpose. His time for mourning would come eventually but for now he had to concentrate on the task in hand. He was taking a chance by not going back to Walthamstow until the evening but if they were doing what he thought they were, then the Makhdoom's wouldn't venture out again until after dark. Setting off early, Frankie decided to pay Bina a visit to see if there was any more information she could provide but he would have to be careful, she had already warned him where her true loyalties would lie if the police got involved. Opening the

door, Bina was a little taken back when she saw who the caller was but none the less she invited Frankie inside.
"I'm sorry to drop in on you like this."
"You're welcome anytime, come through and I'll make us both a drink."
Frankie took a seat at the breakfast bar and as Bina busied herself filling the kettle, he began to speak.
"Is there anything else you can tell me about Adeela's brothers?"
"Like what?"
"Well last night I followed them and to me it seems that they make their living in a less than conventional way."
Bina stopped what she was doing and looking in Frankie's direction, raised her eyebrows.
"If you mean prostitution, I already know about them or have heard the rumours. That's if it's true of course. So, why on earth did you follow them?"
Frankie knew that he had to lie again, that or she would ask him to leave the instant she found out what he was up to and in any case he didn't yet trust her not to warn them all.
"No reason really, I was just at a bit of a loose end. I also went to the place where they found Adeela and laid some flowers. Anyway, when I followed them they seemed to be mixing with a lot of young girls and I do mean young."
Bina placed down two mugs and then took a seat beside him.

"My dear Frankie there are so many things you don't understand about my culture and you probably never will. To Pakistani men, their women are their possessions and are to be kept pure at all costs. On the other hand, there is a faction of men, not all I might add, who view white women as whore's who are there for the taking, to be used however they feel fit. For a long time there have been rumours that my nephews deal in underage prostitution but they would never admit to that. I however am of the belief that there is some truth in the rumours as my sister and brother in law no longer work but they still seem able to run a house on thin air. There is never any mention of what the boys do for a living and to be honest, it's none of my business or yours come to that."

Her words angered Frankie but at the same time they only served to convince him that he was doing the right thing. As if what had happened to Adeela wasn't bad enough, to now learn that they were prostituting young underage girls and getting away with it, was even more horrific. He had thought she of all people would be against this hypocrisy but obviously he had got her all wrong. Standing up Frankie thanked her for her hospitality and then turned to leave.

"But you haven't finished your drink?"

"I'm sorry Bina but I thought after what they did and the love we both had for Adeela, that we had some kind of connection. I now know that I was wrong. In my world we treat all humans the same, especially women and anyone who doesn't deserves exactly what they get."

Frankie walked into the hall and turning the latch could hear Bina calling after him but he ignored her. Getting on the scooter he returned to the pub to make further plans before he once again set off to trail the Makhdoom's.

For the rest of the week Frankie followed the same routine every day. He would start by cleaning the pub, bottle up and then help Karen with the lunchtime trade but as soon as it started to get dark, he would roar off on the scooter in pursuit of the brothers. It became clear after only a couple of days that they always followed the same pattern but he still didn't want to rush things. When he decided to hit them, Frankie West wanted everything to run smoothly. For now he would watch, watch and learn what those monsters were doing and when he felt that the time was right, he would strike and send them all to hell!

CHAPTER TWENTY FOUR

Thursday morning saw Frankie West up and out of bed before it was even light. He liked this time of day as there was little traffic and it was one of the few times that London was relatively quiet. Lighting a cigarette he stood outside taking in the early morning air and for the umpteenth time went over in his mind exactly how things would pan out, or so he hoped. He was not so naive that he didn't know the best laid plans never actually materialized the way they were supposed to, not when other people were involved. After stubbing out his cigarette on the pavement, Frankie went back inside and took a seat behind his desk in the office. Removing the blue book, he again studied his routes. It was bizarre, but the prop and that's all that the book had ever been intended for, had turned out to be worth its weight in gold. Knowing the brothers nightly destinations beforehand had allowed Frankie to find out all the shortest routes, some of which were only accessible on two wheels. This knowledge would assist Frankie in getting from one place to another far quicker than the Makhdoom's could. Had this not have been possible, it would have made things tricky as Frankie knew that he had to strike in one night. By eleven am and just as Karen walked through the door, he was finally ready. Sitting on a stool at the bar he was as jumpy as a cat on hot coals when he heard the door open.

"Morning boss, is everything ok?"

"Of course it is why would you even ask?"

Karen didn't like his tone and as she went to hang up her coat and scarf, whispered under her breath 'fuck me, someone got out of bed on the wrong side'. Karen had kept a close eye on Frankie over the last few days and thought how well he was handling things, maybe too well. When she returned from the back office, he seemed to be in a better mood as he slipped off of the stool and placed a kiss onto her cheek.

"Sorry I'm snappy love, you know how it is when your nerves are bad and since Adeela mine seem totally shot."

"Say no more about it, now I think it's time we set about giving this place the once over don't you? Oh Frankie, I forgot to say, Harry was in here on the war path yesterday. He'd already been in a couple of times and I was able to fob him off but not yesterday. He got really arsy when you weren't here and said to tell you he would be in today and that you'd better show your face."

Harry West was the least of Frankie's worries but it didn't matter as his plans wouldn't begin until nightfall. Within a few minutes the door burst open and Harry marched in with Jimmy Fingers in tow.

"Talk of the devil."

"What the fuck are you on about bitch!"

It was clear to Karen that the big boss was in a bad mood and picking up her mop she scuttled into the back room. Whatever was going on between the two men, she didn't want any part of it. Helping her boss through a bad time was one thing but when it came to Harry West, she would rather stay as far away from the man as possible. Frankie wanted to laugh; Harry always seemed to put the fear of god into everyone apart from him. Oh he knew the man was more than capable of dishing out a good beating but he also knew that if Harry ever laid a hand on his so called nephew, it would be more than his life was worth as far as Bella was concerned.

"There was no need to talk to her like that Harry; she's a good kid and a hard worker."

"Fucking hard worker? What would you know about hard work, you never seem to be here lately? Still seeing that little Asian tart or has she dumped you?"

Frankie could feel his blood begin to boil and he really wanted to punch Harry's lights out but he knew he had to stay calm. What he had planned for later would take all of his mental energy and getting fired up early would do him no good at all.

"Why don't you just fuck off Harry, I'm sure you only come in here to try and wind me up!"

Harry West ignored all that was said to him and taking a step forward, expected Frankie to move back in fear but Frankie stood his ground. Jimmy

Fingers, who had a grin on his face when they had first walked in, now, looked more than a little concerned as to where this would all end. He knew if Harry turned it would be bad and at the same time he couldn't understand why Frankie didn't just toe the line and keep his head down like Jimmy always did. When Karen sheepishly walked back into the bar hoping that Harry had gone, she could feel the tension and was scared that Frankie was going to blow his top. Surprisingly it was Harry who backed down and without another word he turned and walked out with Jimmy Fingers following in hot pursuit.
"That was a close shave Frankie."
"Not really love, he's nothing but a bully and above all else, I hate fucking bullies. Now I think we're about ready to open up don't you?"
"Well we didn't get any cleaning done."
"Does it really matter?"
Karen smiled but didn't answer as she knew the question was rhetorical. Taking their places behind the bar they waited for the first of many customers to come in and for the shift to get fully underway. Three hours later it was finally time to bolt the door and as Karen was about to leave for her afternoon break Frankie informed her that he wouldn't be about later but hopefully this would be the last time and by tomorrow she should be able to have her scooter back.

At seven that night Frankie West was all set

and ready to go. As soon as Karen and the rest of the bar staff arrived for the evening shift, he made his way into the back office. Opening up the safe he removed the nineteen fifty one Makarov pistol that Harry kept for emergencies. From a boy, Frankie had been taught how to clean the gun and had always kept it in tip top condition. Checking the magazine, he made sure that the safety catch was in place, the silencer was correctly attached and after a thorough wipe to remove any finger prints, slipped it into his rucksack. Along with a canister of CS gas that was always kept in the office in case of trouble, it was all systems go. As he rode over to Walthamstow he was strangely calm and parking in an alleyway on Church Lane, he stashed his helmet in the top box and then cut through onto the old Burial Gardens. Originally he had wanted to make a quick exit and be ahead of Safeer and Rashid but last night while he lay in bed going over his plans, he'd decided on a different strategy. With his new plan he would be able to take his time and do the job in a controlled and clinical manner. Going in from Church Lane meant he would cross a large grassy area and approach the monument from behind. As the light dimmed he could see two girls already waiting. Ducking behind a headstone he watched them for a few minutes and when he was sure that no one else was about, he pulled up the scarf from his neck and covered his nose and mouth so that only his eyes were visible. As he walked over, Lindy was standing with Katie Watson, one of the Makhdoom's newest recruits. As they chatted away they didn't see Frankie sneak up behind them. Lindy was moaning to her friend that Safeer was making her work more and more and that she didn't want to do it but arguing with him had only resulted in a black eye.

"I'll tell you something for nothing Katie, I've definitely had a gutful of those wanker's. I know you're still new to all of this but if I could get out somehow I would and I'd tell you to do the same but we're prisoners and there's nothing we can do about it."

"Just tell them you don't want to do it anymore Lindy."

"You're joking aint you, they'd beat me to a pulp. I've seen it many times before with some of the other girls. When I first started there was a girl called Jilly, she was a mouthy bitch but I liked her. She started to complain and then mysteriously disappeared and I'm sure in my heart that Safeer had a hand in her death but he'll never get caught for it."

"How did she die?"

"What poor old Jilly? No one knows for sure but I realised then that there's no getting out of this game, well at least not alive."

The girls both spun round when they heard footsteps and came face to face with a man who, from the scarf on his face, didn't want to be recognised. Lindy swallowed hard and tried not to show her fear but it was evident for anyone to see. The conversation that Frankie had just heard was music to his ears and he was now a lot more confident about approaching them.

"I don't know what you want but we aint got any money and our boyfriends will be here in a minute."

Frankie felt nothing but pity and he knew if he removed his mask it would relax the situation but he had to keep his identity a secret.

"Just listen to what I have to say. I heard every word that you just said and I know you both want out of all this and if you do as I say, I can make that happen. I promise I'm not here to hurt either of you. I need to speak to the Makhdoom brothers and this is the only way I can get close to them. I've been following them for a while and I know what they do and how they force you both to sell yourselves."

Lindy was about to protest but stopped when Katie squeezed her friends hand. It was a signal to let the man speak and for once Lindy Harding did as she was asked and allowed Frankie to continue.

Removing his wallet, he took out two hundred pounds and handed half to Lindy.

"When they get here I want you to go with the two oldest just as you always do. When they drop you at the flat and after you're sure they've gone, go home and never come back to this place."

"But they'll come after us, Safeer will beat me and I

can't take much more."
"You have my word that he won't."
"How do we know we can trust you?"
"In all honesty sweetheart you don't but can you trust those three scumbags either?"
Lindy and Katie slowly shook their heads, things had to change and they had no option but to trust the man or this godforsaken lifestyle would be theirs until they were too old for the Makhdoom's to use any more or until something happened to them like it had to poor Fiona. The girls weren't stupid and when their friend had disappeared without a trace, they both realised that something bad had gone down but neither of them were brave enough to question any of the Makhdoom brothers.
Turning to Katie, Frankie also handed her one hundred pounds.
"Now when your boyfriend gets here."
"He's not my boyfriend, not really. All he did was trick me and I hate him for it."
"Ok ok, well when he walks over and you're sure that the others have gone, I want you to run as fast as your legs will carry you. Don't look back and I swear to you both that all your suffering will end tonight and that is a promise. So what do you say?"
Lindy and Katie vigorously nodded their heads and once more Frankie went over what he wanted them to do. Ten minutes later the cars headlights could be seen pulling up. When the brothers appeared, Lindy stepped forward and heading in their

direction, passed Akram as he walked over to meet Katie. Safeer opened the car door and Lindy got inside, she felt calm as she thought of the mysterious mans words 'all your suffering will end tonight'. After switching on the engine Safeer pulled out onto the road and headed off. Frankie had been hiding behind one of the old headstones waiting for the right moment and when he saw Katie begin to run and heard Akram call out, knew that so far everything was going to plan and it was now time for him to spring into action. Taking off the scarf, Frankie stepped from behind the headstone as Akram began shouting after the girl.
"Hey! What the fuck are you doing girl? Come back do you hear me you fucking little bitch! I tell you girl, you're going to get a fucking beating when I get hold of you."
As Frankie walked towards Akram and when he was within a metre of the man, Akram heard his footsteps and turning around sharply, was surprised to see Frankie West.
"Who the fuck are you and what are you doing...."
Before he could finish speaking, Frankie raised his hand and sprayed Akram Makhdoom directly in the face with CS gas. The reaction was instant, his face felt as if it was on fire and he started to frantically rub at his eyes. Beginning to cough uncontrollably, Akram was starting to have trouble breathing as mucus and nasal discharge began to escape from his mouth and nose and he cried out in pain. Frankie

took a swing at his victim and his fist hit Akram squarely on the jaw knocking him to the ground. A thud could be heard as Akram's head made contact with the concrete path and he was rendered unconscious. Glancing all around, Frankie made sure that they were alone and that the burial gardens were deserted. Grabbing Akram's ankles, Frankie dragged him from the path to behind one of the headstones. The man was a dead weight and it was a struggle but finally when Frankie had Akram where he wanted, he positioned himself on top of the man's chest. Slowly Akram began to regain consciousness and the first thing he saw was Frankie's fist as it made contact with his face. All the anger that had built up over the last few days now suddenly erupted as Frankie reigned down blow after blow and when he finally finished his assault, Akram Makhdoom's face was a bludgeoned mess.

"How's that feel you fucking bastard?"

"Who are you?"

As Akram struggled to speak he coughed and spat blood from his mouth.

"I'm your fucking worst nightmare. I'm the man who loved and adored your sister."

As Frankie stood up, Akram turned and hauled himself onto his knees and with his back to Frankie he began to crawl away. Frankie West reached into his rucksack and placing his hand onto Harry's gun, removed it. Akram hadn't got more than a few feet away as Frankie walked slowly towards him. Placing the tip of the silencer to the back of Akram Makhdoom's head and without any hesitation, Frankie pulled the trigger. A quiet puffing sound was heard as the silencer did its job and Akram's now lifeless body slumped onto the wet ground. Putting the gun and CS gas back into his bag, Frankie then dragged Akram body over to the side of the burial gardens and with a couple of hard pushes with his foot, rolled the body down into a ditch.

"One down, two to go."

Lindy had been dropped off at the flat on the Tyers Estate but she walked a little slower than usual and when she was out of sight in the stairwell, she stopped completely. Being extra careful she peered through a small hole in the main door and smiled when she saw the Mercedes drive off. Deciding to have a cigarette, she would wait just long enough so that Safeer wouldn't see her if he looked out of his rear view mirror. Lindy knew that before long George Sewell would contact Safeer and say that she hadn't arrived so she didn't dare go back home as it would be the first place he would look. Wracking her brains, she remembered there was a small respectable bed and breakfast on Addison Road. The woman who owned it was a kindly sort and Lindy knew that she had taken a few girls in temporarily when the home had been full. Her rates were low and with the hundred that the man had given her, she would at least be safe overnight. The stranger had promised that her suffering would be over but after all that she'd been through, Lindy trusted no one and prayed he had been honest with her and Katie.

Safeer and Rashid picked up Dawn and Janice, Mary Matson was nowhere to be seen but Safeer didn't bat an eyelid, the woman was far too old and as he only wanted young girls for his clients to chose from, he didn't waste his breath asking where she was. Dropping the girls off at Kings Cross, he arranged to collect them later and then the two brothers drove back to the burial gardens. Safeer stayed in the car and Rashid was sent over to the monument to get Akram and Katie. With a new girl this was the usual practice as they liked to keep them sweet, at least for a while. Seeing that there was no one about Rashid called out.

"Come on Akram, put your cock away its time to get going."

Thinking that his brother was behind one of the headstones giving the girl a seeing to, he started to get annoyed when there was no response.

"For fucks sake Akram hurry up!"

Still there was no reply and after walking around for a couple of minutes, Rashid went back to the car.

"He aint there Safeer and neither is the girl."

"That little cunt! I bet he's taken her to a cafe, those whores twist him around their little fingers. I aint waiting about any longer, well get in you Muppet, let's get going! I'll wring his fucking neck when I get hold of him."

Frankie had anticipated their return and dragging Akram's body over to the ditch that ran around the gardens perimeter had been a shrewd move. As it was dark, the trail wouldn't be visible until the morning and hopefully by then it would no longer matter. Frankie then drove over to Kings Cross and knowing that it would be a while before the brothers arrived to wait for the two girls, went to get some food. Parking the scooter and after downing a burger and a cup of coffee at the Rocket pub on Euston Road, Frankie walked to Balfe Street. Standing on the corner of Rail Street, he kept in the shadows as much as he could but he still had a good view of all the cars as they drove down the road. The brothers usually parked in the same spot and Frankie didn't have to wait very long before the old Mercedes pulled up. He decided to hang about for a few minutes to see if they got out but when nothing happened, he slowly walked towards the car. When he was level with the rear doors, Frankie grabbed the handle and was inside and sitting on the back seat before the brothers had time to do anything. At the same time Safeer and Rashid swung around in their seats but when they came face to face with the Makarov pistol, there was only silence.

"Well it seems we meet again, only this time I will do the talking and you'll do the fucking listening,

you pair of low life cunts!. Now I know what you did to Adeela and as much as you feel it was your right to murder an innocent woman, I feel it's my right to seek revenge. You know what they say?"
Safeer just stared open mouthed but said nothing.
"Every action has a reaction dickhead!"
Frankie pointed the gun directly at Rashid's face.
"Turn around you cunt!"
Rashid did as he'd been told without any argument and Frankie placed the pistol to the back of Rashid's head and pulled the trigger. Blood and brains hit the front windscreen and Safeer for all his hard man bravado, began to scream and cry out in desperation. It wasn't because of the distress he felt over his brother's death but purely down to the fear he felt for his own life.
"Please, pleeeeease whoever you are don't kill me. It was my brothers that did that terrible thing to our sister not me, please I beg you."
Frankie felt no sympathy only rage at the man pleading for his life and he wondered if his beautiful sweet Adeela had pleaded for her life, only to be ignored by these animals. Frankie placed his hand in the air and Safeer was instantly silenced.
"Tell me one thing, how did you know about me and Adeela?"
The man was at least engaging in conversation and for a moment Safeer thought that he may have a chance.
"It was her boss, a big man who along with two

heavies came to see me and my brothers a few days ago. He told me what had been going on, even showed me pictures of you and her kissing." Frankie suddenly felt sick, he wanted to vomit but knew he couldn't as this animal would make a run for it and he had to finish what he'd started. Swallowing hard, he lifted the pistol and grabbed the handle with both hands to steady his grip. Frankie West pulled the trigger one last time and shot Safeer Makhdoom right between the eyes. Blood and brains again hit the windscreen as the back of Safeer's head exploded outwards and then his body slumped forward. Frankie knew he had to get a move on, he'd spent far too long as it was and with so much blood everywhere, he risked drawing attention to the car. Pulling up the collar of his jacket he laid the gun onto the backseat, calmly stepped from the car and after taking off his gloves and putting them into his pocket, walked off as quickly as he could. Heading in the direction of Caledonian Road and when he felt he was a safe enough distance away, he stopped and rested against a wall to compose himself. His heart was racing for all its worth and it took a few seconds to get his breathing under control before he could continue on his way. He seemed to be in a trance as he made his way back to the scooter and he felt as if a hundred pairs of eyes were all watching him. It was nerves pure and simple and he chastised himself for being so stupid. Everything was whirling around in his mind and he was finding it difficult to accept that Harry, the man he had once called dad, could have betrayed him in such a way. Sure they didn't get along that well but to instigate the killing of an innocent young girl was hard to take. Frankie knew the kind of acts Harry was capable of but this, well this was something else altogether. By the time he pulled up into the pubs backyard, he knew what he had to do. Tomorrow would mean the end of his life as he knew it, but then without Adeela, he didn't feel as if he had a life anymore.

CHAPTER TWENTY FIVE

Harry West sat at the kitchen table drinking his morning coffee as Bella entered wearing the expensive cream silk dressing gown he'd given her last Christmas. He studied his wife and couldn't help but notice, that without makeup she was looking very tired, almost as if she was worn out. Bella's skin colour was pale and she had dark circles under her eyes making Harry wonder if she was sickening for something. Things between them were slowly starting to get back to normal but it had taken some time and he knew he had to tread carefully. Usually after an argument they would kiss and make up within a few hours but this time it had taken days and Harry knew he was skating on thin ice. If his wife ever found out what he'd done regarding the Asian girl and Frankie, well it would be the end of his marriage but then again he couldn't see how she could ever find out. Today he had more than enough to worry about as the biggest and last delivery of the long firm was taking place. By tonight all the stock would be moved from the warehouse and British Electrical Wholesale trading Co would cease to exist. Everything had been planned out with military precision and if his men did as they'd been told, things should run smoothly and without a hitch.
"Morning Babe, sleep well?"

"No not really, you?"
"I aint slept well for weeks, there's a lot going on with my work and laying in the dark at night, well it all seems to just go around in circles in my head."
Bella walked over to the coffee machine and raised her eyebrows as she poured herself a drink. Normally she would have wrapped her arms around her husband; kissed him tenderly and told him not to worry so much but right at this moment she really couldn't be bothered. Bella knew he meant the long firm, something she was dead against but she had learnt early on in their marriage not to get involved in her husband's business. Taking a seat at the table she looked into his eyes and when he winked at her and squeezed her hand, she finally relented and smiled at him. Harry West was the love of her life, always had been and always would be but sometimes he could try the patience of a saint. About to speak, she was silenced by Helena bounding into the room demanding to know what was for breakfast.
"Young lady, you are big enough and old enough to pour yourself a bowl of cereal."
Helena plonked herself down at the table and folding her arms in an indignant manner, she let her bottom lip drop.
"I will just have to go to school hungry then; I bet all the other girls' mothers prepare their breakfast."
"Please yourself. I might have given birth to you but I wasn't put on this earth to wait on you hand

and foot and I doubt very much that your friend's parents wait on them either. Anyway, I think it's about time you started to do your fair share of chores around this house young lady, for one thing you can tidy up that pigsty of a bedroom."

Harry hated it when his wife and daughter had an argument and he could see that this conversation would turn into exactly that. Walking over to the cupboard he removed a bowl and a packet of cereal and put them down onto the table in front of Helena.

"There you go sweetheart."

Placing a kiss on her forehead, he then bent over to kiss his wife but Bella turned away so that his lips only skimmed her cheek. Harry had too much on his plate today to deal with all this pettiness. Just lately there was always a battle of wills going on between the two women in his life and he was fed up to the back teeth with it all. Walking into the hall he pulled on his jacket and picked up his briefcase. He made a mental note to buy some flowers on his way home, hopefully Bella would have calmed down a bit by then.

Jimmy Fingers was already waiting outside and as Harry fastened his seatbelt Jimmy was bursting to reveal all that he had heard. Pulling away from the kerb, he started to speak in a casual way that he hoped would intrigue his boss.

"I bumped into Kelly this morning boss. He reckons he was down the Cross last night having a drink in the Rocket and saw your Frankie in there."

"He aint my Frankie and where that twat chooses to drink aint none of my concern alright? Anyway stop fucking running on and concentrate on your driving ok?"

Jimmy didn't know whether to do as he'd been told or continue to inform Harry regarding what he knew. For once the urge to relay some juicy information was too great and he couldn't help but continue.

"Maybe it aint boss but Kelly reckons an hour or so later the area was swarming with Old Bill. Well Kelly being Kelly, the nosey cunt, walked over to have a gander at what was going down. Seems a couple of them brothers we went to see had just got their fucking brains blown out. Kelly said he knew it was them as he recognised that old Merc they drive about in."

"Why the fuck would I be interested in a couple of Paki's getting topped?"

Jimmy didn't add any more but when he quickly glanced sideways at is boss; he could see that all the colour had visibly drained from Harry's face. The rest of the journey was taken in silence and when Jimmy dropped his boss off outside the warehouse, Harry got out and slammed the door shut without a word. It was signal enough that he had said to much and so he decided to keep his head down for the rest of the day. He wouldn't be needed until tonight, when along with Kelly and a couple of others, they had been instructed to collect five high top transit hire vans for the removal of the stock.

Frankie hadn't slept a wink and strangely it didn't concern what he had already done but rather what he was about to do. There was little love lost between him and Harry these days but Bella was a different story and he knew that the outcome of his actions would break her heart but there was no way he could let things go. Hearing someone bang loudly on the front door he hauled himself out of bed and went downstairs. He didn't look at the large station clock that hung on the wall in the bar and when he opened up was a little surprised to see Karen.

"You're early love."

Barging past him she marched through to the back room and spoke as she walked.

"No Frankie, you're late and if we don't pull our fingers out we will never be ready for opening time.

Frankie now glanced at the clock and couldn't believe that it was already ten thirty. He hadn't been able to sleep through the night and had laid in the dark reliving all of the previous evening's events. Just before it was time to get up he must have dozed off and now he had a disgruntled member of staff because of it. When Karen returned with a mop and bucket full of hot soapy water he could tell by the look on her face that she was pissed off with him. Grabbing her keys from the bar, he smiled as he handed them to her.

"Thanks for loaning me your bike."
Karen Jones immediately softened; there was just something about Frankie, that no matter how hard she tried, she couldn't stay mad at him for long.
"Fancy a coffee?"
"But Frankie we need to get on."
"Does it really matter if the fucking floor goes unwashed for once?"
Karen looked around, the place was always pristine and their daily cleaning sometimes really wasn't necessary.
"It's actually the second day Frankie."
"So? Like I said does it matter?"
"Well no but if Harry comes in he won't be happy, you know how particular he is."
"You leave Harry to me; I can honestly say that pretty soon he won't be bothered what sate this place is in."
Totally out of character Frankie then took Karen by the shoulders and hugged her to him.
"I want to thank you for all that you've done girl, you really have been a true friend."
"Have been? I still am aint I?"
"That's what I meant."
Her friend's slip of the tongue hadn't gone unnoticed by Karen. Walking around to the other side of the bar, Frankie poured two coffees and hoped that his last remark was enough to convince her, although in all honesty it had been the truth and after today he was very doubtful that he would

ever see his friend and confidant again.

At eleven am Karen went to unbolt the front door and turning around, was surprised to see Frankie standing in the bar wearing his jacket. Handing her an envelope, he kissed her on the cheek and then walked from the pub. He really was acting strangely today but Karen assumed it was down to the shock of loosing Adeela. Past experience had taught her that some people cried nonstop, some hid themselves away to mourn and others, like Frankie, just acted plain weird. Sitting down for a moment, she tore the envelope open and gasped as she removed a wad of twenty pound notes. After slowly counting them, Karen put her hand to her mouth when she realised that Frankie had given her a thousand pounds. A small post it note was attached and the message, though short, worried her to the core.

'My dear friend, just a small thank you and an apology in advance as the days ahead will be upsetting to you and for that I am sorry. Frankie xx'

Suddenly Karen began to shake but she didn't know why, surely he wouldn't do anything silly and try and harm himself. She didn't have a clue where he had gone and there was no one she could contact. Harry wouldn't be interested and she didn't want to worry Bella unnecessarily when she didn't know for sure what was going on. As the first customer came in she stuffed the money into the pocket of her jeans. There would be time for worrying later but for now she had a job to do.

Frankie hailed a cab and asked to be taken to the Old Billingsgate Market. Walking around the iconic building that was now used for events, he could feel his nerves begin to set in. His mind was racing and just for a moment he had doubts regarding what he was about to do. In the distance he saw two women walking in his direction and one of them was wearing a hijab. Frankie knew there was no way it could be Adeela but just for a second his heart skipped a beat and it was enough to convince him that he had to carry out his plan. Reaching the warehouse he pulled open the door on the shutter and walked inside. It was eerily quiet and as he walked along the isles his footsteps echoed making the place sound hollow. Suddenly a voice called out.

"Who's there?"

It was Harry, and Frankie could see quick glimpses of the man through the racks, as he ran along the isle parallel to where Frankie was standing. As he came into full view, Frankie noticed that Harry was sweating profusely and knew that the years of high living had done nothing to aid his fitness.

"It's only me Uncle Harry; I've come to give you a hand."

"Well fucking wonders will never cease, anyway you're too early as the deliveries aint until this afternoon."

When Harry was almost level with him, Frankie

pulled out a knife and held it directly towards him. For the second time that day all colour drained from his face and Frankie could instantly see by his actions that Harry was scared. There was nowhere for Harry West to run to, so raising his hands he decided to try and talk his way out of the situation.
"Now come on son, what's all this about?"
"I aint your fucking son! You've reminded me of that enough in the past. All this, is about you stirring the shit and getting Adeela killed."
Harry slowly nodded his head.
"So it was you who killed the Makhdoom's. Fuck me boy I never thought you had it in you, but it seems you've finally grown a pair of balls. Well I must have done something right then."
"You've never done anything for me you cunt!"
Harry took a step forward and Frankie raised the knife to throat height which was enough to stop Harry dead in his tracks.
"Aint I? Well who took you in, paid for that fancy school, all your education and spent hours running you from one club to another when you were growing up? Who fed and clothed you? You were part of my family and now look at you."
"Yeah you did give me everything and then you snatched it all away again and abandoned me. I'd have been better off living with my mother, she may have been a druggie prostitute but at least she loved me."
Harry began to laugh in a sarcastic way and Frankie

could feel the anger begin to build up inside. "Fucking loved you? Yeah she loved you alright; she loved you that much that the slag sold you to me. I could have been a fucking paedo but she didn't care, all she was interested in was getting cash so that she could pump that fucking shit into her veins!"

Frankie didn't want to hear anymore, there was no point and right at this moment he hated the very sight of the man standing before him. It felt like slow motion but in reality it was very quick. One step forward and the six inch blade went straight between Harry's ribs and directly into his heart. For a short moment in time Frankie held onto Harry and as the colour drained from his face for the last time, their eyes locked onto one another. As Harry was released his body slid down into a crumpled heap on the warehouse floor. Frankie West didn't move an inch and could only stare down at the man he had once called Dad, glad that it was all finally over. Mesmerised, he watched Harry's life blood flow from his chest and form a deep red pool on the cold concrete. Frieda Parker was sitting in the office when she heard raised voices and without thinking, she ran straight into the warehouse. The sight that greeted her made her instantly stop as she thought about her own safety. Frankie looked up and the slight glimmer of a smile could be seen on his lips. It was something Frieda would never forget and something she would repeat over and over again in

court. Shock had her rooted to the spot but when Frankie spoke she looked into his eyes.
"I think you need to call the Old Bill don't you?"
Running back to the office Frieda dialled nine nine nine and her words came out in a stammer as she relayed that her boss had just been murdered. In hindsight she should have ran a mile as she was probably now looking at a hefty prison sentence for her involvement in the long firm but it didn't cross her mind, well at least not until after the squad cars and SCO19, the special firearms command, had arrived. Frankie sat on a wooden crate and waited, the knife was still in his hand but he immediately dropped it when told and holding up his arms, walked slowly forward. Forced to the ground, he was read his rights, handcuffed and taken to Bishopsgate police station to be charged.

CHAPTER TWENTY SIX

Arriving at the police station, Frankie had gone through the usual routine of being booked in. He was charged with murder, his clothes and shoes were taken and he now found himself dressed in a paper suit sitting in a cold cell. As far as he was concerned it was all a stupid exercise as they wouldn't need any forensic evidence; he was going to plead guilty. He'd been caught bang to rights but that was the way he had intended it to end all along. Still he gave them no trouble and did everything they asked of him without question. Detective sergeant Garry Mace was in charge of the investigation and he had decided to delay the interview until his team had gathered as many facts as possible. Detective Bob Coe had been sent over to Harry's club with three uniformed officers to begin taking statements and at the same time two uniformed constables along with a WPC, went to Harry's home in Belsize Park to inform Bella West of her loss. At Rosie's club Kelly and Jimmy had been waiting to hear from their boss and when Jimmy opened up to let the Old Bill in he was instantly on his guard. Bob Coe introduced himself and then asked Jimmy who he was and what he was doing at the club. When Jimmy explained that he worked at Rosie's club, Bob had to break the news to him of Harry's demise.

"I'm sorry to inform you, that a body was reported at a warehouse in the old Billingsgate market. We don't as yet have any formal identification but we strongly believe that the body was that of one Mr Harry West."
"Harry!"
"Yes Sir and furthermore, Mr West was murdered. A person by the name of Frankie West is at present being held in custody and helping us with our inquiries. That leads me to my first question, what can you tell me about the men, did they have an argument?"
Jimmy was shocked to the core but he didn't let it show. His guard was now well and truly up and he said what anyone in his line of business would say.
"Look governor, I just drive the man, as to anything else I aint got a clue. Harry was a very private person and this has all come as a shock so if you don't mind I'd like to be left alone. If I think of anything that might help I'll be sure to get in touch."
Bob Coe had expected nothing less, he'd been on the force long enough to know that these kind of people lived by a code and talking to the Old Bill was taboo. Still he'd followed orders and in all honesty he would rather get back to the station to start the interview, after all they had their man and it wasn't as if he was denying his actions.
"Is there anyone else inside that might be able to shed some light on things?"
"Sorry governor but I'm the only one here."

Jimmy Fingers hadn't let the officer go any further than the bottom of the stairs and holding open the front door, now waved his hand in a silent gesture that told Bob Coe to get out. With the door firmly locked Jimmy ran up the stairs and burst into the office. To begin with he found it difficult to get the words out but finally he relayed all that he'd just been told to Kelly. The two men were stunned and couldn't believe that their Boss was dead and now their livelihoods had come to an abrupt end. For a while they talked about Frankie, trying to work out what had happened but an hour later they were no nearer to an answer. The men decided that whatever happened they wouldn't say a word to anyone about the events of the past few days and after shaking hands, they locked up the club and walked off in separate directions.

On Belsize Park Constable Ian Greenwood had taken the lead and had informed Bella West of her husband's death. This part of the job he hated but someone had to do it and on this occasion, he was the one that had pulled the short straw. Ian couldn't stand all the crying and wailing and he loathed having to show a sympathetic side, especially when it had to do with a known villain like Harry West. Bella immediately broke down sobbing but when the WPC stepped forward to offer her some comfort, Bella sharply pushed the woman away. Things dramatically changed when Bella was also informed that they had her son

Frankie under arrest for the crime. The tears instantly dried up as shock took over. Twenty minutes later and the three officers were sitting back in the car not quite able to take in what had just happened. Bella West had swiftly stopped crying and had then coldly informed them that she would go and identify the body but at the moment she was extremely busy, so if they wouldn't mind going so that she could get on with things it would be much appreciated. Harry had always said that you never showed any emotion in front of the Old Bill and she was now angry with herself for letting him down. When the front door was firmly closed it was a different story. Bella sobbed until she thought her heart would actually break in two. Harry, her Harry the love of her life was gone and as her whole body shook, she didn't have the first idea how she would live without him.

   Three hours later Frankie was finally led into the interview room. Gary Mace and Bob Coe sat on one side of a table and a uniformed officer stood at the back of the room in case Frankie caused any trouble. The tape was switched on and after introducing themselves, the detectives began to ask their questions.

"Why have you refused a solicitor Mr West?"
"There's no point, aint like they can get me off with it and in any case I wouldn't want them to. I'm guilty so there really aint any need to carry on with this charade and waste your time now is there?"

Gary Mace had been on the force for over twenty years and had dealt with several murders but this one was strange, the man was polite, seemed to know his rights but wanted no help whatsoever.
"It doesn't really work like that I'm afraid. What we need to know, is why you killed Harry West?"
Frankie was tired, the day had taken its toll and he felt as if he could sleep for a week. Running his hands through his hair, he looked directly into the eyes of Detective Mace.
"Look you can save yourselves a lot of time if you just end this now or you can continue for the next god knows how many hours but the outcome will still be the same. I killed him but I won't tell you or anyone else why, so do we carry on with this because I'm not going to comment any further?"
Detective Mace looked at his partner and shrugged his shoulders. Concluding the interview he switched off the tape but as with all human beings he was intrigued and really wanted to know what had happened.
"So now the tapes switched off are you going to explain?"
"I've told you all you need to know, I killed Harry West and that's an end to it."

Since the double murder had been discovered all leave had been cancelled at Bishopsgate police station. The place was manic and two investigation rooms were in use at the same time which was highly unusual. The bodies of

Safeer and Rashid Makhdoom were awaiting formal identification and autopsies but the investigation had begun in earnest. Forensics had been over the car with a fine toothcomb but apart from an enormous amount of blood, skull fragments and brain tissue, there was little else. The gun had been removed from the back seat but as the serial numbers had been ground off and there were no prints, it was of little help clue wise. The cars registration had been entered into the central computer and within a few minutes the identity of the owner had been confirmed. Detective Tommy Abbott had been instructed to pay a visit to the Makhdoom family home to inform the next of kin.
Yasmeen had just finished clearing away the plates from lunch and she was on tenter hooks worrying as to why her boys were still not home. When the knock came at the front door she could only stare in her husband's direction. Anwar removed his oxygen mask and his words were sharp as he spoke. "Well answer the door woman!"
Yasmeen did as she was told but only opened the door a fraction. To begin with she didn't know who the strange man was but when she spied WPC Tracey Wilmot standing beside Tommy Abbott, she had to hold onto the doorframe to steady herself.
"Mrs Makhdoom?"
Yasmeen could only nod and after Tommy had introduced himself and asked if he could come in, Yasmeen slowly led the way through to the front

room. Anwar's eyes opened wide when he saw who their visitors were and when Tommy took a seat and asked Yasmeen to do the same, the Makhdoom's realised that whatever the man was about to say it would be serious.

"Mr and Mrs Makhdoom, I am detective Abbott and this is WPC Wilmot. I'm afraid we have some bad news for you. Last night there was an incident at Kings Cross where the bodies of two males were found in a car. We have reason to believe that one of the victims was your son Safeer."

Unusually it was Yasmeen who spoke.

"What about Rashid and Akram?"

Tommy Abbott assumed the second victim was also a son but he didn't have any idea regarding the other name that Mrs Makhdoom had mentioned.

"The second victim was possibly another of your sons but I'm sorry Mrs Makhdoom, I have no information regarding a third."

Anwar removed his mask and with laboured breath, began to speak.

"This is all because of that whore of a daughter; my boys would be alive now if it wasn't for her."

Tommy glanced in Tracey's direction and raised his eyebrows; this investigation was becoming more intriguing by the second.

"Could you explain Mr Makhdoom?"

Before Anwar had a chance to reply Yasmeen took over. Even though Anwar glared at her as she spoke, for the first time in their marriage she totally ignored him.

"Our daughter ran away several days ago. The dirty whore had been sleeping with a white man and unlike people from the west, that behaviour will not be tolerated by a good moral Pakistani family. The man she was sleeping with came looking for her and I know deep in my heart that it was him who has carried out this terrible revenge on my sons."

"Revenge?"

Anwar removed his mask, he was now worried that his wife was about to incriminate them regarding what had happened to Adeela.

"Woman!"

Yasmeen instantly clammed up and apart from giving Frankie's full name to Tommy, she wouldn't say anything else. The couple were informed that they would need to go to the morgue at some point to identify the bodies but apart from that there really wasn't anything else to say.

Outside Tommy was about to speak to Tracey Wilmot when he thought better of it. This was turning out to be complex and he wanted to do further digging before he spoke to anyone about his ideas. He decided to knock on a few of the neighbours doors and just ask if they knew anything about the girl. His questions received a mixed reception and he could see fear on the faces in front of him. Most just didn't want to get involved but there were one or two who were quite helpful and they described Adeela as a very pretty, quiet girl. One neighbour, who asked not to be named, also described the brothers as evil and that he had seen them hit the girl on several occasions. Returning to the station, Tommy took a seat behind his desk in a bid to make some sense of all this and when news filtered through that a body had been found on the Old Burial Gardens over in Walthamstow and that the method of murder was the same as the two Makhdoom brothers, Tommy realised that he was definitely onto something. Hearing the revelations he thought back to the young woman found burned to death a few days ago and his gut instinct told him that it was Adeela Makhdoom. Deciding to take this to the Detective Inspector, Tommy tentatively knocked on Ken Palmers door.

"Enter."

"Sir I wondered if I might have a word, I think we may have a link regarding the events of last night that I'm currently investigating."

Tommy then proceeded to relay all the events of the last twenty four hours.

"Sounds like an honour killing to me and also the possible revenge of a spurned lover. What have you found out about the boyfriend?"

Tommy was a little embarrassed as he had come to his superior without the full facts.

"Not a lot as yet but I was intending to visit him this afternoon."

"Well get on with it man, you know time is of the essence in a murder inquiry."

Tommy Abbott entered the investigation room that was dealing with the double murder and asked his partner to accompany him to Rosie's pub. Geoff Arnold had worked alongside Tommy for the last five years and knew that when his partner had the bit between his teeth there was no stopping him. Tommy's record was exemplary and his result rate was second to none when it came to solving crimes. By the time they arrived at the pub it was two thirty in the afternoon and Karen was up to her eyes in customers. Tommy introduced himself and then asked if they could have a word in private.

"I aint being funny darling, but as you can see, I'm a bit busy at the moment. This lot will create bloody murder if I stop serving now. We close at three so if you want to come back or you can wait if you want, then I'll be happy to talk to you."

Tommy ordered two pints of larger and then he and Geoff took a seat at one of the tables. Thirty minutes later Karen finally placed the bolt across the door and walked over to join them.

"So how can I help Officer?"

"We are investigating an incident that took place in Kings Cross last night and before we speak to your boss we would like to ask you a few questions."

Karen's guard instantly went up, she wasn't about to discuss Frankie with anyone.

"So what is it you want to know?"

"Have you ever heard of a family by the name of Makhdoom?"

"Well if you mean Adeela then yes, although I haven't seen her for several days. Look I don't mean to be rude but I have a lot of work to do and sitting here talking to you won't get the shelves restocked ready for opening. Officer I only work here, I don't poke my nose into things that don't concern me so you're wasting your time if you think I have anything to say."

For the second time that day someone had clammed up on him. Tommy Abbott knew he wouldn't accomplish anything as Londoners always held their tongues when the police started sniffing about. If this woman knew anything, she certainly wouldn't share it with him.

"Fair enough, now where could we find Frankie West?"

Karen began to laugh; this really was the icing on the cake.

"Don't you lot speak to each other? Frankie was arrested this morning and is being held at your station."

Tommy looked in Geoff's direction and his expression was one of amazement and anger. The police had been made to look like idiots and all because there was a lack of communication.

Tommy and Geoff returned to Bishopsgate station to confirm the barmaid's revelation and when Tommy was notified that Frankie was indeed

installed in one of the cells and had already been questioned, he was none too pleased. Reporting straight to Inspector Palmer Tommy informed him of the developments and the fact that they could possibly be holding the suspect of several murders without even knowing it. Gary Mace and Bob Coe were summoned to the inspector's office where everyone in the room was given a tongue lashing and told to get their acts together. It didn't go down well with any of the detectives who were all blaming each other but finally things calmed down and after Tommy Abbott had passed over all the information he had, Frankie was once again brought to the interview room. There were now three detectives in the room and as Frankie was led in and told to sit, he wondered just how long this was all going to take. It had been decided in advance that Tommy would take the lead although it was a job that Gary Mace would have liked to have done. He hadn't got much joy with the earlier interview and this time he had hoped to crack Frankie West.
"Mr West, what can you tell me about Adeela Makhdoom?"
For a second Frankie was taken aback but he did well in hiding his shock.
"Not a lot, I had a relationship with her for a while but I haven't seen her for a couple of weeks now."
"And her brothers, what can you tell me about them?"
"Never met them."

"Oh come on now, you don't expect us to believe that do you?"

"Believe what you want, anyway I'm tired of all this. I've held my hands up and admitted what I've done so unless you want to charge me with anything else, I suggest we finish up here."

Tommy Abbott called a halt to the interview and switching off the tape, left the room. Making his way up to the Inspector's office he handed over everything that the team had managed to get together. Tommy was told to take a seat while Ken Palmer looked through all the documents.

"Do you think he's guilty Tom?"

"Without a shadow of a doubt, it's too much of a coincidence."

Inspector Palmer sagely nodded his head and after another scan of the evidence he finally came to a decision.

"Charge him."

As Tommy entered the interview room Gary Mace and Bob Coe were still seated at the table facing Frankie. Tommy silently walked over and after restarting the tape, looked directly into Frankie's eyes as he spoke.

"Mr West I am formally charging you with the additional murders of Safeer Makhdoom and as yet one other unidentified male. Do you now wish for legal representation?"

Frankie's face was blank; he showed no emotion or shock, unlike Gary Mace and Bob Coe who just stared open mouthed at their colleague.

"No."

"Do you have anything at all to add?"

"No."

"In that case I am suspending this interview while we investigate further."

Nodding to the uniformed officer standing at the back of the room, Tommy told him to escort the prisoner back to his cell.

The following morning matters took a turn for the worse as over night the CPS had studied the evidence and dropped the charges of murder regarding the Makhdoom brothers. If further evidence should come to light then the case would be looked at again but until that time they had advised that it was a no go.

    At ten am Frankie was taken before an emergency court and remanded. He didn't say a word or try and fight for bail because as far as he was concerned this was now his life, one long round of being told what to do by the establishment. Sent to Pentonville prison until sentencing, Frankie was given a single cell. Most other prisoners avoided murderers at all costs and even though he was allowed association time, the ensuing weeks felt like he was in isolation. The only person that came to see him was Karen and on her first visit he thanked her over and over again. Frankie West hadn't imagined that he could feel so lonely and his only consolation was the fact that he knew sooner or later he would eventually get used to it. Karen didn't ask him why he had murdered her boss and for that he was grateful, instead she gave him all the local news about what had been happening down the lock and what the punters had been up to. He was glad that she still had her job and when she informed him that Bella had taken over the pub he smiled.

"I bet she's a right task mistress and no mistake?"

"Actually Frankie, apart from you, she's the nicest boss I've ever had. She even makes that brat Helena come in and do some work but the girl is sneaky and I wouldn't trust her as far as I could throw her."

Frankie was desperate to ask a question but for the next hour and although he was chomping at the bit, he was able to contain himself. When the bell rang out to signal that visiting was over, he couldn't hold back any longer. Standing to kiss her on the cheek, she already knew what he was about to say.

"Karen, does Bella ever mention me?"

Slowly she shook her head but Karen's next sentence at least gave him hope.

"Nor does she slag you off! I was quite surprised when I first saw her, she looked so drawn and I expected her to hate you with a vengeance but nothing was said and I didn't feel it was my place to ask her any questions. In all honesty Frankie I was just pleased to still have a job to go to. Oh I forgot to mention, Bella's thinking of selling the club, whether she will or not I don't know, its early days

yet but she said she'd always hated the place and would be glad to see the back of it, bless her."
"I can't say I blame her, a lot of nasty things went down in that place."
"Well I don't know about any of that and I suppose it sounds selfish on my part, but I just thank god that she's decided to keep the pub."
Back in his cell Frankie thought of all that Karen had said and picking up a pen and a sheet of paper, he began to write. By the time it was lights out the bin was full of balled up letters, none of which would ever be sent. Over the next few weeks it was mandatory for psychiatric reports to be carried out but as Frankie refused to engage in conversation on every visit, the report would end up containing very little when handed to the court.

CHAPTER TWENTY SEVEN

It was a further three months before Frankie finally appeared at the Central Criminal Court, or as he knew it The Old Bailey and as he was led into the dock his eyes desperately searched the room for Bella. He knew deep down that she would never forgive him but just a shred of hope remained that she would be here today. She wasn't and the only face he recognised was that of Karen Jones. Looking at her he smiled sadly and even from across the court room Frankie could see the tears in her eyes. The hearing didn't last more than an hour and due to his guilty plea, there was no need for a jury. There was also little need for evidence to be produced but the Crown Prosecution Service still showed the Judge, the Right Honourable Lord Digby Moss, the weapon and insisted that Frieda Parker spoke of what she had witnessed. The Court Usher called out her name and taking the stand Frieda was sworn in. Listening to her words and seeing the fear in her eyes made Frankie feel guilty. He never intended for any innocent party to get involved and had he have know that she was at the warehouse that day he would have planned things differently. The judge listened to her account with interest and just as he was about to tell her to stand down, he decided to ask one more question.
"Can you tell me Ms Parker, if when you came face

to face with the accused, you felt frightened for your own life?"

Frieda paused before she answered and staring over at Frankie she wondered for a moment, just like so many others had done, why he did what he did. Harry West was a complete bastard and not one to be crossed but she also knew that he loved his family more than anything in the world, or at least his wife and daughter. Frieda had heard on the grapevine, well via Jimmy Fingers actually, that Harry had adopted Frankie as a small child but regarding their relationship, she didn't have a clue. Shortly after the murder she had bumped into Jimmy Fingers, who had taken great pleasure in telling her all he knew. The man sitting in the dock, even though he didn't have the same blood, was for all intent and purpose Harry's son. If Jimmy Fingers revelation was to be believed, whatever could cause someone to kill their own father?

"Ms Parker, would you like me to repeat the question?"

The moment was broken and Frieda looked back at the judge and shook her head.

"No thank you your honour. In all honesty, the answer to your question is no. For a second when I saw someone holding a knife and with Harry, I mean Mr West, dead on the floor, then obviously I was scared but when I looked up into his eyes, no I can honestly say I did not fear for my own life."

"Thank you Ms Parker, you may step down."

As there was no legal representation on Frankie's behalf, Judge Moss could only address the prosecution. Known at the Old Bailey for being a fair man, he didn't want to rush into sentencing and ordered a recess for lunch to give him time to consider what course he would take. Frankie was taken down to the cells and offered food but he wasn't hungry. The outcome of this could only end one way and he wished with all his heart that they would just get it over with.

At two pm the court resumed and Judge Digby-Moss addressed the legal team and the few people in attendance before he handed down his sentence. Frankie was told to stand and as always he did as he was asked.

"Mr West, I find this a strange and disturbing case. You openly admit that you carried out this horrendous act but you will not reveal your reasons why. From this I find myself in a bit of a quandary. Did you commit this crime as a cold blooded killer who took the life of an innocent man?"

A loud gasp was heard from someone in the public gallery and the Judge's face was stern as he glared in Karen's direction.

"Or, did you act out of some kind of misguided believe that you were wronged in some way. The facts are clear and you have admitted your guilt saving this court a lot of time and money for which I commend you. That said, you still saw fit to take another man's life and have offered no just cause as to why you did so. There are no psychiatric reports available due to your refusal to assist the doctors but given that you are of previous good character and that I feel you are not of any real danger to the general public, I prefer to accept the latter conclusion."

Frankie was starting to get fed up, the Judge was rambling on and on to such an extent that his words were going in one ear and out of the other. This was not going to end well, so why this geriatric arsehole was dragging things out baffled him.

"Frankie West, I am passing a sentence of fifteen years and may you spend that time reflecting on the atrocity you carried out, an atrocity that has left a woman without her husband and a child without her father. Take him down."

Driven to Belmarsh, Frankie expected the place to be much the same as Pentonville but he was in for a shock. The category A prison, Belmarsh was home to inmates who had mostly been convicted of very violent crimes, much like his own but in his mind Frankie didn't consider himself like the others. The High Security Unit housed some of the country's most dangerous criminals. Spies, terrorists and top drug dealers all lived under one roof and luckily for Frankie West, he didn't have to be on that particular wing. That said, D wing wasn't much better and even though Frankie was one of the forty percent who were lucky enough to get a single cell, it was still a very dangerous and volatile place.

Karen continued to visit as often as she could and while she didn't use every visiting order that he sent her, Frankie never let it bother him. Five weeks after his incarceration and on the first Saturday of September, Frankie received exciting news of today's visitor and it wasn't Karen. At long last Bella had contacted the prison and inquired about paying a visit. When asked, Frankie had readily agreed and her order had been forwarded to the pub under the care of Karen Jones. He thought it was more than a little strange but then maybe Bella didn't want Helena to find out that her mother was going to see the man who had murdered her father. Now he was being led through the numerous gates with all of the other prisoners and his thoughts and emotions were mixed with nerves and trepidation. Glancing all around the visiting room, he couldn't see her anywhere and when he was shown over to a table and saw Bina Raja sitting there, his face fell.
"How did you get here?"
Before Bina replied she lashed out and slapped Frankie sharply around the face. Instantly a guard ran over but as he held his cheek with his right hand, Frankie put up his left and waved which told the officer that all was fine.
"I had to do that, had to express how much pain and misery you have caused me and my family. As for getting in here, I pleaded with your friend Karen. It took some persuasion but eventually she gave me your prison number and agreed to let me apply for

a visiting order in your mother's name. I couldn't take the risk of you refusing to see me."
"So you've come all this way just to reprimand and slap me, does it make you feel better?"
"No and I don't really know why I came. It's not anything to do with the murder of my nephews and don't try to deny that you had a hand in that. They were monsters and deserved exactly what they got. I also no longer have contact with my sister and brother in law but once again that is of no great loss."
"So why strike me?"
Bina rubbed at her forehead with the palm of her hand and Frankie could see that the normally immaculate woman had been through the wringer. She was still smartly dressed but today she wore no makeup and the dark circles under her eyes were clearly visible.
"I'm sorry about that; I suppose I just needed to release my frustration at the utter waste of it all. I suppose coming here to see you was a way of trying to feel close to Adeela, I miss her so much Frankie."
Frankie didn't know how to reply to that and his disappointment that Bella wasn't here was clearly evident to Bina.
"Does your mother ever visit you?"
Frankie sadly shook his head.
"And all I did was to build up your hopes with my deceitfulness. I'm sorry Frankie; you've gone through so much lately. We all miss Adeela terribly

but you were in love with her and that is something very special."

Bina stayed for the remainder of the visit and they talked nonstop about Adeela and what she had meant to them both. Bina shared memories and sometimes Frankie smiled as he imagined his girl as a child and all the things she probably got up to. When the bell rang out and it was time for Bina to leave, Frankie would have done anything to spend just a few minutes longer with the woman. While they were talking it felt as if Adeela was somehow still alive and now he had to go back to his cell, he felt a fresh wave of grief.

Over the following few months Frankie got into several scrapes with people that had known and carried out business with Harry West. One beating he received was so severe that he had to be hospitalized but he always stood his ground and tried to give as good as he got. Gradually things began to quieten down and eventually Frankie settled into a routine, a routine that would stay with him for the next fifteen years. It was whilst in Belmarsh that Frankie West was given the opportunity to attend a study course. Apart from the few years spent at the public school, studying was something he had loved and over the years, had missed terribly. He threw himself into every course available and it opened up a whole new world to him. With all the pain he was going through and the stress of prison life; it was the only thing that seemed to keep him sane. Proving to be a model prisoner and student, he had taken three exams in the first couple of years and had passed all of them with distinction. He didn't hear from Bina again and Bella never did visit. As for Karen, her friendship stood the test of time but after five or six years her visits had diminished to two or three times a year. He didn't blame her; people's lives were moving on, all except his own which was fixed in an institutional madhouse.

CHAPTER TWENTY EIGHT
Wormwood scrubs
(Cell of Frankie West and Sonny Higgins)

Frankie West stretched out his arms and yawned. Recounting his version of past events in every tiny detail had made him not only emotionally drained but also physically tired.
"And that Sonny boy is my story, warts and all."
"So killing those brothers, well what I'm trying to say is that you're racist aint you?"
"Racist? I'm the least racist person you are ever likely to meet Sonny. What life has taught me, in the worst possible way I might add, is that there really are good and bad people. It's not the race; it's the people themselves no matter where they are from. It wouldn't have mattered if the men who killed my girl had been white, Chinese or from Mars come to that, I would still have killed them all."
There was silence for a moment and as Frankie looked in Sonny's direction, he just caught sight as the young man wiped away a tear with the cuff of his sweatshirt. Not realising that he'd been seen, Sonny then puffed out his cheeks in a sign of astonishment. It had taken over two hours for Frankie to tell the boy his story and in all that time Sonny hadn't interrupted once. It was the first time in twelve and a half years that Frankie had spoken to anyone about what had happened, the last being

Bina Raja and even then it hadn't been in any great detail. With each word that was relayed, Frankie had felt pain as if it had only happened yesterday. He could still picture his beautiful Adeela's face just as vividly as the last time he has seen her, still see the fear in Safeer Makhdoom's eyes a second before he had shot him and splattered his brains onto the cars windscreen and he could still see the blood as it oozed from the wound to Harry West's chest as he lay on the cold concrete floor.

"But you must regret it? I mean you've wasted your fucking life man."

Frankie smiled in a knowing way but Sonny didn't understand.

"Not one bit of it and I would do it all again in a heartbeat. That's probably one of the reasons I've never applied for parole, that and the fact that I know I deserve to be here. You see if I'd have gone in front of a parole board and if they had asked me if I was sorry for what I did, then my answer would have been a polite 'no'. It would have been a complete waste of their time and mine."

Sonny Higgins listened but he was still having a hard time understanding. At twenty one years old, he couldn't imagine what it must have been like being locked up for all that time.

"So you'd kill again, I mean you really would kill the same people?"

"Of course I would, wouldn't you commit the same crime that you're in here for?"

Sonny frowned; he couldn't believe what he was hearing.

"No I fucking well wouldn't."

Frankie stood up and walking over to Sonny, placed his hand onto the young man's shoulder.

"Then my work is done!"

"What are you talking about Frankie, you aint making any sense man."

"Look, when you got banged up with me, I told you that you made the choice to come in here by committing that crime remember? Then you said to me that I did the same and I told you it was totally different. I didn't set out to rob an old man, that's despicable."

"No, you just killed four people."

"But I didn't set out to live a life of crime, I would have been happy to have a life of pipe and slippers as long as I had Adeela by my side. Only when you meet the love of your life Sonny, will you truly understand what I'm talking about and the lengths you are prepared to go to no matter what the cost."

Sonny gently nodded his head, it seemed that what Frankie had been trying to tell him, was at last beginning to sink in. There were crimes committed purely out of greed, no matter who got hurt and then there were crimes of love, which he now understood were totally different.

    The next few months passed quickly, and Sonny wanted to be in the company of a man he now looked up to and admired. It wasn't anything

to do with Frankie's crimes and being friends with someone who others were afraid of, because he actually thought Frankie's actions, though he now understood why, had still been vicious. No, Sonny wanted to learn from the man, Frankie was smart, knew how to behave and Sonny realised that this man had morals and principles. It was all beginning to rub off on Sonny and for the first time in his entire life he was experiencing an inner calmness. It was totally alien to him but none the less he liked the feeling. At every opportunity the two would spend all of their time together in what appeared to others, to be deep and meaningful conversations. The transformation in Sonny Higgins attitude hadn't gone unnoticed and when the wing governor received reports on the young man, he gave himself a pat on the back for placing Sonny with Frankie West in the first place. At the fifteen month mark Sonny Higgins was called before the governor where he received news that due to his good behaviour, he was being granted an early release. Running back to his room, he couldn't wait to tell his cell mate the good news.
"Frankie, Frankie you'll never guess what, they're letting me out!"
Frankie smiled and sagely nodded his head. There was no doubting that he would miss the young man but he was also very happy for him.
"Now don't mess up Sonny, you've got a real chance to do something with your life and learn from your

mistakes."

By breakfast the next morning Sonny was packed and waiting to be released. At nine am he hugged his dear friend one last time and was then escorted to pick up his belongings. Collecting his release payment, Sonny now found himself standing alone outside the prison gates. It had only been a few months since he'd looked up at the sky and been free but it felt like years ago and that realisation made him think about Frankie. True the man only had just over a year left to serve but it was still a long time and Sonny hoped that one day, Frankie West would find happiness, or at least some kind of real peace.

Walking to Hammersmith underground, Sonny boarded a train on the Piccadilly line. Everything still seemed strange and he couldn't help but stare at the other passengers, it felt as if he was seeing other human beings in a different light for the very first time. At Piccadilly Circus he changed onto the Bakerloo line and emerging from Lambeth station, stopped at a stall to buy flowers. The first bunch he chose were peach roses, his mothers favourite and the second was yellow chrysanthemums. Sonny remembered always seeing a bunch on Gladys Bateman's sideboard and he guessed they were her favourites. Reaching the flats, he gently tapped on the door and when old Gladys opened up her face was a picture.

"Well bless my soul if it aint young Sonny Higgins.

Come on in son; don't stand there like a spare part. It's so nice to see you and you look so well!"

Doing as he was asked Sonny walked along the hall and into the front room. The flat still smelled of old people, but strangely he now didn't mind. Handing Gladys the flowers, he smiled warmly at the neighbour who had always taken great care of him.

"I want to apologise for my behaviour Mrs Bateman. I've been a jerk and I'd just like to say....."

"You listen here, there aint no apologies necessary. We all go off the rails at one time or another but as long as we get back on them then it's all that matters. Have you seen your Mum yet?"

"No not yet and to tell you the truth I'm a bit nervous."

"Bleeding nervous of seeing your own mum? I've never heard anything so daft in all my years. Mercy will be over the moon, you mark my words."

"Well I suppose there's no time like the present and once again Mrs Bateman, I really am sorry."

Gladys laughed and as she saw him to the door, tenderly placed a kiss on his cheek.

"I always knew you were a good boy at heart Sonny, now you make that mother of yours proud and keep out of trouble."

"I will Mrs Bateman, I promise."

Standing outside his own front door, Sonny waited until Gladys was back inside her flat before he knocked on the door. He hoped his mother would be pleased to see him but after almost a year and a half he wasn't totally sure. Mercy had occasionally visited but not as often as she could have. Sonny had thought it was down to the shame but in reality it was due to the fact that each time she had been to the prison, it had torn her apart and had taken days for her to get over it. After knocking, Sonny nervously stepped from one foot to the other as he waited for the door to open. Once it did, all of his fears vanished and Mercy hugged him to her like she never wanted to let him go. Sobbing, she found it almost impossible to talk and Sonny didn't push her, there would be time for talking when the tears had dried and for now he was happy just to be home. Over dinner Sonny told his mother all about Frankie West and to begin with she wasn't happy about her son mixing with a convicted killer but as Sonny relayed all the things the two men had talked about, she could see that this Frankie person had been a good influence on her boy. Sonny didn't go into any detail about Frankie's crime, he felt that the man had confided in him and he wasn't about to let Frankie down but Sonny did tell his mother about the studying and that he also wanted to make something of himself. By eight o'clock he was totally worn out and after kissing his mother goodnight, Sonny headed in the direction of his bedroom. About to switch off the hall light, he was stopped by the sound of someone tapping on the front door. This area of Lambeth wasn't safe after dark and he was cautious as he opened up but

when he saw the caller was his old friend Pingo, he relaxed. The two embraced before immediately parting, embarrassed by their actions.
"So how are you doing man?"
"Good Pingo, I'm good thanks and you?"
"Well ducking and diving as usual, you know how it is. Anyway, I'm here to see if you're interested in a job I've got lined up?"
Unbeknown to Sonny Mercy was behind the front room door listening. She was afraid of what her sons answer would be and dropping to her knees, prayed to god for help.
"Sorry Pingo but I aint into all of that anymore. I've learnt the error of my ways so to speak and I really want to make something of myself."
Pingo laughed out loud and in the front room Mercy made the sign of the cross. She had been sure that her son would relent and go off with that good for nothing Pingo.
"I need to get to bed now mate; maybe I'll see you around sometime."
With that Sonny closed the front door and went to his room. Mercy was still kneeling on the floor, only now the tears were falling thick and fast as she thanked the lord over and over again.

  In the next few days life was busy as Sonny had parole visits and several job interviews lined up. Malcolm Doughty, Sonny's probation officer, had been so impressed with the young man's manners and attitude, that he had gone out on a limb and contacted as many companies as possible in the hope of getting Sonny Higgins employment. Within a week things had paid off and Sonny had raced home to tell his mother that he had not one but two jobs.

"Oh baby, that's brilliant news. I'll put the kettle on and then you can tell me all about it."

"It's not anything special mum but it is a start. I've got three regular days work at the local builder's yard and two nights a week delivering for the pizza parlour on the high street. They provide a moped and everything so it's not too bad."

"Baby what do you plan to do with your future?"

Clasping his mother's hand in his, Sonny stared deep into her eyes and Mercy knew that whatever he was about to say, he would mean with all of his heart.

"I want us to leave London and start somewhere again fresh."

His words shocked Mercy. This definitely wasn't something she'd expected to hear but even though it was a surprise, it was something she had dreamed of for years.

"So where are you or we, hoping to go?"

"Jamaica."

"Jamaica! Sonny you've never even been there before, why on earth would you want to go now?"

"Because you always said how much you loved it. I don't expect you want to see your family so maybe we should treat it as a holiday to begin with.

If things work out then we can stay. I plan to work my arse off for the next few months and get as much money together as I can. We can sell off everything, because I know that even if it doesn't work out over there, there's no way we're coming back to this shithole."

For a moment Mercy didn't speak, she was trying to take in the enormity of her sons words.

"And can I have time to think about it?"

"Of course you can mum, take all the time in the world. I know I've been a disappointment to you but I've changed, really I have and London doesn't feel like home anymore."

Mercy leaned over the table and kissed her son, right at this moment she couldn't have been any prouder of him. The next two days passed without any mention of Jamaica. Even though Sonny was desperate to hear his mother's decision, he didn't want to force her to do anything she wasn't comfortable with. It was over their evening meal on Friday night that the subject was raised but surprisingly it wasn't by Sonny. Mercy had cooked a special meal of brown stew chicken, ackee and salt fish with pepper pot soup. Calling her son through to the kitchen to eat, Mercy waited for his response. The dishes were all authentic Jamaican food but as Mercy had only ever cooked English, Sonny had never eaten anything like it before.

"What's all this?"

"This my darling, is the kind of thing that you will

be eating when we get to Jamaica, so I hope you like it."

Standing up Sonny hugged his mother tightly and then lifting her from the floor, carefully swung her around.

"Let me down boy you're making me giddy. So when do you think we can go?"

"Well if we give ourselves another six months to save, I think we should have enough money to see us through the first few months at least. Mum, are you going to contact your family?"

This was a question Mercy had asked herself many times over the last couple of days and she still hadn't reached a decision. Deep down she would love to see them all again, especially her father.

"I'm still thinking on that one, maybe, I don't know."

The food went down a storm and when Sonny had gone to his room to listen to music, Mercy removed a notepad from the sideboard drawer and began to write.

'Dear Mama and Papa

I know this will come as a shock but I am returning to Bull Bay in a few months and wondered if I could come and see you? I will understand if you still feel the same way as you did when I left but Oh my, you should see my boy, he's almost twenty three now and a more handsome boy you aint never set eyes on. Listen to me running on like the proud mother but that's exactly what I am, proud of my boy and no matter what hurt we felt all those years ago, I wouldn't change a thing not if I had to be without my Sonny. Anyway, I will give you time to think things over and I will contact you nearer the time to let you know what flight we will be on. As I said earlier, if you don't want to meet up then I will understand.

With all my love

Your daughter Mercy xx

Mercy Higgins sealed up the envelope and placed it into her handbag. Her hands shook as she handed it over at the post office the next day, now it was all up to her parents and she crossed her fingers as she walked home. Deep in her heart she knew that whatever happened, whatever her family's decision was, she and Sonny would make a new life for themselves but she prayed that it would include them all.

CHAPTER TWENTY NINE

It had taken nine months for Sonny and Mercy to save enough money for two flights to Jamaica. Sonny knew that if his grandparents didn't want to see him or his mother, then they would need extra cash for accommodation. Unbeknown to Sonny, Mercy had also been saving hard. It went totally against the grain to do it but she hadn't been paying any of her household bills towards the end. Normally Mercy Higgins would pay her bills as soon as they dropped through the letterbox but knowing she wouldn't be returning, she had decided to forgo what she would normally consider as essential requirements. In her opinion they were all a rip off anyway. Along with selling almost everything in the flat and that included personal items that had over the years, come to mean a lot to her, the Jamaican fund was growing steadily. Getting her son away from temptation was top of her list and when she finally admitted what she'd been doing; Sonny kissed her tenderly on the cheek. Within a few hours of the revelation, Sonny had headed down to the travel agents on the high street and booked two one way tickets to Kingston. Before they knew it, mother and son and the few personal effects they had allowed themselves to take, were boarding flight British Airways 2263 from Heathrow and were on their way to Jamaica.

Mercy was nervous for the whole journey but she tried her hardest not to show it. If her parents didn't want any contact, it would break her heart. Oh it wasn't anything to do with her, she had resigned herself to being alone many years ago but what would hurt, was the fact that they didn't want to see her boy. As soon as the flights had been booked she had written to her father to let him know the details but there hadn't been any reply and now Mercy felt in a state of limbo.

Thirteen hours later and the Boeing seven three seven touched down on Jamaican soil. Descending the steps, Mercy felt the warm air on her skin and she inhaled the salty smell of the sea. She couldn't help but smile when memories came flooding back and when Sonny saw her face, he gently squeezed his mother's hand.

"Well we've made it Mum!"

"Yes we have baby, I've finally come home and it feels good."

"Mum, I've never said this before, but I'm so proud of you."

Mercy smiled and nodded but she didn't reply she knew in her heart exactly what he was referring to. When their luggage had been collected and they had passed through customs, the two entered the main foyer. Mercy was nervous beyond belief, it was years since she was last here and if there was no one to meet them, then she didn't have the first clue about where to go. Thankfully Mercy wasn't

privy to the fact that Sonny had only purchased one way tickets because if she had found out it would have caused her even more worry. Sonny was determined that things would work out and if they didn't, well he wasn't going to think about that at the moment. Slowly Mercy glanced around and when her eyes fell upon a grey haired man holding up a sign with the word 'Higgins' printed on it she began to cry. He had wrinkles and had put on a bit of weight but there was no mistaking him, Mercy would have recognised her father anywhere. Dropping her bags she ran as fast as she could into his arms and Winston embraced her in a bear hug. It felt like he was never going to let go and as he sobbed on her shoulder, Mercy couldn't remember a time when she'd felt happier. Eventually they parted and Mercy beckoned for Sonny to come over. He had guessed who the man was and striding forward, held out his hand. Winston Higgins brushed his hand away and then gave Sonny the same loving bear hug that he'd given to Mercy. Pulling away, Winston held both of Sonny's hands.
"Let me look at you boy, what a fine looking young man you are. You've done a good job raising him Mercy girl, a good job indeed."
"Thank you Papa, shall we get a coffee and talk about what happens next?"
Winston nodded his head and pointed to a seating area that provided hot drinks. Sonny went to the counter and while he waited to be served, watched

his mother and grandfather.

"So how have you been girl?"

"I've been good Papa, it was hard at first but we managed. I suppose you heard all the gory details from Uncle Donovan?"

"Baby I take whatever that man says with a pinch of salt, I always have done."

"I'm glad and hopefully I'll get to tell you my side of things but not now, now I just want to look at you. Oh Papa, so many years have been wasted and for what?"

Mercy could see that her words were causing her father pain and that was the last thing she wanted to do, so she quickly changed the subject.

"How's Mama? Is she still angry with me?"

Sonny arrived back with three coffees and the conversation was momentarily interrupted.

"Thanks son, so Papa how is she?"

"Oh Mercy baby, I have so much to tell you and it aint all good. As your brother grew up he became troublesome and turned bad. Baby we aint seen him for over ten years. The last I heard he was in prison for mugging an old lady but where he is now, your guess is as good as mine. It broke Tandy's heart; I mean you remember how she was with him."

His grandfather's words had cut deep and as Sonny sipped at his drink, he turned away. He knew that his mother would never reveal his past crime but at the same time he was filled with guilt and remorse at what he and Pingo had put old Harold Wells through.

"I'm sorry to hear that Papa, it must have been so hard for you and Mama?"

"Baby you'll never know how hard, I don't think your mother has ever gotten over it and I think that's one of the things that caused her stroke."

"Stroke!"

"Yeah, five years ago it was and it's left her very poorly. She's in a wheel chair and she can't do much for herself. If you listen carefully you can make out what she's trying to say but her speech is very slurred. I had to give up my job to care for her so things have been a struggle, not that I'm asking for anything but if you do both stay and get jobs, then it would help a lot."

"So does she know we're coming?"

Winston grabbed Mercy's hand and as he squeezed she could see fresh tears begin to fill his eyes.

"Indeed she does baby girl and she can't wait to see you."

The thirty minute drive to Bull Bay was mostly taken in silence as Mercy and Sonny took in the sights. For Mercy it felt as though all those wasted years were falling away and every time she saw a building or a sign that she recognised she squealed in excitement. Sonny was constantly laughing and although he'd never experienced what his mother had, he really liked the look of the place. Pulling up outside the house, Mercy's jaw dropped but she tried not to let her father see her disappointment. The brilliant whitewash had long since faded and the hanging baskets on the front porch, that her mother had always lovingly tended, now swung in the fading afternoon light, their contents nothing but dried up grass.

"You don't have to try and hide any expectations you may have had Mercy, I know it aint what it used to be but I'm just too old and too tired to do it anymore."

"Maybe you are Papa but there's a strapping young man sitting behind us and I'm sure if he sets his mind to it, this place will be back to its former glory in a few days. Now let's get inside and see Mama."

The front door creaked as Mercy pushed it open and in the middle of the room, sitting in her wheelchair, was Tandy Higgins. She now wore an ill fitting wig and her right arm hung loosely in her lap as a result of the stroke but when she saw her daughter, the biggest grin filled her face. Mercy ran over and kneeling down in front of the wheelchair, took her mother's hands in hers. Tandy slowly began to speak and even though it was only four little words, they instantly had Mercy in floods of tears.

"I'm so sorry baby."

Mercy placed her index finger onto her mother's lips and then leaning forward, embraced her lovingly.

"Sonny, come and say hello to your grandmother."

As he stepped forward Tandy was shocked at the size of him and mouthed the word 'handsome' which made Sonny blush. Looking at the old woman in the chair it was hard to imagine the tyrant that his mother had spoken of but he wouldn't let that cloud his mind, from now on the memories he and his mother would make would only be happy ones.

Just as his mother had said, Sonny carried out the repairs and completely repainted the outside of the house. After Mercy had replanted the baskets with deep purple bougainvillea, Tandy's chair was pushed outside and the sight made her gasp. Once again her home was beautiful and it was all because her daughter had come home.

It didn't take Mercy more than a few days to find a part time job at the local supermarket. Every day after her shift ended, she would return home to prepare the evening meal. Their arrival had taken a lot of the stress and strain from her father's shoulders and bit by bit she noticed her old Papa returning, Winston was laughing again and he even had time to take Tandy out for walks in her wheelchair. Evenings were spent sitting out on the veranda sipping cool lemonade and watching the world going by. To begin with Mercy had worried that there wouldn't be enough for Sonny to do but he seemed so happy just being around his new found family that he hadn't even tried to make any friends. Getting a job proved difficult as he wasn't a

Jamaican citizen but that didn't deter him and every day he would walk miles asking for work. Eventually he was taken on at a local garage as a cleaner. It wasn't his dream job but it was at least something and would do for now. Working in the hot sun doing menial tasks like cleaning the showroom and forecourt was hard work but it beat prison hands down and not once did he complain to anyone. One evening as he sat watching the sunset, he suddenly turned to Mercy and asked a question, it was a question she'd been dreading since their arrival.

"Tell me about my Dad."

His mother, grandmother and grandfather all stared open mouthed and when Tandy politely coughed, Winston stood up and wheeled her into the house. This conversation was private and mother and son needed to be alone.

"What do you want to know?"

"Oh I don't know, do I look like him, did you love him, where does he live? That sort of thing I suppose."

Mercy gazed in the direction of the beach and for a moment she was a girl of sixteen again, climbing out of her bedroom window to go and meet a boy. It was all so clear and she could even remember the clothes that she wore. Sighing and with a heavy heart she spoke and hoped with all hope that the little she had to tell him would be enough.

"Yes you do look like him Sonny only you're far

more handsome. Did I love him? I thought I did but at sixteen I didn't really have a clue what love was about. I suppose it was more of a fascination, just a young girl who was looking for romance. As for where he lives, I really don't have a clue son. As soon as I got pregnant I was sent to England and I don't even know if Junior was aware that you were on the way. I can't say he was a bad person Sonny because looking back, like me he was only a child. Do you want to try and find him?"

Sonny thought for a moment, and then shook his head. The two of them had managed just fine on their own for all these years and he didn't want anyone else on the scene now. Mercy stood up and taking her boys hand, led him down the steps of the veranda.

"Where are we going?"

Mercy just smiled but Sonny followed her all the same. Within five minutes they were standing at the water's edge listening to the wave's crash before them. The sun had almost set and the lights of Kingston could be seen twinkling in the distance.

"I forgot how much I loved this place."

"Yeah, it really is beautiful. God, you must have had a real shock when you landed in London."

Mercy didn't reply but pointed to a small building a few hundred yards along the beach.

"Remember I used to tell you about the bar? Well that's it."

It wasn't much, just a wooden structure about

fifteen feet square.
"Come on Mum, let's go and see if it's still open." Arm in arm they strolled along but when they reached the little shack, Mercy's heart sank. The windows and door were boarded up and the locks were so rusty, that it must have been that way for a long time.
"Ah well, nothing lasts forever but in its time it really was a great place. Come on lets go back it's starting to get chilly."
Sonny Higgins began to spend more and more time at the beach. He was in his element just walking and swimming in the sea. He loved the peace and quiet and the beautiful sunshine but most of all he loved the freedom, the kind of freedom that he'd never felt in London. Occasionally he thought of Frankie West and wondered how the man was doing; hopefully he was fine and would soon be free to start a new life just as Sonny had done.

CHAPTER THIRTY

Finally, the day of Frankie West's release arrived and as he walked along the landing carrying a clear plastic bag with his possessions inside, the slow sound of clapping could be heard. To begin with it was just a couple of inmates but by the time he reached the first set of gates, the whole wing could be heard applauding him. It was something set in stone in a prisoner's code, that when a lifer served his time and was finally released, they were looked upon with respect, as if they were some kind of hero. Anyone that could stick the regime for fifteen years without going off the rails was a god as far as the others were concerned. Frankie didn't turn or wave but as he passed through the gate he slowly shook his head and laughed. After walking through the iconic arch he was at a loss as to where his future was going. Although his release had been looming for some time, now that it was actually here the realisation that he was totally alone was starting to sink in. Deciding that there really was only one place to go but not knowing what kind of reception he would receive, Frankie started to walk. He had to find out if any of his personal items were still there or if they'd been discarded and even though Rosie's pub wasn't a place he wanted to go to, he had no choice.

At East Acton underground station Frankie caught

the central line to Tottenham Court road. If it all seemed strange to Sonny, it was a million times worse for Frankie. As the train clacked along the rails he studied all the people on their mobile phones and marvelled at how small the devises were. It made him think back to the one he'd given Adeela, at the time it was top of the range but now, well now the youngsters would probably look upon it as an antique. Changing trains, he walked through the tunnels to the northern line and boarded a link train for the next leg of his journey. As the carriage grew closer and closer to Camden Town he began to relax and emerging into the bright sunshine he stopped for a moment and surveyed the road. Nothing much appeared to have altered and suddenly he set off at speed, desperate to see his old home. When the pub came into view, Frankie could feel a lump in his throat. He had always loved this part of London and never more so than today. Standing outside, he looked up at the building he'd called home for most of his adult life, well at least until he was incarcerated. He placed his hand on the highly polished finger plate but for several seconds didn't go any further. What if Bella was inside, what if she had a new manager that had no idea who he was? Puffing out his cheeks Frankie decided to take the bull by the horns and find out. It was still quiet as the lunchtime trade hadn't come in yet and his eyes slowly scanned the bar. The interior had changed beyond belief, contemporary taupe paint covered the walls and stylish leather sofas and chairs surrounded low oak tables. Even the lighting was softer, it cast gentle shadows onto the walls which gave a warming effect and all in all Frankie liked the renovations. Making his way to the bar he waited for the woman behind the counter to turn and when she did she let out a gasp. Leaning over the highly polished wood, Karen planted a big kiss on his cheek.

"Oh Frankie it's so good to see you, how are you love, when did you get out?"

"It's good to see you to Karen. I got out this morning and I'm fine thanks. To tell you the truth I was a bit nervous about coming in, you know, I didn't know if Bella would be here?"

"No worry on that score love, she made me manager and basically leaves me to get on with things."

Karen was momentarily embarrassed when she realised that she now had Frankie's job.

"Here let me get you a drink."

"Only a half Karen, remember I aint had any alcohol for over fifteen years. Any more than a half and I'll be off my face."

"Now that, I really would like to see."

Karen poured the drink and then waited to hear what her old friend had to say, she knew he wasn't in the pub for a social visit and just hoped that whatever the reason, it wouldn't cause any more trouble. Frankie took a mouthful of his drink and let out a contented sigh.

"Ahhhh, it tastes so good."
"I bet you really missed that?"
"You can say that again, inside when it was hot I used to lie on my bunk dreaming about this moment. Right Karen, down to business. Do you know if Bella has kept any of my stuff or did she throw it all out?"
Karen walked around the bar and taking his hand, led him through the door and up the stairs. When he entered his old room Frankie West couldn't believe his eyes; everything was just as he'd left it.
"After it, well after Harry died, she wouldn't let anyone up here, wouldn't let them touch a thing. For the first few weeks she would spend hours holed up in here alone, it was so sad Frankie. Finally she got her act together but I'm still the only one she allows to come up here and that's only to clean which she insists is done once a week even though there's been no one living here.
"Would you mind if I stayed, just for tonight and then after that I'll pack my stuff and be on my way."
"Of course not, it's your home. Are you going to see Bella before you leave?"
"I aint decided but if she phones, please don't tell her I'm here or even that I'm out yet, I need to handle things in my own time."
"I promise, now I need to get back downstairs before the regulars start arriving. Call me if you want anything."

By the time Karen came in for her shift the following day, Frankie had already gone. Rising early he'd packed a rucksack, retrieved his passport and bankbooks from the safe and set off for Belsize Park. All night long he had struggled with his conscience, should he go and see Bella or should he just disappear. Finally he had come to the conclusion that she at least deserved to see him, deserved to smack his face and rant and rave if that's what it would take to quell her anger. The area hadn't changed much and when the house came into view he felt a lump form in his throat for the second time in as many days. Some of his happiest moments had occurred in that house but also some of the worst and he thought back to the day Harry had told him to leave. Last night as he lay in the dark this had all seemed like a good idea but now in the cold light of day he was scared. If Bella, the only woman he had ever known as a mother, slammed the door in his face, he didn't think he'd be able to take it. This was ridiculous, of course she wouldn't want to see him, her husband had died at Frankie's hands, what the hell did he think he was doing here. About to turn and walk away, something deep inside stopped him, he had to see her and at least try to explain why he murdered Harry in cold blood. Slowly he walked up the steps and pressed on the brass bell. It took several moments before he saw the silhouette of a figure through the frosted glass and when the door opened he gasped. Bella West's hair was silver grey and she now walked with two sticks. Gone were the stylish clothes and perfect makeup and she now looked all of her, god Frankie realised that she must now be in her early seventies. So many years had passed, so many years wasted and they had all taken their toll on his poor old mum. For a few seconds the two just stared at each other before Bella turned and walked back along the hall and into the kitchen. The one glimmer of hope for Frankie was the fact that she had left the front door wide open. Cautiously he followed her and without a word took a seat at the table. Nothing had changed, the furnishings and decor were still all the same and it felt as if he'd stepped back in time. Bella rested her sticks against the worktop and began to fill the kettle as she spoke.

"I wondered if you'd come and see me when you were released, when did they let you out?"

"Yesterday. Mum, how is Helena?"

His sister had always been a brat but at the same time he had loved her since the day she'd been born. Bella lifted the tea tray from the side and Frankie stood up to help her but she waved him away.

"I have to do as much for myself as I can or my pins will give up altogether."

Hobbling over, she placed the tray onto the table.

"I wouldn't have a clue, aint seen her for over five years. Not since I sent her packing with a flea in her ear. After her dad, well you know, she went off the rails."

Frankie's face fell and for a second Bella's heart went out to him.

"Now don't go blaming yourself, it had been on the cards for years. It started with binge drinking in her last year of school. Helena got in with a bad crowd and gradually slipped into drugs. It all came to a head when she stole the watch I'd given to Harry the Christmas before he died. The little cow pawned it and it was then that I realised she didn't give a flying fuck about me or how I felt. We argued and a lot of harsh words passed between us, not to mention tears but she couldn't see what she'd done wrong. I honestly think for some strange reason she believes the world owes her something. Personally I blame Harry, he was too soft on her and in the end she was all take take take. Do you know she didn't shed a tear at her own father's funeral? I tell you love, she may have been the one I gave birth to but she means far less to me than you do. If I'm totally honest, it was always that way although I would never have dared reveal that to Harry."

He had never expected this, never even dared to hope for a reconciliation and her words had shocked him to the core. He could feel the emotions rising up from within and did his best to hide the tears of love and relief but he didn't do a very good job.

"So what about you Mum, how have you been?"

"Not so bad, me old arthritis is playing me up but apart from that I mustn't grumble. The quack offered me a new hip but I aint going to have it done, I'm far too old to be pulled about and besides, I aint got that long left so it might as well go to someone younger."

Frankie smiled; she always had a way of lightening the situation no matter how grave it was.

"Anyway, let's get down to brass tacks, why have you come round? It certainly aint to enquire after my health, I do know."

Frankie placed his elbow on the table and held his head in his hand. Taking in a deep breath he started to explain but he wasn't sure Bella wanted to hear what he had to say.

"I wanted you to know why I did it, why I wrecked your life; Helena's and my own come to that."

"And will it make any difference?"

Frankie rubbed at his brow with the tips of his fingers.

"No but hopefully you might understand that it wasn't over something petty."

"I never thought it was. So what was it over? Harry was the love of my life, he was also a complete and utter bastard and that's where Helena gets it from. To begin with I imagined that it might have had something to do with your mum."

"But you're my mum."

"Ok, I mean your birth mother. Shortly after Harry's death Jimmy Fingers came to see me.

I wondered why because we aint never exchanged more than a polite hello or goodbye. To tell you the truth I never liked the man, always found him a bit shifty if you know what I mean. Anyway, he said he had something on his mind and couldn't rest without telling me. He told me, that a year after you came to live with us Harry had your mother killed, so I suppose it was poetic justice in the end."
"It had nothing to do with my mother, I didn't even know about that until now."
"Has it upset you?"
"How could it, I never even knew her? No mum this was a different thing all together, I fell in love."
"In love!"
"Yep, hook line and sinker, with the most beautiful girl in the world and even today my heart still yearns for her."
Frankie began to tell Bella all about Adeela, how beautiful she was, how much he loved her and how they were only a day away from being together forever. He explained about the Makhdoom brothers and how they prostituted young girls and how when they found out their sister was seeing a white man, they had burned her to death. For the entire time he talked, Bella listened intently and would occasionally nod her head. When he got to the end, or what she thought was the end, Bella had tears running down her cheeks.
"Oh my poor baby, you must have been heartbroken and that poor girl, god bless her little

heart, she must have been in agony."
Bella didn't think there could be much more left to say but when Frankie revealed that the reason Adeela was killed was all down to Harry, the tears suddenly stopped. Now Bella West wore a hard look and for a moment Frankie couldn't tell if she had believed him or not.
"Then that nasty cruel bastard deserved everything he got Son, I'm only sorry I didn't know this sooner. I always said there was more to it all than I knew but no matter who I spoke to, there was never any reason to explain it or at least none that anyone had the balls to reveal."
Now Bella's tears once again began to fall and standing up, Frankie walked over to her and placed his arms lovingly around his mother.
"I'm so sorry Frankie, if I'd have known I would have visited you. It's my own fault, I always knew deep down that my boy would have to have a very good reason to kill someone and now we've wasted all these years."
Mother and son hugged for a long time, neither wanting to let go but eventually Frankie released her and reaching behind him, handed Bella a tissue to wipe her eyes.
"So my darling, now what are you going to do?"
"Well, I need to get away for a while, just to get my head together and get used to living in the real world again."
"Promise me you'll come back, you're all I have now

Son."

Frankie smiled lovingly at the woman he thought would hate him forever.

"Of course I will."

"Wait here, I've got something for you."

Grabbing her sticks, Bella hobbled into the hall and out of site. He could hear her going through drawers and cupboards and guessed she was in Harry's old study. A few minutes later she returned and whatever Bella had been up to, Frankie could see that it had taken its toll on her as her breath was laboured.

"Here we are."

Bella handed Frankie a large manila envelope.

"Well go on then, open it."

Pulling out what looked like a legal document he scanned the first few lines and then with a shocked expression, stared up into his mother's eyes.

"This says that I'm the legal owner of the pub?"

"That's right; I transferred the deed of ownership a couple of years back. I wanted you to have something to come home to, keep looking there's more."

Frankie flipped through the document and attached to the last page was a signed undated cheque for five hundred thousand pounds.

"I can't take this!"

"Oh yes you can and you will, it's the least you deserve after what Harry and I did to you."

Frankie placed the papers onto the table and taking

Bella's tired old hands in his, stared deep into her eyes.
"Harry maybe, but you Mum never! All you ever gave me was love and I was to blind to see it but not anymore, from now on we're going to make up for lost time and be the family we always should have been. That's a promise."

By the time Frankie was released, Sonny and Mercy Higgins had been in Jamaica for three months. Sonny was still working in the garage and Mercy at the supermarket. They weren't short of money but that said there wasn't much left over for luxuries. Still they were all happy in their own way and since Mercy's return her mother had come on in leaps and bounds. The wheelchair was only used if they left the house but inside Tandy had learnt with the guidance of her daughter, to walk with a stick. Sometimes Winston thought he was dreaming and on several occasions Mercy had seen a tear in his eye but she'd never questioned her father and instead had given him hugs and reassurances that they were here to stay.

One Saturday in June, when Sonny had finished his shift cleaning and was enjoying a beer on the veranda, a strange car pulled up outside the house. A well dressed man stepped out and tipped his hat in Sonny's direction. Whoever this visitor was, he looked official and Sonny Higgins began to panic. It was a stupid idea but not completing his parole had always worried him, still Sonny doubted very much that anyone would come all the way from England to arrest him.

"Mr Higgins, Mr Sonny Higgins?"

"That's me Sir, how can I help you?"

Henry Morgan walked up the steps and onto the veranda. Holding out his hand he introduced himself and then took a seat.

"I work for the law firm of Thomas Gregory and sons in Kingston. A couple of months ago we were instructed to carry out a strange request, that request was asked by a client in England. We had to locate you and give you something and I would like to add Mr Higgins; you were not a very easy man to find. Anyway, I have been told to pass this envelope over to you. Please don't ask me about its contents as I am as mystified as you must be. Good day Mr Higgins and I hope that what I have brought to you is good news."

With that Henry Morgan stood up, once more tipped his hat and then left. Sonny looked down at the envelope with bewilderment. He didn't have a clue what it was all about and he could feel his whole body begin to tense up as he slowly opened the envelope a little bit at a time. The first item he pulled out was a hand written letter.

'Hello my friend

I hope you are happy with the contents of this package. Sonny I want you to prosper, please be good to your old mum and when you meet the love of your life, be happy as I wish I could have been. Your friend F

Sonny Higgins pulled out further pieces of paper, the first was a cheque for two thousand pounds which on his reckoning amounted to, oh Sonny couldn't work it out but it was certainly a lot of Jamaican dollars. The note attached said it was to be used for stock which puzzled Sonny for a moment. All became clear with the next document he removed, the little boarded up beach bar was now owned by one Sonny Higgins Esquire. Suddenly Sonny began to scream and jump up and down, he made so much noise that Mercy came running out thinking that her son was hurt. When she saw him hopping about she wore a frown and was about to get angry when he trust the letters towards her. Mercy read on and couldn't believe what she was seeing.
"Oh baby, Oh baby bless my soul."
Soon she was also jumping for joy and all the commotion brought Winston outside but as he stared at his daughter and grandson doing some kind of weird dance, he could only shake his head.

    Over the next two weeks Sonny began painting and doing repair works to the bar. He didn't want to hand in his notice at the garage until the place was ready to open, so daylight permitting, he was at the beach for every spare hour that was available. He occasionally even roped in his grandfather to help and Winston would wheel Tandy's chair down onto the sand so that she could watch the transformation and tell them when they were doing things wrong. Finally the day arrived when they were ready to open and within two months the bar was heaving with tourists and locals alike. Soft pastel shades made the place seem larger than it actually was, fairy lights had been strung inside and around the entrance and a few nice tables and chairs had been set out on the sand to provide extra seating for when they were busy, which happened to be most nights. The hypnotic beat of Reggae music played nonstop and as Mercy cleared away the empty glasses she would sway to the rhythm of the music. It was a sight her son loved to see and one the regulars would all join in with. The place was filled with laughter and Sonny was so happy that he often had to pinch himself to make sure that he wasn't dreaming. He never saw or heard from Frankie West again, but he often thought of his friend with fondness. Sonny was so busy that he didn't notice the bearded stranger wearing sunglasses and a straw hat as he walked along the water's edge and passed by the bar but it didn't matter. Looking up at the sign and seeing 'Frankie's Bar' in bold black letters made the man smile. He had achieved what he'd set out to do and now it was time to return to London, to his own bar and his dear old mum. Now it was time for Frankie

West's life to begin all over again.

THE END

Printed in Great Britain
by Amazon